HOW SAFE IS NEUTRON TWO?

Dr. Andres Kudirka
His reputation as an expert earned him the key position at the Neutron Two atomic reactor. But his private thoughts made him, quite possibly, the most dangerous man on earth.

Mariko
She fled from nuclear holocaust with the help of Andres Kudirka. She became his wife, only to find that he had married to ease his conscience—not to love and be loved.

Yale Pollack
The National Security Service agent would not give up his investigations. He had to know about the secret past that Kudirka kept hidden from public scrutiny. He had to know more about the mysterious explosion at Neutron One. And he had to guess what Kudirka was up to at Neutron Two—before it was too late!

IT'S ONLY AS STABLE AS THE PEOPLE WHO RUN IT!

NEUTRON TWO IS CRITICAL

A NOVEL BY

Lawrence Dunning

AVON
PUBLISHERS OF BARD, CAMELOT AND DISCUS BOOKS

NEUTRON TWO IS CRITICAL is an original publication
of Avon Books. This work has never before appeared in
book form.

AVON BOOKS
A division of
The Hearst Corporation
959 Eighth Avenue
New York, New York 10019

Copyright © 1977 by Lawrence Dunning
Published by arrangement with the author.
Library of Congress Catalog Card Number: 77-84309
ISBN: 0-380-01775-X

First Avon Printing, October, 1977

AVON TRADEMARK REG. U.S. PAT. OFF. AND IN
OTHER COUNTRIES, MARCA REGISTRADA,
HECHO EN U.S.A.

Printed in the U.S.A.

NEUTRON TWO IS CRITICAL

1

IN THE EXTRAVAGANT leather-bound diary he had bought before leaving New Mexico, Kudirka wrote hurriedly in mathematically straight lines of small, precise script, as if he might not have time to get it all down:

11 August 1954, 0500—Aboard the U.S.S. *Farrell* anchored off Peliea Island. We are standing here on the top deck—the physicists and chemists and electronics people from Los Alamos and, of course, the Navy personnel who transported us to this vast and mostly uninhabited part of the South Pacific—looking like some contingent of Martians in our thick dark goggles. The Director keeps reminding us about the ultraviolet and infrared radiations, as if we were children. And perhaps, in some ways, we are. Though this is my first atomic test shot, it is not the first for many here, yet we all seem tremendously excited and even anxious, as if perhaps someone has miscalculated the effective yield and this ship should be anchored not 7 but 12, or 50, or some undetermined number of nautical miles further away from the dark tower at the western end of the island. Nature rears its head; I have an overpowering need to pass water, yet I dare not leave

7

the railing for so much as a second, for fear I will miss some minute aspect of the shot. I am thankful to have been asked to come along, yet this, too, I fear is a mistake—some not unusual mix-up in the personnel office. My feelings at this moment are unexplainable, a blending of elation and childish anticipation mixed with something darker, a worrisome nagging deep in my being that the event itself—supported by all this technological sorcery—is utterly wrong and wasteful and somehow demeaning to the human spirit. I feel almost disloyal as I write these words, disloyal to the ideals of my adopted country and the many advantages it has offered me, but still I cannot escape my unscientific emotions.

"Well, Andres, any minute now, eh?" one of the technicians standing close by the huge automatic cameras said to him. "What is that, a diary? The Director doesn't like us writing down unofficial things, you know. I suppose he worries about security—but then I suppose I would, too, if I were him."

"Do not concern yourself, Alex, I am no spy," Kudirka said, the inflections of Eastern Europe still easily detectable in his speech. Nevertheless, he put away his pencil and slipped the diary into the pocket of his light jacket. "Let me borrow your binoculars a moment, will you?"

The technician handed over the glasses and Kudirka held them to his eyes, surveying the western tip of the island. There was just now beginning to be enough light to make out the shape of the two-hundred-foot tower —spindly metal legs, on the top end of which sat a jury-rigged ten-foot-square shed with corrugated iron sides and roof and an iron-grating floor. Not a thing of beauty, but it didn't have to be; the only necessity was that it be high enough off the ground to minimize the tendency of the fireball to suck up tons of highly radioactive debris. Various pipes snaked from the bottom of the shed toward instruments that would measure the radiation intensity only milliseconds before the instruments themselves would be vaporized. A simple tower, and because of the electronic communication with the control panels and switches on the ship riding offshore, there were no dangling wires, no visible equipment, really, of any kind. But inside the shed, resting heavily on the iron grating, a wired cylinder waited like an unhatched egg for the proper time to release its unimaginable energy to the atmosphere. Kudirka had seen it there, had been involved in its connections, had in fact had much to do with its very design and construction over many months at the New Mexico laboratories. In a little while this metal child of his brain would give itself up to one voluptuous moment of excess, and then would exist no more.

Kudirka breathed heavily as he swept the glasses over the purplish shapes of the island's trees and rocks and sandy beaches. People had lived here once, had maintained their homes and families and lived out their simple lives on those sandy beaches. Had lived here, some of them, as recently as three days ago, when the last of the holdouts had been forcibly removed to another chain of islands some seventy-five miles to the southwest. Which was worth more, Kudirka wondered, to the orderly continuation of human civilization—the thatched-roof huts and monotonous lives of the simple people who had lived on Peliea, or the hard scientific facts that would shortly be recorded on marvelously sophisticated instruments, the functions of which those transplanted islanders could not even begin to imagine? Which, indeed?

Beside him, the camera technician Alex cursed and

slammed his fist against an electronic box covered with switches and lights. "I'm not getting any juice to number-two sequencer!" he shouted to someone further up the deck. "Jesus Mother of God! If that little pecker doesn't light up in the next thirty seconds we'll have to scrub the shot."

He was joined immediately by two other technicians, who hovered over the control box, clicking switches and alternately cursing and praying as they probed the circuits. A light no larger than a flashlight bulb eventually flickered and apparently decided to stay on. "No sweat," one of the technicians announced, "the sequencer was okay, it was just a faulty connector."

As Kudirka continued his vigil through the binoculars, a brilliant green flare released over the shot tower momentarily blinded him. A great cry went up from everyone on the ship as the loudspeakers crackled into action: "Five-minute warning . . . five-minute warning." He returned the binoculars to Alex, who was now making a last-minute check of the battery of giant cameras aimed toward the island. A tall man in the uniform of a Navy lieutenant commander stopped by and rested his hand briefly on Kudirka's shoulder. "Exciting, isn't it?" he said. "I hope your shot goes well, Mr. Kudirka."

Kudirka smiled. "I thought it might be rather like the old joke about sex."

The officer frowned. "I don't believe I follow you."

"You know—that all shots are good, but some are better than others."

The officer chuckled pleasantly and wandered off toward another group of men hugging the railing. Kudirka glanced at his watch and stared across the patch of water now glowing dully with the first gray-orange indications of sunrise. "He's right, this is exciting," Alex said to him. "I wish my boy could be

10

here to see this—he dreams of becoming an engineer someday. 'Just keep up the math grades,' I tell him. What about you, Andres—do you have any kids who want to be engineers so they can rule the world?"

"No," Kudirka said. "I am still a bachelor, and it looks as if I may remain one all my life."

"Oh, you're still a young man—some fine girl will get you yet, wait and see."

"But I am no longer young, not really," Kudirka said, thinking, Is thirty years of age old? Sometimes he felt ancient, sometimes he thought he must have been old at birth. And yet someone had mentioned to him that he was the youngest member of the task force from Los Alamos on the ship.

A flicker of light from the island caught his eye and then the one-minute red flare burst over the shot tower. "Minus one minute . . . minus fifty-five seconds . . ." the ship's loudspeaker droned. Kudirka moved along the railing to a point where he could watch the shot controller at his panel of lights and switches and meters. At minus forty-five seconds the controller activated the automatic timer that Kudirka knew would rapidly and precisely trigger the circuits on the device atop the tower. At minus thirty seconds a tiny light on a voltmeter winked on, indicating that the firing unit was now fully energized.

"Minus twenty seconds . . . minus fifteen seconds . . . minus ten seconds . . ." The noisy, chattering crowd of scientists and military people whose duties were not directly involved with the firing had by now hushed to the point that Kudirka could hear his own breathing. At minus five seconds the huge automatic sequencing cameras began clicking off shots at the rate of ten thousand every second, recording each separate micro-event of the shot for future study. During the next few seconds Kudirka stared across the water at the island and weighed all the old arguments about whether or not they had any right to be doing what they were doing. He reached no conclusion.

"ZERO!" the loudspeaker boomed. In a purely reflex action Kudirka's knuckles curled around the cold railing of the ship until both hands were white as shrouds.

An incredible intensity of light was the bomb's first impact on Kudirka. In a moment there would be waves and waves of searing heat, followed seconds after by thunderous, tangible sound. But at first there was only the light, like the beginning or the ending of the world. . . .

It began with no more than a brilliant pinpoint that suddenly burst in all directions and poured laterally into a rolling sheet of God's own fire, turning everything visible into a bleached panorama of unbelievable whiteness—the island, the ship, the men clustered no more than a few feet away. Kudirka's brain, like some crazed computer, regurgitated bare facts: temperature at ground zero four times the temperature at the center of the sun, the shot itself equivalent to one hundred thousand tons of TNT.

Initially centered on the flimsy shed suspended two hundred feet above the island, the fireball assumed the shape of a bell as it hurtled downward toward the ground, the edges flattening out and beginning to pick up great quantities of molten earth. Simultaneously, those on the ship were assaulted by the thunder of the mountainous shock wave that came rolling at them across the now pitifully inadequate stretch of water separating the ship from the island. At the perimeter of the huge pinkish-orange fireball, Kudirka thought he could distinguish black spikes that might be parts of the vaporized shot tower. The fireball gathered into its enormous center thousands of tons of boiling sand and dirt and coral, in the process turning deep red and then ominously dark, as if perhaps its gluttony failed to satisfy it. The fireball then shot upward, bursting into new flame at odd moments and places from the incandescent gases at its core, until at forty thousand feet its top flattened and the stalk of radioactive dust trailing down toward the water gave it the look of a malignant mushroom. Surrounded by a purplish halo of ionized air, the deadly cloud began to drift southwestward, away from the ship. That had been planned carefully by batteries of meteorologists. What had not been planned was the awful roar and churning of twenty-foot waves as the entire western end of the island broke off and slid into the sea.

"My *God!*" one of the young sailors said.

Another scientist clapped Kudirka on the back. "Better than we'd hoped for, Andres. It's still an incredible sight, isn't it? This is my third. Jenkins over there was just saying that, according to his calculations, what we've seen this morning was caused by the fissioning of only about a gram of plutonium. Imagine —*one gram!*"

"It is incredible," Kudirka said softly.

The Navy lieutenant commander came by again, arguing with a junior officer. "I *told* Dr. Wilkins, I told *everybody* how stubborn these natives are. Can you imagine such stupidity? From the tribal leaders on down, no one wanted to get off the island, even after we explained what would happen to them if they didn't."

The junior officer shrugged. "I suppose it's hard for the uncivilized mind to grasp such technology."

"Especially," Kudirka cut in, unable to hold back the thoughts that had been troubling him for three days, "especially when they do not speak much

13

English. Civilized or not, these people have no homes now—Peliea is off limits to them, forever."

"That's not the prognosis from our Human Factors people, and you know it," the senior officer said. "In ten years or so—maybe even five—human beings and birds and animals will be able to move back to Peliea and live normal lives, as if we'd never come here today."

Kudirka stared at the man. "Would *you* want to live there?"

The officer snorted. "That's hardly the question, Kudirka." Both officers scornfully dismissed him as another of those lunatic scientists who were always meddling in things that didn't concern them and about which they knew nothing at all—particularly the fine art of handling an alien people.

The camera technician was scouring the coastline of the island with his binoculars. Suddenly he put the glasses away and cocked his head, as if unable to believe his eyes, then raised the glasses again and began pointing and shouting. "God-almighty, there's somebody coming off the island! Look, I'm not crazy . . . two people, two women, and one of them's carrying a baby. God-almighty . . . they're just walking out into the ocean!"

By now everyone who had binoculars was straining to see the impossible sight the technician had described. It was true, there were two women struggling through the boiling surf, the older one desperately clutching a form recognizable as an infant.

"Get the launch going, you men!" the senior officer ordered. He conferred hastily with several of the scientists and a plan was devised to send out two boats, one towing the other at the end of a hundred yards or so of rope. The scientists feared the women's clothing and bodies might be so contaminated with radioactive

14

ash that anyone coming close would suffer radiation poisoning. The women would be towed back to the ship in the second boat; they would somehow have to manage to get *into* the little boat by themselves.

The plan worked. The older of. the two women, and her twenty-year-old daughter and baby son were towed out to the ship, where, after Geiger counters showed that their presence would not contaminate the task force personnel, they were hauled aboard. The baby was dead. The daughter was in shock but otherwise appeared unharmed. The mother was severely burned over most of her body and, screaming in agony, was taken to the ship's infirmary, where she died in horrible pain later that day.

The captain of the ship and his senior officers hastily conferred and decided to take the daughter to the chain of islands where the other former natives of Peliea had been transplanted.

"As I see it, we have very little choice," the captain told the Scientific Director.

"I'll admit our options are limited," the Scientific Director agreed, puffing on his pipe.

"In a way it's too bad she didn't, ah, expire like the old woman and the child," the captain continued. "The other natives are a superstitious lot. When they find out she was on Peliea when it blew and somehow lived through all that, they'll probably stone her to death as a witch."

"And if she lives she'll talk," the Scientific Director said, "and there's always a chance word will eventually get back to the mainland about what happened to her family. A mistake like that on our record could close down our operations for years. I wonder . . ."

"Yes?"

"You realize I'm just thinking aloud now—noodling the X factors, as we sometimes say back at Los Alamos.

15

Do you think your ship's doctor could be convinced to give her a shot of something that would solve our problem permanently? Something quiet and painless, of course."

"Of course," the captain said. "It's a feasible plan, except Doc is one of those ethical old bastards you're always reading about in *Reader's Digest*. I don't think there's any way you could get him to do that—not even if I threatened to court-martial him."

It was Kudirka who finally solved their dilemma. He had been one of the first to help the women aboard the ship, even before the Geiger counter readings were completed. The girl was frightened out of her mind, he could see that, and he could also see immediately that there was nothing anyone could do for the baby or the older woman. He had held the girl's trembling hand tightly in his own, and on the way down to the infirmary had used all the soothing phrases he could think of, speaking by turns in French, Lithuanian, Polish, and finally, with success, in English. After arriving at the medical facility, he stayed wth her and consoled her as best he could. This pathetic situation seemed to sum up all the things about the bomb test that had made him so uneasy the entire trip. He felt a kind of personal obligation to the one survivor who might be able to use his help, and would not leave the girl alone for a minute.

When he finally came up on deck to report that she was sleeping soundly and peacefully, everyone—particularly the captain and the Director—wanted to know if she had said anything that he could understand. And Kudirka reported that she had. Her name was Mariko; her father had been Japanese, her mother Micronesian. She had not been killed by the thing that glowed like the sun because she had been hiding in a deep trench at the opposite end of the island, protected by many yards of earth. Her father, mother, and baby brother had not been so lucky—whether they had ventured out of hiding at exactly the wrong time or what, Kudirka was not sure. The girl did not want to be taken to where the other islanders had been transplanted because she feared what they would think and what they would do to her.

Kudirka patiently reported all this information, then threw in his own complication: he had promised to take her back to the mainland with him. "I will assume full responsibility for my actions," he told them, seeing their incredulous expressions. "But if you make trouble about this I assure you I will go straight to the press and explain to them how we Americans murder innocent islanders with our bombs."

There was a hurried consultation among his superiors and the ship's officers. "Something of a *quid pro quo* might be in order here, Andres," the Director finally said in a conciliatory tone. "We won't tell if you won't, and if you guarantee that *she* won't. What I mean is, as the good doctor here has just pointed out to me, we might very well want to observe this young lady over a period of years, study the effects of the bomb on her body, et cetera, since she was inadvertently caught in this unique position. And although she survived, at least has until now, she obviously took a normally lethal dose of radiation. It would be useful to have her near at hand for this continuing study."

The Director puffed thoughtfully at his pipe. "On the other side of the coin, I have a certain influence in scientific circles, as I'm sure you're aware. It would not be at all difficult to arrange things so that you would never be offered a decent job again, anywhere, under any circumstances. If you wish to consider this blackmail, you're probably right to do so. But another way to look at it is that we're offering you a chance

17

to save both your own life and that of the girl. In any case, Andres, you're a splendid physicist and engineer and Los Alamos can ill afford to lose you."

The captain nodded his head in agreement, and Kudirka thought, They make a lovely pair.

"All we're asking, really," the Director concluded, "is that you have a slight case of specific but permanent amnesia. Do you think you can manage that, Andres?"

Kudirka thought of the girl Mariko lying below on a white cot, and remembered with what horror he had helped her mother onto the ship and seen at close range the awful bubbles of her charred skin. There was nothing he could do now for the dead members of Mariko's family—not by going to the newspapers, not by shouting from rooftops, nothing. But something burned inside him just the same.

"Yes, all right," he told them finally, "as long as you know my true feelings about this, as long as you realize how it disgusts me."

The Director smiled. "I'm glad you've decided to be sensible, Andres. I really am."

The angry sea was still roiling with its deadly new cargo of radioactive coral when the ship eventually pulled away from what remained of the island of Peliea and headed for home, its mission entirely successful.

2

IN MIDAFTERNOON Yale Pollack gathered up the documents strewn about his untidy desk, stuffed them hurriedly into a manila folder, and walked down the main hallway to his division chief's office. His lanky frame bounced easily on the balls of his feet as he walked with the agility of a man who, twenty years earlier, in the mid-1950s, had played passable singles in the all-Army tennis tournament in Seoul. Now, if someone had bothered to ask him, he wouldn't be able to remember the last time he had played tennis or any other game. He was not, as his superiors sometimes liked to remind him, a game player.

He stopped before a heavy, solid wood door and knocked twice, producing a satisfying thud that Reitzman had no doubt specifically ordered to give the casual visitor an image of rock-hardness and impregnability. In contrast, rather ornate gold lettering spelled out the name and the occupant's organization: SIMON REITZMAN, INDUSTRIAL BACKGROUND INVESTIGATIONS DIVISION (IBID). How like me, Pollack thought idly as he waited with folder in hand, to have ended up in an organization whose acronym means 'do it over again.'

"Come in," Reitzman called out from behind the door, and Pollack, never knowing what to expect from the man, entered carefully. The room always impressed him as somewhat spectacular for a government office, certainly one as circumspect as the National Security Service. One entire wall, eight by seventeen feet, was covered with a stark black-and-white abstract collage involving soaring curves and abrupt parallelograms. Pollack had been in the room perhaps a dozen times before it struck him: the irregular blobs of acrylic and painted burlap were in reality intricate repetitions of the letters S and R, standing of course for Simon Reitzman. He and the decorator must have been great friends.

"What is it, Pollack? I'm busy as hell and I've a visitor coming at three," Reitzman said, pushing his chrome aviator glasses up on top of his long, carefully styled dyed black hair and leaning back irritably in the leather executive chair. He stared at Pollack without smiling and slowly crossed one seventy-dollar shoe over the other on top of the polished teak desk. "How are you progressing on that Congressional inquiry, by the way?"

"Oh, it's done—Maryanne's typing it, or was before lunch. Simon, I've run into something else that I thought you might be interested in."

Reitzman swiveled slightly and raised an eyebrow as if to say that would be a novelty.

"Anyway," Pollack continued, "at first I thought it was just a routine five-year updating of a nuclear plant operating engineer's license—you know, those A.D.A. things."

Reitzman nodded, his handsome, lined face as deeply tanned now, in October, as it ever was in July. "The Atomic Development Agency usually means trouble, one way or another. Go ahead."

Pollack opened the folder and glanced at a neatly typed background sheet. "He's an engineer, physicist, all-round scientific fellow, apparently. Name's Andres Kudirka—a Lithuanian." Pollack glanced up at Reitzman to see whether there was any readable expression on his face, but of course there wasn't; Simon Reitzman almost never showed any normal human emotional reactions to anything. "Born 1924 in Vilna; son of a language professor at the university there. Had one sister who was killed during the German occupation in 1942. Persecuted because there was a question about whether his maternal grandmother was part Jewish. He and his mother and father escaped to Sweden, where he attended the University of Uppsala and apparently first became interested in the study of atomic physics."

Reitzman played with a small black-and-gold replica of a samurai sword he kept on his desk to open letters and, occasionally, to clean his perfectly clipped and polished nails. "Sounds ordinary to me, Pollack. The same background could go for half the atomic scientists in this country."

"But there's more," Pollack continued. "Kudirka came to the U.S. and went to the University of Chicago in 1944 and '45—he seems to have haunted the abandoned squash court under Stagg Field where Fermi achieved the first sustained nuclear fission chain reaction back in 1942. Through his contacts with the University of Chicago physicists—who, incidentally, thought him brilliant in certain conceptual areas—he moved to Los Alamos in 1945 to work on the tag end of the Manhattan Project. This was about two months before Hiroshima—Kudirka was only twenty-one when Hiroshima and Nagasaki were destroyed. While he was at Los Alamos he got to be known as something of a brooding loner, kept pretty much to himself most of the time, but was considered by his superiors to be a technical expert in the nuclear weapons design field. In 1954 he was part of a task force that went out to Micronesia to test a new bomb he had designed.

Worked for A.D.A. at Los Alamos until 1965, then took a post as associate professor in the nuclear engineering department at Stanford. He stayed there five years, then in 1970 left to travel and lecture on neutron bombardment and particle physics at various colleges across the country. But the record's cloudy from then on. There's not much else, except that whoever did this initial background investigation somehow found out that Kudirka likes straight Polish vodka, no ice, and that at Los Alamos he was several times known to have drunk ethyl alcohol from the laboratory stock, mostly as a joke."

Reitzman studied the tiny dagger in his hand. "And what's Mr. Kudirka's present position?"

"He's the chief operating engineer at that new nuclear power plant north of Denver—the one Rocky Mountain Power Company runs for A.D.A. They call it an L.M.F.B.R., whatever that is."

"Liquid-metal fast breeder reactor," Reitzman said automatically, and Pollack had occasion to marvel again at the thousands of discrete facts the man could recall instantly.

Reitzman got up from the desk and went over to the ten-cubic-foot aquarium which was his special prize. It was said by office gossips that the aquarium was fitted with every fish-keeping device known to man, including elaborate electric, gas, and filtration controls to ensure unvarying temperature, lighting, oxygen content, and laboratory purity of the water. Reitzman's special pets were a half-dozen ugly piranhas that he pampered like babies. He stood by the tank watching for a minute, then reached into a small cooler nearby and took out a handful of raw hamburger which he began to feed the razor-toothed little creatures bit by bit, lovingly, from his fingertips. He seemed to enjoy the way they tore the meat to shreds before devouring it, just as they would have torn his fingers to shreds if he had failed to move them quickly enough. It was a kind of game with him, to which the obvious danger seemed to add the necessary spice.

"Pollack, I really don't see what you're upset about," he said. "It seems like a perfectly straightforward dossier to me; you must have seen hundreds like it since you've worked for us."

"Not exactly," Pollack said. "For one thing, as I told you, this is a five-year renewal of his operator's license. But there's no record here of anyone issuing the *first* license—the one A.D.A.'s supposed to be renewing. There's not even a record of where he might have picked up what I imagine is rather specialized knowledge of how to run something as complex as a nuclear reactor. I suppose he might have done similar research work at Los Alamos, in between working on the bombs, but there's no mention of it. There are just too many holes, Simon. I have a distinct feeling there's something funny about Kudirka."

Reitzman shook his head. "Witches under the bed again, Pollack? You know as well as I do there's something 'funny' about nearly everyone these days—judges, for instance, who give proven long-haired criminals a pat on the back and expense money back to college, women who let their dugs hang out like so many cattle and picket West Point to be allowed to carry sabers into combat. . . . Of course I realize the media are mostly to blame for the screwing up of sexual roles, and even when Hollywood or the networks occasionally try to straighten things out the critics destroy them."

Pollack smiled; this was Reitzman's old bugaboo. "You mean there aren't enough Clint Eastwood and Charles Bronson movies, where the hero wins because he spills the most blood and smiles while he's doing it?"

"Don't scoff at things you don't understand. It isn't becoming."

"All right, Simon. I still say there are big gaps in Kudirka's employment record that I can't explain, and I don't like it."

"Then check it out with A.D.A., like any investigator who's worth having would do. Use your head, man—you don't need my permission for that, even though my own opinion at this point is that it will simply be a waste of time."

"Maybe, maybe not. There's something else strange about Kudirka that I didn't mention before. He's married, has a foreign-born wife, but there are no immigration papers that I can find."

"Well, good Lord, Pollack, that's Immigration and Naturalization's worry, not mine! What are we paying you for, anyway? Listen, I have a budget meeting later this afternoon, and I fully expect to be told that Congress is making noises about cutting our manpower allocations again. I needn't remind you that your last efficiency rating wasn't all it might have been. If you'd like to keep your job I suggest you get busy on that towering backlog of cases we have to dispose of before the next fiscal quarter."

"The hunger motive," Pollack said quietly. "There's just one more thing: I'd like to check with the Office of Naval Intelligence in the Pentagon. They were involved in those South Pacific atomic shots and might very well have a file on Kudirka."

"Then by all means do so, Pollack, do so."

Pollack nodded. "I'll need a D.O.D. bus pass."

Not even trying to conceal his exasperation, Reitzman opened a drawer in his desk and took out a pad of printed blue passes. He scribbled his name on one and handed it to Pollack with obvious distaste. "Try not to get lost," he said as Pollack was leaving the room.

Pollack walked two blocks to the bus stop and waited for the special Department of Defense bus that carried people authorized by the little blue D.O.D. passes into the tunnels under the Pentagon. On the way over he reviewed his discussion with Reitzman and decided he probably hadn't won any points or lost any, either. No matter what he did, Reitzman was never going to like him very much, which made his career with N.S.S. rather tenuous and less than a barrel of laughs.

When the bus stopped Pollack hurried out and up the stairs to the main concourse, past the bank and the candy shop and the flower shop and the ticket agency, to the information booth, where a pleasant but harried young woman listened with one ear to his request for directions and handed him a little white map of the building on which she had marked the path to his destination with a red felt pen. He went to the bottom of the ramp, where he had to show his National Security Service identification to a bored guard—something new since that unidentified idiot had blown up a rest room. Then he took the stairs to the fifth floor, after only two wrong turns found the proper corridor, went to the C ring, turned left, and at room 1103 saw a small sign with the initials "O.N.I." tacked to the door. Inside, a Navy officer in civilian clothes asked if he could help him.

"I'd like to see your file on Andres Kudirka, if it's not too much trouble," Pollack said pleasantly. "He's a nuclear scientist, naturalized citizen of the U.S., born in Lithuania. I need some information about his wife and I rather imagine your files could help me." As he talked he pulled his ID card from his wallet and laid it on the counter between them.

The young officer picked up the card, checked the picture, and looked at Pollack to see that they matched. "N.S.S.," he said, as if it were something new to him and not nearly as interesting as such other ingredients in the bureaucratic alphabet soup as C.I.A., F.B.I., and even D.I.A. "We haven't seen many of you fellows over here," he said.

"That's good," Pollack said. "Proves how sneaky we are."

Looking pained, the officer went to a bank of file drawers in an alcove behind some desks. He manipulated the combination lock until the drawer opened, and after searching through a number of folders pulled one partway out of the drawer. A bright-red vinyl strip was pasted along one edge of the folder. Fingering the red marker, the officer looked over his shoulder at Pollack and immediately disappeared into another room, taking the folder and Pollack's ID card with him.

Pollack leaned against the desk and stared around him at the drab, infinitely depressing surroundings. He knew people who had worked at the Pentagon for years and never gotten used to the absence of windows in most offices, the dull uniformity of the walls and floors and ceilings and furniture that reminded Pollack of etchings of nineteenth-century slave-labor factories he had seen at the National Museum. He also knew people who thought the Pentagon must be a fascinating place to work, but these without exception were people who had never been inside it. Maybe it had something to do with his own antiregimentation sentiments, Pollack thought, or, even more likely, the terrible months he had spent in the Army. The only thing he had ever found even remotely pleasing about the Pentagon was the small parklike grass courtyard in the middle of A ring where, sometimes at lunchtime in the summer, a band played in a terribly out of place red-and-white gazebo.

Pollack heard snatches of conversation from the room where the officer had gone. "The hell with that!" a voice said angrily. "Tell him to get lost."

The officer reappeared shortly. "I'm sorry, sir, but I'm afraid there's nothing in our files that would be of any interest to you."

"Well, now," Pollack said, "why don't you let me be the judge of that?"

"I'm sorry, those are my orders," the officer said brusquely, handing Pollack's ID card back to him. "In any case, you're not even D.O.D."

"Is that something like not having clearance from God?" Pollack said. "Thanks for nothing." He stalked out of the room, leaving the officer standing there holding the file folder with the red vinyl special precautions tag next to Andres Kudirka's name.

3

THE GIRL COULD NOT have been more than twenty-two years old. Small, articulate, beautifully dressed in a green pantsuit and red scarf and looking like a sexy Christmas tree under the bright halo of her shag-cut blonde hair, she might have been a model for any of the young women's magazines on the newsstands. Sometimes Kudirka wondered why she wasn't, with her obvious combination of beauty, poise, and vivaciousness; the public relations department of the Rocky Mountain Power Company must pay better than one would imagine.

"Kids today," Smitty, the reactor control engineer on duty, said to Kudirka. "They can't be more than fourteen or fifteen years old but look at the guys, will you? They're creaming in their jeans over Miss Hotpants."

The girl was leading a group of thirty junior high school students and their middle-aged male science teacher to the security desk, where the uniformed guard made a production of having each of them sign into the plant. "That special passageway we just came through from outside—the one with the two thick doors—is called an air lock," the girl explained. "There's never a direct opening to the outside, and although you can't see them, special filters scrubbed all of us as we walked through the passageway. The purpose of the air lock is so that no tiny particles of any kind can enter or leave the plant unless we want them to."

"You mean radioactive particles?" a girl asked.

"Yes, that's possible, but of course we have other instruments all through the plant to detect any loose particles floating around. We're very clean here—so clean, in fact, that as soon as you've signed in and have your visitor badges pinned on I'm going to take you right over there to that supply room where we'll all get our own white cotton shoe covers. That's one of our rules here—you have to wear shoe covers whenever you walk around in the plant."

"Stupid rule," Kudirka said, looking down at his own shoe covers as the entire group marched over to the supply room. "If they're going to cover anything I would suggest that it be their hands. Children are much more likely to go poking into things with their fingers instead of their toes."

"It's mostly for show anyway," Smitty said. "Just another gimmick the P.R. people thought up to show how careful and safe we are around here."

Kudirka scratched at the shaggy gray hairs of his beard and sighed wearily. "I wonder how long it will be before we no longer feel we must lie to the public about everything."

Smitty shook his head. "Don't forget, old buddy, Rocky Mountain Power has a couple of bucks tied up in this place—they need public support."

The tour guide had put on her own shoe covers, which made her look somewhat ridiculous, as if she were dressed to appear in a school play about floppy, cuddly rabbits. "While the rest of you are getting set I'll tell you something about what we're going to see today," she said cheerfully. "The plant is called the Handley Pond Nuclear Generating Station. That's a long name, and some of the engineers who work here have another name for it—Neutron Two. Do you all know what a neutron is? It's one of the elementary particles in the center of an atom, and it carries no electrical charge. You can remember that a *neutron* is *neutral*. Your teacher probably told you that Handley Pond is the first full-scale commercial breeder-reactor power plant in the United States, and we're *very* proud of it. Actually it's an L.M.F.B.R.—that means 'liquid-metal fast breeder reactor.' The liquid metal we use here to cool the reactor is sodium."

"I thought sodium was like, you know, salt," a tall red-haired boy said.

The P.R. girl smiled. "That's sodium in combination with chlorine. Pure sodium is a metal, and it's a bad actor—it reacts violently with air and water and some other things, which is why we have to be very careful how we put it into the reactor and take it out again."

"Why don't you use something safer?" someone asked.

"Because sodium carries away heat much better than other things—like water, for instance. And we need to carry away the heat generated by the reactor as quickly as possible. You see, that's what makes a nuclear power plant—or *any* power plant, for that matter—work to bring us electricity. In the old-fashioned kind of plant we burn coal to heat up a lot of pipes full of water, and the water gets so hot that it turns to steam. The steam shoots out of nozzles against the blades of a giant turbine generator, sort of like the pinwheels you used to spin by blowing on them when you were little kids. The generators turn very fast and make electricity, and lots of wires carry the electricity to your house and mine. Now, a nuclear power plant is really exactly the same thing, but instead of using coal to heat water to make steam to run the

30

electricity generators, we use the heat from a controlled nuclear-fission reaction inside the core of the reactor. The reactor heats the sodium, and that heats the water to make steam to run the generators. You see how simple it is?"

She looked at the bright faces of the group for some kind of reaction but there was none. In fact, a good many of the children were paying no attention to her at all, but instead were clomping around in their shoe covers pretending to be spacemen or perhaps mummies recently escaped from some ancient tomb. "That boy, the short one with the heavy glasses," Kudirka said, watching. "He has a question he wants to ask her, and it is killing him until he can ask it. I imagine it is a good one, too, if only that fuzzy-brained whore would pay attention to the people she's supposed to be educating. Did you hear that abominable over-simplification she was feeding them, about how there is no essential difference between Neutron Two and a coal-fired plant? My God, she ought to be strangled!"

"Take it easy, Andres," Smitty said. "Remember, you leave the tours to them and they in turn leave the engineering to us."

"I know, I know. That is decent of them, isn't it?"

The teacher smiled at the P.R. girl. "Miss, could you tell us something about—hey, knock it off, you kids, and try to learn something!—about what goes on inside the reactor?"

"Certainly," she said, smiling in the professionally cheerful way she must have been taught by the public relations director. "There are about two tons of uranium and plutonium inside the reactor vessel, which is made of prestressed concrete five feet thick lined with steel. The control engineer first lowers the twelve hundred and fifty-two fuel pins into the reactor and then slowly raises some of the forty-eight control rods—these are made out of a substance called boron carbide that soaks up neutrons and can stop the reaction completely. When the fuel rods and the control rods balance properly, the plutonium starts to fission in a chain reaction. The neutrons jump around into the uranium 238 that's wrapped around the plutonium like a blanket, and then the *uranium* starts to fission, and do you know what happens to the uranium? It breaks down into plutonium again, which makes more fuel to keep the chain reaction going and have some left over. Those two men you see sitting at the control panels over there," she said, pointing to Kudirka and Smitty, "can push the right buttons and pull the right handles to make the control rods do exactly what they want them to."

Smiling cynically to himself, Kudirka fingered one of the control levers that, pulled back slightly, would raise a control rod by hydraulic machinery ten stories above where they were sitting and set in motion a nuclear excursion, the dreaded runaway nuclear fire deep in the bowels of the reactor. He actually pulled the lever back a fraction of an inch, watching a needle on one of the dials on the panel in front of him begin to climb slowly toward a red line.

"For God's sake, Andres, what the hell are you doing?" Smitty yelled as he too saw the needle advancing toward the danger area. He grabbed automatically for a duplicate control lever on his side of the panel, but by then Kudirka had reset the control and the needle began to drop to its former position.

"Your nerves are not very good today, Smitty," Kudirka said, laughing a little. "You know the reactor and everything else would shut down automatically before anything dangerous could happen. Anyway, my habits are so strong and deep that even if I *wanted* to cause an accident my reflex action would no doubt

32

cause me to grab the scram handle. I expect I can beat the automatic system, if you'd care to gamble."

"Jesus, man, you're crazy to pull stuff like that. You want to get us both canned?"

"No," Kudirka said, thinking about what that might involve. Glancing at Smitty, who was again concentrating on the lights and dials of the huge, complex control panel, Kudirka reached into his pocket for two amphetamine capsules and a small bottle of liquid he had secreted there earlier. Tossing back the shock of unkempt gray hair that perched uneasily atop his largish head, he swallowed the capsules quickly and washed them down with two gulps of raw ethyl alcohol that he had taken from the plant maintenance shed. The alcohol, roughly 198 proof, burned his throat and momentarily brought tears to his eyes until its soothing warmth spread through his blood. The combination of alcohol and amphetamines would no doubt eventually kill him, slowly, by degrees, but that no longer mattered.

It had been a real temptation and not just a dangerous joke when he had raised the control rod just now. Tempting, to see the excitement it would cause; more than once he had thought it was probably the only way to get their attention and perhaps stop this mad rushing toward larger and more deadly nuclear power plants, particularly the breeders, the most deadly of them all. Someone had estimated that there might be as many as four hundred of them in operation by the year 2000. Of course he wouldn't be around to see them, and that was all right, too. There had been a time, back in his student days at Chicago, when he thought it would be marvelous to live into a new century, but now he realized that January 1 of the year 2000 would be just another Tuesday or Wednesday and no different, really, from the day before.

33

No, he thought, Andres Kudirka will not even be a memory when that great day arrives.

The tour guide had arranged the children into a manageable group and had moved into the center of the open space beside the control panels. "Now, for your notebooks," she said, "I can give you some figures that probably won't mean very much to you. For instance, this plant is more than ten stories high, took six and a half years to build, and cost one point eight billion dollars. Its reactor was initially fired up in April of 1974, and was designed to have an optimum output of one million five hundred thousand kilowatts of electricity. The plant is shut down periodically for maintenance, and then the electrical output has to be shunted to some other plant. As a matter of fact, the Handley Pond plant is due for a two-week maintenance shutdown period in a few days, so you kids got here just in time."

Kudirka shifted his bulk uncomfortably at the control panel and listened to the girl raving on like a lunatic about things she didn't even begin to understand. The only thing she had said so far that made any sense was that the plant would be shut down for a while, and then she had given the wrong reason. Normal shutdown inspection wouldn't have been for another six months, but he and some of the other engineers had discovered several cracks in the outer casing of the supposedly impregnable reactor wall, and now they would have to shut down and decide what to do. The power company would no doubt vote for something cosmetic. And above all, secrecy. Hairline cracks could become large gradually, though they might not grow visibly until someday the whole plant blew apart. But Kudirka was glad for the break in routine; he needed the rest badly, although they were still likely to be calling him out here every other day.

But at least there would be no night work—that had already been decided by management, who claimed they could not afford the overtime.

Kudirka was tired all the time these days—and bored to distraction. He was miserable sitting inside these windowless walls day after day, knowing that outside, no more than twenty-five feet away, there was a beautiful October day and country air filled with migrating birds, colorful blowing leaves, and the delicious hazy smell of autumn. Also, he thought, frowning, perhaps there were a few particles of plutonium—say, one ten-thousandth of an inch in diameter or so—that might or might not be detected by the perimeter air-filter monitors but in any case would never be reported, not even to the Atomic Development Agency. One of these undetected particles would eventually come to rest on a grassy knoll, and a cow would eat the grass, and a human being would eat the cow *and* the particle, which would lodge somewhere in the human's body and wait silently, almost dormant, for ten or twenty or thirty years before blossoming forth as a deadly carcinoma. The particle had all the time in the world; the radioactive half-life of plutonium—the time needed for it to decay to half its initial potency—was 24,360 years.

"As you can see," the P.R. girl was saying, "I carry in my pocket this little tubular instrument called a dosimeter, which measures any tiny bit of radiation that might be present anywhere in the plant. Now, this is nothing to worry about—as most of you know, we encounter radiation every day of our lives. Why, even our own sun gives off radiation, and those of you who have watches with dials that glow in the dark are able to see the dial because of radiation. So, I repeat, radiation is nothing to fear if you understand it. Handley Pond was built to be as safe as any plant possibly could be, but if anything should ever go wrong with the equipment or the reactor, why, we have all kinds of Geiger counters and sensors and gauges all through the plant that would automatically shut down the reactor in seconds. And of course our control engineers are always on hand, too, and they know just what to do to take care of all this equipment. All operating engineers must be licensed by A.D.A.—that's the Atomic Development Agency—and their licenses must be reviewed and renewed at least every five years."

The short boy with the heavy glasses could stand it no longer, he had to ask his question. "Ma'am," he fairly shouted, "I wanted to ask you—could this plant ever explode like an atom bomb and kill everybody in Denver? I mean, it's only twelve miles away, and my mom is kind of scared about it."

The P.R. girl's nearly permanent smile faded slightly. "Your mother's being foolish," she told the boy. "No, absolutely not—there's no way this plant or *any* nuclear plant could ever explode like a bomb. Now come along—we're all going way up there, ten stories up, so you can see how the very top of the reactor controls look. Stay all together, won't you? And don't anybody trip and fall down."

As the group began to disappear up the first set of white iron stairs Kudirka felt his head spinning. He caught it in both hands and closed his eyes, praying that the dizziness would stop. But still there was the buzzing in his ears, like millions of angry hornets, and the dreams, the waking nightmares, returned . . .

The structure was on the side of a mountain where the pine trees were thick and their needles carpeted the earth, and the smell was enough to make a man's senses reel in ecstasy. One day the earth trembled and the structure rocked and three people died, and a dog, and no one mourned their death. He had seen ten thousand suns rupture in the awful splendor of a South Pacific dawn, and people had been killed, needlessly, and it was not his fault; but the other thing, unplanned, was horrible, and not splendid at all . . .

"Kudirka!"

He realized the security guard was calling him from the desk in the foyer. "There's a call for you, from your wife. Line six. You want to take it here?"

Frowning because Mariko never called him at the plant, Kudirka went out to the security desk and took the receiver from the guard. "Hello?" he said cautiously, instinctively moving out of the guard's hearing range.

"I am very sorry to bother you at work, Andres. However, there is something I believe you should know. A man has been here, asking personal questions about you and your work. He wanted to know about me, also; I did not know what you wished me to tell him, and so I told him nothing. Was I correct?"

Kudirka's mind raced over the possibilities. "Yes, Mariko, you did exactly the right thing. I will be home very soon and we will discuss this further. Do not worry."

He put the telephone down and glanced at the guard, who was filling out some papers at his desk. Kudirka continued to stand with his hand on the cradled receiver for a moment or two, trying to think who could possibly be asking questions about his past, but there was no one, absolutely no one who should be at all interested. His hands began to tremble uncontrollably as the nightmare thoughts returned.

4

AT HIS DESK in the office on M Street, Pollack dialed the number of Dr. J. Welles, head of the Industrial Liaison Office at A.D.A. headquarters in suburban Maryland. One thing he had learned in eleven years with the National Security Service, and before that with the Army, was that if you were in a hurry and, without much agency authority, needed information or action the day before yesterday, you don't go straight to the head of an organization but a level or two below him, where all the work was done and most of the important decisions made. Sometimes this was dangerous but it usually worked. In this case, Dr. J. Welles was the functional division chief, on a level comparable to Pollack's own division chief, Simon Reitzman. Welles was definitely the man to contact.

The number rang twice and was answered by a stiff secretarial voice that announced the caller had reached the Atomic Development Agency, office of Dr. J. Welles, and could she be of any service?

Pollack laughed at the precision in her voice. "Yes, you can," he said. "My name is Yale Pollack. I'm with the National Security Service, and I'd like to talk with Dr. Welles, if I may."

"National Security?" the secretary repeated. "Sir, is this a secure communications line? Is your handset equipped with an electronic scrambler at your end?"

Pollack laughed again, though he sensed it wouldn't win him any points. "No . . . no scrambler here. Actually, I'm not a spy, I only do background investigations. Now, if I could just speak with Dr. Welles—"

The secretary cut him off. "I'm sorry, sir, but our rules on that are very strict. If you wish to speak to Dr. Welles about any security matter you'll have to come to the Maryland office in person, any day between eight and four. Thank you, sir." She hung up.

Muttering under his breath as if he didn't run into the same senseless bureaucratic revolving door twenty times a day, Pollack checked a District of Columbia bus schedule for the next express to the Maryland suburbs southeast of the city. Even if he ran all the way to the bus stop he would barely have time to make the next bus. D.C. bus service was good—very good for a city of its size and complexity—but runs to the outlying suburbs weren't all that frequent or reliable. With the briefcase containing the file on Andres Kudirka tucked under his arm, Pollack jogged down the street, thankful that N.S.S. kept its people in good physical condition—occasionally by workouts in the basement gym at the headquarters building, but more often by forcing its agents to run all over the district vainly trying to flag down buses that had no intention of stopping.

There were few people on the bus at this hour and the ride went faster than he had expected. Within forty-five minutes he was deposited in front of a complex of long, low buildings that stretched at various angles toward infinity. Within another thirty minutes he had located, quite by accident, Dr. Welles' office. The outer-office secretary was unquestionably the one he had spoken to earlier on the telephone; it seemed entirely typical that after he had given her his name and affiliation she showed no sign that she had ever heard of him *or* N.S.S.

"Dr. Welles is busy at the moment," she said without interest. "Would you care to wait?"

She was beginning to make him tired. "No," he said, "I like riding buses all over hell's half-acre . . . it's sort of a hobby of mine, puts me in touch with the common people."

"As you wish, sir," the secretary said, simultaneously pushing an obscure button on a small metal box occupying one corner of her desk. A tiny red neon light came on beside the button, and Pollack wondered with more curiosity than alarm if this were some kind of warning signal or if, perhaps, all sound in the reception room was now being monitored elsewhere.

The secretary ignored him and Pollack studied his surroundings—a habit of his that had once or twice helped to extricate him from very sticky circumstances. But the characterless room gave up no information about itself or its occupants. The only item of any real interest was the box on the secretary's desk and an interior door marked DR. J. WELLES.

Thinking to undo his roughness, Pollack smiled at the secretary. "What's the J. stand for?" He nodded toward the door.

"I don't know," the secretary said, obviously not much interested in his question.

"You mean you prefer not to tell me."

"I mean exactly what I said, sir. No one here knows what the J. in Dr. Welles' name stands for. Why don't you ask Dr. Welles yourself?"

"I certainly will," Pollack said, knowing that would be absolutely the worst thing he could do, given Welles' obvious sensitivity about it. He amused himself for the next fifteen minutes thinking up oddball names that began with J.—Jacobus, Jobadiah, Jip, Jingo. The list was endless. Growing tired of that game, he stared for a while at the wall behind him, on which was a poster showing some kind of industrial plant surrounded by lush fields of green grass and grazing cattle and a small boy fishing from a clearly inviting pond. The lettering on the poster read: "This is a breeder-reactor facility. It is just as clean as it looks, and fits quite nicely into its environment. With this kind of generating plant you can start with two pounds of plutonium fuel, use two pounds, and still *have* two pounds—truly a modern engineering miracle." The boy fishing in the pond was wearing a straw hat and a broad smile.

"Dr. Welles will see you now," the secretary said.

Pollack entered the inner office and closed the door behind him. The woman standing behind the open chrome-and-glass desk was short, somewhat stooped, with close-cropped iron-gray hair and heavy steel-rimmed glasses. She extended her hand to Pollack without smiling, and said, "I'm Dr. Welles. Please sit down."

Pollack shook her hand and sat in the chair that had been placed in front of the desk, directly across from Dr. Welles. She sat and stared at him intently a few moments without speaking and he, in turn, stared back, taking in the shapeless brown sweater and wool skirt and, beneath the desk, the gray cotton stockings and brown oxfords that he imagined, from the look of things, she probably wore day in and day out.

"You're Mr. Pollack—one of Reitzman's bright young men," Dr. Welles said.

It wasn't a question but some sort of reply seemed called for. "Not that young, I'm afraid," he said politely, "and not always that bright."

"What exactly can I do for you, Mr. Pollack?"

Pollack opened his briefcase on his lap and extracted

41

a sheaf of papers, which he riffled through but didn't look at because he knew their contents by heart. "I'm looking for a few missing pieces of background information on one of your former Los Alamos scientists —Andres Kudirka. I believe he's now the chief engineer at the nuclear reactor plant near Denver."

Dr. Welles frowned at mention of Kudirka's name. "Kudirka . . . yes, I place him now. Lithuanian, originally—came over to give us a leg up on the Manhattan Project back in the 'forties, I understand. Of course, I wasn't here at the time. We've all come from somewhere else."

"You're British, aren't you?" Pollack said. "One of the brains that drained from Harwell Laboratory in the 'fifties."

Dr. Welles almost permitted herself to smile. "You must have been reading that old *Time* magazine article."

"But Kudirka does work for you now?" Pollack persisted.

Dr. Welles adjusted the steel glasses upward on her nose. "Mr. Kudirka is an employee of the Rocky Mountain Power Company. Since the Handley Pond facility north of Denver is the first liquid-metal fast breeder reactor plant in this country, we naturally have a great interest in its operation. And since Mr. Kudirka is the chief engineer of that facility, we do have a certain connection with his work. I assume, Mr. Pollack, that you've been steered onto this as a result of the standard request for renewal of Mr. Kudirka's nuclear operating license, or something of the sort."

"That's exactly right, Dr. Welles. But there seem to be gaps—nothing specific, and probably they're simply gaps in our information processing rather than anything mystifying about the man himself, but still you understand we have to check. Do you, for instance, know anything at all about his wife?"

"Nothing. You could talk with R.M.P.C. about that."

"Rocky Mountain Power Company? Yes, thank you, I'll do that. The thing that bothers me most of all, though, is that I don't find anywhere in his file that Andres Kudirka went through any sort of training or apprenticeship for the kind of work he's apparently doing now. Why is that, do you suppose?"

"Mr. Pollack," Dr. Welles said, letting out a sigh of exasperation directed, Pollack guessed, at the entire nonscientific world. "You do not ask a scientist, an engineer of Mr. Kudirka's obviously superior qualifications, to serve an apprenticeship like some common tradesman. He was at Los Alamos for twenty years, very well thought of in the nuclear weapons design group. He had access to a great deal of technical information and practical hands-on experience during that time in all sorts of fields allied with producing power from atomic fission. His main concern, naturally, was bomb power, but the underlying principles are the same in any case. I can't think of a better man to have running our Handley Pond plant."

Something about Dr. Welles' statement rang false to Pollack. "What happened to Kudirka between Los Alamos and Handley Pond?" he asked her. "Our records on him during that period are skimpy in the extreme."

Dr. Welles' thin lips drew into a smile. "I should have thought Simon Reitzman's people would have been more efficient than that. However . . . I'm afraid I can't help you much there. Kudirka left Los Alamos to lecture at several American universities—there again you could check the specifics with R.M.P.C. in Denver. I believe he worked for a time in private industry as a consultant on nuclear fracturing of ore-bearing rock for Columbine Mining and Smelting. He traveled extensively—exactly where I'm not at all sure since he rarely made it a habit to send us picture postal cards. For all I know he may have spent months on end counting dandelion spores. May I ask you something?"

"Yes, of course."

"Why do you have such a powerful interest in Mr. Kudirka at this particular moment?"

"I told you—his nuclear operator's license is up for renewal within the next thirty days. This is all pretty routine, really. I just don't like feeling ignorant about one of my cases."

"Well, I'm sorry. Sorry I can't help you more, Mr. Pollack, but I really know nothing further. When our Handley Pond plant was approved for construction we sought out the best people we could find, and one of them was Andres Kudirka. He agreed it was an exciting project and he's been with us ever since."

Pollack nodded, stood up, and shook hands once again with Dr. Welles. "You've been a big help. I won't keep you any longer."

"Give Simon my regards," she said, standing behind her desk with her hands flat on its polished surface, watching Pollack go.

The secretary flicked a button in response to a blinking on her multi-eyed telephone. "Yes, Dr. Welles?"

"Get me Richardson at the Rocky Mountain Power Company in Denver. And stay on the line—I may need you."

The secretary dialed the number and spoke to Richardson's secretary in Denver. After a moment he came on the line. "Richardson here," he said, the last word sounding more like "heah" in his Deep South drawl.

"Henry, this is Dr. Welles. There was a man here just a moment ago from the National Security Service, asking a lot of questions about Andres Kudirka. He said it was because of the license renewal, and I suppose that is what started it, but he seems to want to carry it further than that. I don't like it, not one bit. I warned you we should have plugged up those gaps in his chronology."

"Now, now, I think you may be overestimating our watchdogs," Richardson said. "They don't feel important unless they find one or two skeletons to rattle. But *you*, dear lady, are not going to tell them anything, and *I'm* certainly not, so what is there really to worry about? I'm sure this will all blow over in a day or two."

Dr. Welles frowned into her telephone. "I'm not at all sure, Henry. In any case I'm sending you a transcript of every word he spoke in my office—I want you to get that off this afternoon, Miss Blaine—because I'm positive he'll be calling you to verify what I've told him, and he'll also try to sniff out anything else he can about Kudirka. He even wanted to know about his *wife*, for God's sake! The agent's name is Pollack, Yale Pollack. He's trouble, Henry. I don't want him picking up any loose threads, because he seems the sort of chap who could probably weave a noose out of them."

"All right, I'll be on the lookout. But doesn't this Pollack have a superior at N.S.S.? Someone we can get to in a reasonable manner?"

"He does . . . he does indeed," Dr. Welles said.

5

"I *do* WISH you'd learn to listen to me," Reitzman said, neatly clipping the end from a tiny black cigar and lighting it with a jade-inlaid lighter one of his people had brought him from Okinawa.

"The spoils of peace," Pollack said, smiling at the lighter.

Reitzman scowled. "You do remember, I suppose, what I said about A.D.A. not being any help to you?"

Pollack cleared his throat, which often, in discussions with Reitzman, took the place of some dangerous expletive. "I talked to Dr. Welles, the head of the Industrial Liaison Office. She didn't seem to care much about my problem with Kudirka—in fact she acted about the same way you did, suggesting that there really wasn't any problem. Incidentally, she seems to know you from somewhere."

"Who, Welles? Yes, she's a dear, isn't she? Somewhat butch for your tastes, I rather imagine—but then your tastes as I remember run mostly to chorus girls and those poor creatures you can buy on the street."

"Each to his own," Pollack said testily. "What sort do your tastes run to?"

Reitzman folded his arms carefully so as not to disturb the military-style creases in his checked Oxford-cloth shirt made specially for him by former President

Kennedy's personal Washington tailor. "Did you have something particular on your mind, Pollack, or did you just stop in for an idle chat?"

"A couple of things, Simon. I hope they won't bore you."

"Try me."

"I called our Denver man, George Davis, last night to see what he'd learned, if anything. He went out to Kudirka's house and talked to his wife Mariko, and I guess he checked with some of the neighbors, too. Davis has the feeling no one is very close to Kudirka or knows much about him, not even his wife. Of course, Davis isn't my idea of the perfect investigator and never has been, so whatever he tells me I take with a large grain of salt."

"Why, Mr. Pollack, that sounds very much like a roaring case of professional jealousy. Is it, do you suppose?"

"No. Anyway, the second thing is, I'd like your permission to fly out to Denver and follow up on this Kudirka thing personally."

Reitzman sighed heavily, tapping the ash from his cigar into a cut-glass bowl on the desk. "Really, Pollack, you are beginning to get tiresome. I believe I've mentioned to you before that we're under the microscope of the Security Council's budget committee, and they don't like everything they see by any means. No, I'm afraid such a trip is out of the question."

Pollack smiled at his superior. "I promise you, I'm serious about this."

"So, dear boy, am I."

"No, listen to me, Simon, I'm not giving up on it until I'm reasonably satisfied that we have all the answers. Would the budget committee like to hear that you blew a chance for one of your agents to get the information that would close a case, simply because you refused to okay a couple of hundred for travel expenses?"

"But of course they wouldn't find out about that, would they, Pollack?"

"I'm afraid they would."

Reitzman studied Pollack's face a long while. Finally he rose from the desk and went to the aquarium where he began feeding the hungry fish. "You'll have to stay in a second-rate hotel, eat hamburgers, take the bus . . . And your travel voucher for per diem reimbursement will have to be a little masterpiece of accuracy and detail—you'll be spending more time keeping records of where every penny goes than you will working on your so-called case. What I'm saying is that your voucher and trip report will have to be a great deal better than your work for me has been the last several months."

"That isn't fair, Simon, and you know it."

"Fairness has never been one of my hang-ups, Pollack. Have your request in for my signature within half an hour, will you? And give my regards to your friend George Davis."

In his bachelor apartment in Georgetown, Pollack hastily packed the few things he thought he would need in Denver—one suit in a hang-up plastic bag; two soft shirts, slacks, pajamas, changes of underwear and socks, and a toilet kit in a small overnight bag; and a thick black briefcase into which he had crammed the folder on Andres Kudirka and a sheaf of notes to himself about what he should look for and how. In the bottom drawer of his dresser he came across the tiny Argentine .38 in the god-awfully uncomfortable leather rig that allowed it to be strapped between his legs and held tight in his crotch. The beauty of this arrangement was that even professional friskers would miss it ninety percent of the time, and if anyone *did* find it there you'd already be in big trouble.

He weighed it in his hand and decided impulsively that he wouldn't need it. Basically he was anti-gun; it had been his observation that most people in his line of work who were shot by a gun were also carrying a gun at the time, and though he had never been able to find a strong causal link between these two facts, he didn't doubt that one existed. Sometimes he wondered what he was doing in such a ridiculous business. It seemed wrong to take his job too seriously, and yet he knew that *not* taking it seriously could conceivably get him killed. Mostly, he realized, he got a certain amount of pleasure from wrapping up hundreds of loose ends in a detailed report, and that was about all he could say concerning his time with the National Security Service.

The phone rang, and when he answered it a girl's voice said, "I called your office and they said you were on your way out of town. You could let a person know."

"I'm sorry, Joan," he said, "I didn't know myself until this morning."

"I was hoping you'd take me out this weekend. As a matter of fact, I was hoping it so much that I foolishly went all the way over to Kennedy Center and got tickets for the symphony."

"Joan, what can I say? I imagine you can find someone else to take to the symphony. Anyway, I thought we'd decided you could find someone else to do a lot of things with from now on."

There was a long silence on the line. Then she said, matter-of-factly, "You're a bastard, Yale—I don't know why I bother with you at all."

"I don't know either," Pollack said. "If I were you, I wouldn't." He hung up the phone quickly before he

49

became even more deeply bogged down in the meaning-
less rhetoric of an impossible affair.

On the way to Dulles Airport he stopped by a
branch of the Washington Public Library and checked
out a book at the business reference desk—*United
States Public and Private Corporations Established
Since 1900*. In front of the Statler-Hilton he caught
the Dulles shuttle bus and dutifully marked down in
a small red notebook, "$3.75—bus downtown D.C.
to Dulles—28 Oct." It was picky, childish stuff, but
he was determined not to give Reitzman the pleasure
of finding an error or oversight anywhere in his
voucher.

The plane was not crowded and he had a three-
seat section all to himself. He chose the aisle seat.
About ten minutes after they were airborne the pilot
came on the intercom and announced that the plane
they were flying in was a United DC-8—a "stretched
eight"—that they would be cruising at an altitude of
about thirty-seven thousand feet, and that if all went
well they should reach Denver in about two and a half
hours. Just about time for a drink and a quick lunch,
Pollack figured. He had stored the overnight bag under
the seat in front of him and left his suit bag hanging
in a little closet by the galley. The briefcase he kept
in his lap, locked.

For a while he let the sensations of motion overtake
his body. He liked to fly and always had; often he
regretted not having spent his service time in Air
Force flight training instead of Army demolition, but
he had never seriously considered obtaining a civilian
pilot's license.

A trim, full-bodied stewardess, taller than most,
passed by his seat and stared down at him with huge
dark eyes underscored with blue mascara. The next
time he noticed her, she was bending over his seat

telling him that the sign was on to fasten his seat belt. "Slight turbulence up ahead," she explained.

"Jasmine?" he asked her, catching the scent of her perfume as her flight blouse parted slightly to reveal a lovely rounded breast.

"Yes, how did you know?" she said, looking pleased and more interested than before.

He considered asking her where she was staying in Denver, or whether, perhaps, she went on to the coast, but decided against it; something told him she was all body and no brain. When she served drinks he asked for Pernod, the French licorice-flavored liqueur, for which he had acquired a taste in Korea, of all places. But of course they didn't have Pernod— even in cosmopolitan Washington, D.C., they mostly didn't have Pernod on the shelves of most bars—and so he settled, as he usually did, for unnamed Scotch and water.

Somewhere over southern Ohio, between the Scotch and a prefabricated economy-class lunch, he unlocked the briefcase and took out the library book on U.S. corporations of this century. He found the Columbia Broadcasting System, and he found the Columbus (Ohio) Dairymen's Association right under it. But there was nothing in between, no mention at all of Columbine Mining and Smelting. Perhaps Dr. Welles had been mistaken, or had misremembered, but he didn't think so—her mind had been as sharp and pointed as a marlinspike. No, it was apparent to him that Kudirka had at one time worked for an outfit Dr. Welles *preferred* to remember as Columbine Mining and Smelting.

He closed the book and stared out the window at a billowing white cloud thousands of feet below the airplane. Whatever the reasons for the official run-around he had been getting, he was now more determined than ever to search out the answers—if, indeed, there were any answers. He was beginning to wonder exactly what it was he had stumbled upon.

6

By THE TIME Kudirka reached his house at the south-eastern edge of Denver, the mountains to the west had already taken on the deep rose and purple hues of the setting sun. Mariko was waiting for him, sitting perfectly still in a straight-backed chair in one corner of the small, sparsely furnished living room, her hands folded in her lap. When he came into the room she stared up at him out of gentle, anxious eyes.

"Now, tell me again about the man, Mariko," he said, pronouncing each word distinctly, as if he were talking to a small child. "What was his name?"

"George Davis. I wrote it down—the paper is there on your desk."

"Did he say for whom he works?"

"I do not remember, Andres. I told you, when he said your name I became excited and confused. I thought something bad had happened to you."

"Perhaps it has. What did he say, exactly?"

Mariko studied her hands. "He said it was very important, that I must tell him what he asked or there could be much trouble for both of us."

"And . . . ?"

"I do not know, Andres. He asked many questions, about your work, about your life before I knew you. I tell him I do not know these things, that he must ask you."

"Did he say he would ask me? Think, Mariko—it is most important that you remember everything that happened."

"I am trying! He said nothing about meeting you . . . yes, I am sure of that. He asked many other questions, however. About our life together, you and I, and how we met . . ."

"Mariko, you didn't tell him *that*, did you?"

"I remembered what you have always told me, that I must not speak to anyone about Peliea or the atomic bomb or . . . my family. And so I tell this man what is not true—that my home was in Tokyo and that I came to the United States of America and this is where I met you at Los Alamos. Was that a good thing to do?"

Kudirka took an amphetamine capsule from his pocket and placed it under his tongue. For several minutes he paced the floor in front of Mariko like an accusing prosecutor. Suddenly he stopped and pointed his finger at her. "Why did you have to mention Los Alamos? What did you imagine this man, this . . . this spy, this agent, would think when you try to have him believe a young girl from Tokyo comes to the United States for the first time and immediately goes to an obscure village in the Jemez Mountains of New Mexico, where there just happened to be the most sophisticated nuclear weapons assembly plant in the world? Stupid! It was *stupid*, Mariko."

His wife looked up at him, unblinking, as the tears ran down her olive cheeks. "I did not *know* what to say! Do you think I am a kind of machine that can invent stories about my life to please you, when you have not told me what I should invent? The man asked many questions. I was confused, I tried to think only of your good, but the questions continued and the man would not give me time to think—"

"Because he knew his business! Ah, God, Mariko —you do not understand, do you?" With the uncoordinated motions of a mortally weary man, Kudirka sank heavily into his worn brown leather chair and held his head in his hands.

Mariko stared at him. "You are correct, Andres. I do not understand when you are this way. You used to be . . . different. You were so gentle in the beginning, so kind to the poor island girl. But you have changed into something I do not know, something hard and bitter. You never tell me about your work or your plans. Do you remember the times you tried to explain things to me, secret things about your work on the bombs at Los Alamos, and you said if anyone ever found out what you had told me we would both be dropped in the sea for the sharks to eat? Do you remember, Andres?"

Kudirka shook his head. "Foolish—such a foolish thing to have done . . . I was a young man then, Mariko, who wished to show off his newfound knowledge to someone, *any*one."

She brushed the tears from her face. "Andres, do you remember the house that belonged to us in those days of Los Alamos? On the little mountain . . . so clean, everything clean and growing and at peace. Our lives were at peace then, as they have not been since. I cry, Andres, to think of that house and the man and woman who lived there—the important scientist Mr. Kudirka and his loving wife Mariko. Do you remember these foolish, sad things?"

Kudirka looked at Mariko and sighed, his fingers touching his lips through the gray beard that he had grown years ago to give his face character, and that now he tolerated as one might tolerate an ugly, troublesome growth on some other part of the body. His wife was old now, her skin perhaps prematurely aged by the radiation at Peliea. But her eyes—large, wet, un-blinking—still occasionally scraped at the very core of his being. He had once been in love with her, but even then, at the beginning, he never knew how much of his emotion was based on real affection and how much on deep guilt over the circumstances of their meeting.

"Yes, I remember the house at Los Alamos," he said. A moment later he was unsure if he had spoken the words aloud.

The house was made of adobe bricks the way houses had been made in this part of North America for centuries, whitewashed so that the exterior efficiently reflected the sun's rays and kept the interior cool. This ancient construction was leavened with entirely modern touches, like the soaring glass windows that afforded breath-taking views of Redondo Peak and the Jemez Mountains to the west and the broad lush bowl of Valle Grande down below. The area surrounding the house was heavily wooded and still relatively wild; Kudirka was often able to shoot small game from his front yard, and had once brought down a whitetailed deer with a single blast from a slug-loaded shotgun only fifty feet away from the kitchen freezer where the beautiful animal eventually reposed. He had installed a fourteen-inch astronomical telescope in a kind of balcony appended to the roof of the house, and had designed an enormous sun dial which local craftsmen had installed in the exact center of the walkway connecting the front of the house with the winding dirt road leading back down the mountain to the town of Los Alamos.

It had been a good house. He and Mariko had studied and approved the building of every inch of it. Despite the vast difference in their cultural backgrounds, their tastes were similar in the basic things, both of them preferring simple lines, and an abundance of light. There had been almost no arguments about the house's final appearance as, they were certain, there would have been between any other husband and wife. The truth, of course, was that they knew almost no other husbands or wives who would lend substance to their theory—their lives were as uncluttered and isolated as the house, intentionally so.

When he had first come to Los Alamos in 1945, fresh from college and bursting with enthusiasm, he had naturally gravitated toward other young men of roughly similar age and temperament from among the five thousand or so scientists and technicians working at the experimental facility. They lived, in those days, in rough barrackslike buildings and ate Army food, and though they were technically under the Army's jurisdiction they took every opportunity to rebel against the military way of doing things. There was the snow project, for instance. Once, after a heavy snowstorm, a group of young scientists including Kudirka brought a considerable amount of the white powder inside their barracks building, packed it to a depth of about a foot along the entire length of the main hallway, and held the world's first indoor unidirectional nonelevated championship ski races. That is, until the snow melted, flooding their rooms and spilling down the front steps in a miniature waterfall that was not appreciated by the camp's commandant.

Another time—it could have been the same year— two friends of Kudirka sneaked into a rival barracks one deserted noontime and wired every metal cot to a series of automobile spark coils attached to batteries hidden outside their own barracks. That night after lights-out they connected the wires, with Kudirka serving as lookout and eager accomplice. The ensuing

57

shock nearly turned into furious combat when the men whose beds had suddenly begun sparking discovered where the wires led, and there would undoubtedly have been bloodshed if the duty officer hadn't called out armed MPs to control the riot. . . .

No. The images were blurred, confused. The indoor snow had been while he was at the University of Chicago, one winter in the dormitory. And there had been no riot following the wired-bed episode because someone had discovered the wires almost immediately and simply ripped them out. It was difficult to concentrate these days, even more difficult to remember with any accuracy. . . .

The Army command, with some justification, had considered nearly all the Los Alamos scientists reckless, childish screwballs. Even the eminent Dr. Robert Oppenheimer was not immune. Shortly after his arrival as Chief Scientist on the project, Dr. Oppenheimer requisitioned from the Army—through channels and on the proper government forms—a nail for the back of his office door on which to hang his hat. The Army in due time notified him in writing that a standard wooden hatrack had been ordered and would be delivered to him. When the requisition was eventually filled, the Army received a brusque memo from Oppenheimer stating that while he appreciated the wooden hatrack he would still like them to honor his original request for a nail. The nail was delivered and installed to Oppenheimer's specifications, and no one cracked a smile.

Scientists were, after all, different. The very air which Kudirka and the others breathed after Hiroshima and Nagasaki was a heady atmosphere of numbers, of scientific formulae, of educated guesses about all sorts of preposterously complex concepts. There were many kinds of human alliances at "The Ranch," as Los Alamos was known by those who lived and worked there during the early years. Because of his Lithuanian and Swedish background, Kudirka was sometimes associated in people's minds with the more famous scientific refugees and expatriates working at the center, which from time to time included George Gamow (Russian), Stanislaw Ulam (Polish), Edward Teller (Hungarian), Enrico Fermi (Italian), and Hans Bethe (German). It was a United Nations in microcosm before the real United Nations existed, but even these justifiably famous people could, on occasion, show petty vanity about their reputations, awards, and previous academic posts. In any case, Kudirka's foreign origins hardly qualified him for entree into the rarefied atmosphere of genuine Nobel prize winners, and finding himself in the same room with one of the forbiddingly eminent scientists would usually terrify him so that he found it difficult to speak.

The high-spirited conviviality with other young scientists that Kudirka had initially reveled in gradually dropped off, then all but disappeared as, over the years, he found the work becoming a steady, predictable grind. The people he worked with no longer seemed so amusing or interesting. He began avoiding other people as much as possible, and was aware that by doing so he was gaining a reputation for being a loner, an outsider, an unsociable young man with no particular hobbies or interests except his daily work in the laboratories. By the time he brought Mariko back to Los Alamos after the bomb test at Peliea he was already a pariah in that small, inbred community. Had anyone ever asked questions about his wife or her background? He couldn't remember that they had, so there was never any need to explain. It had only been during the last year or two at Los Alamos that he had begun wondering whether his self-imposed isolation had ruined both their lives. Mariko, of course, never complained; he sometimes wondered whether their lives might not have been different, better, more fulfilled if she had asserted herself even once during all those years. But now, such speculation was useless.

"You evidently miss the old days more than I do," Kudirka said aloud. When Mariko didn't answer, he swung around in the leather chair and saw that she was kneeling before her shrine. Set into the little alcove off the living room, it gave off a pungent odor of incense that was now quite strong throughout the room. He knew it would be useless to continue talking to her, since she was obviously lost in some communication with the small carved wooden figure she had had the first time he had seen her, hanging from her neck by a woven reed chain—the only possession she had saved from the island. Lately she spent more time talking to the little Buddha-like figure than she did talking to him.

Shaking his head in disgust, he got up from the chair and opened the bottom drawer of his desk, from which he took an old medicine bottle filled with laboratory ethyl alcohol. He drank from the bottle in short sips, the spiraling ridges of glass made to accommodate the bottle cap pleasantly cold against his lips. The alcohol burned terribly for an instant, until, by a complicated internal chemistry, it began to mellow and warm his whole body and smooth over the jagged edges of his nerves.

Dimly he became aware that Mariko was staring at him and he turned to face her, the bottle still in his hand.

"That is not medicine, is it?" she said. The tone of her voice made it clear that she had no doubts.

With a final bow toward her icon she rose gracefully and went toward the bedroom. Kudirka, unsure about exactly what he wanted, stumbled after her, but she was too quick for him and managed to shut the door before he could enter. He stood silently in the hallway outside the bedroom, enraged but still unwilling to force the issue. Gradually he became aware that she was crying, and his righteous indignation left him. "Mariko . . ." he called softly.

"No, Andres," she said between sobs. "You have changed, I no longer know you. You are not even a man. . . ."

Kudirka closed his eyes and leaned against the wall beside the door. After a while he went back to the living room desk and sat in its small, uncomfortable chair and raised the medicine bottle to his mouth. His brain felt wet and mushy, a poor rag that would no longer do even simple polynomial equations. He stared at a framed photograph, taken shortly after he had gone to work at Los Alamos that summer of 1945. He and two other men, young and healthy-looking, stood beside a 1939 Chevrolet sedan in which they had just transported, from Los Alamos down to the Trinity site northwest of Alamogordo, some of the electrical components of what two weeks later would be the world's first atomic bomb. . . .

But that was ridiculous—they would never have trusted one of their newest young men with a mission as important as that. He must have been mistaken about the picture. The people standing beside the car could have been anyone—he had no names to give them, could no longer even remember whose car it had been. Another error from the past.

Beside the photograph was a Bible, which Kudirka had lately begun opening at random, reading several pages rapidly as if searching for some urgent message that would change his life. When he picked it up now and thumbed its gilt-edged pages, the book fell open to a passage in Romans where, at some previous time, he had underlined part of a verse: *"For it is written, vengeance is mine; I will repay, saith the Lord."* The words seemed to leap across the synapses in his brain and he read the verse over and over again, marveling at the simple, direct beauty of it: *"Vengeance is mine, saith the Lord!"*

He drained another two ounces of raw alcohol from the bottle and let his hand fall to the desk, noticing for the first time the scrap of yellow paper on which Mariko had written the name of the man who had interrogated her. George Davis. Oh God, he thought, why couldn't they leave him alone? This Davis was someone he had never met, never heard of, and yet was someone who obviously wanted to do him harm. More frightening still, he had no way of knowing who the man worked for, what kind of information he wanted. Was it something to do with Neutron Two, he wondered, or was it about some period of his life before that? It could be so many things.

Sighing heavily, he looked at his watch and saw that it was very late. Well, no matter, he thought. He reached for the telephone book and looked up "Davis, George." There were four of them, along with several Davises identified only by the initial "G." He picked up the telephone receiver and dialed the first number, knowing that nothing at all would be settled by his talking to this George Davis, whoever he was. But sometimes it helped to know the voice of your enemy, if not his face.

7

SIMON REITZMAN picked up the bright green telephone —one of three on his desk—and after hearing the tone signifying the electronic scrambler was in operation dialed the number of the Atomic Development Agency. "Dr. Welles, please," he told the answering secretary. While he waited he ran two virgin pencils through the electric sharpener, then laid them carefully side by side so that their beautifully conical ends pointed southeast, in the direction of the White House.

"Ah, Justine," he said when she finally came on the line, "this is Simon returning your call. Sorry I was out."

"Hah! Probably out chasing some gorgeous young man, if I know you. And I wish you wouldn't call me that hideous name."

"Justine? But it *is* your name, love. I can see you'll never forgive me for having ferreted it out of London's security files."

"Never mind that. I wanted to know about this bucky you've somehow put on my tail—what's his name, Pollack, Yale Pollack. What the bloody hell do you think you're doing?"

Reitzman pursed his lips thoughtfully. "I know perfectly well what I'm doing, dear. We have a routine background check to update Andres Kudirka's security clearance, and it just happened to be assigned to Pollack. I couldn't very well take it out of normal job channels and run the risk of stirring up nasty suspicions, could I?"

"How you run your office is no concern of mine. Your junior bloodhound was over here yesterday acting like James Bond and driving me round the bend with his questions. I had the impression he didn't believe a word I said."

"Now, now, you mustn't let him upset you. Pollack's a bright enough fellow, I suppose, but I've always put him down as a bit of a drudge. He's the only one of my agents who's likely to still be in the office at six o'clock of an evening. A bit headstrong, especially when he thinks he's onto something, but I can handle him."

"That's a bloody comfort."

"Anyway, you don't have to worry about him coming around your place seducing the secretaries again anytime soon. He left on a plane to Denver this morning."

"God's blood, Simon! What could you have been thinking of? I *knew* that's where he'd be poking round next—I could feel the way his brain was vibrating in my office."

"Ah-ah . . . you're stepping over the line into my territory again, Justine. I told you I couldn't very well force him to abandon a legitimate lead—or at least something that looks legitimate to him—without raising his suspicions. He's an old hand here, he knows his business and he also knows where some of our more putrid bodies are buried. He wouldn't hesitate a minute to go over my head if he thought he needed to."

"You're not restoring my confidence, Simon. We're sitting on a powder keg and you know it."

"Yes. That's an apt metaphor, powder keg . . . isn't it?"

"Don't tell me *you're* starting to buy the blather of these raging ecologists. That *would* give me a laugh."

"Would it, love?" As he talked Reitzman removed a locked briefcase from his locked bottom desk drawer and took out a folder marked "Kudirka, Andres." He riffled through the papers containing investigative reports, cross-references to names and places such as Welles, Dr. Justine; Richardson, Henry; Handley Pond; Columbine. At the bottom of the pile was a personal memo to himself that no one else had ever seen, about the handsome young Navy lieutenant who, assigned to Washington after sea duty on the U.S.S. *Farrell* two decades and more ago, had for a time shared an apartment with the young Simon Reitzman, already ambitiously clawing his way up the Washington security ladder. The Navy man had been a drinker, his career dogged by that flaw so that he never rose above the rank of lieutenant commander and now occupied a dismal backwater shore desk at Subic Bay, P.I. In one of his drunken stupors he had let slip the entire story of the rogue atomic bomb at Peliea in the '50s and the tale of the lone survivor and Andres Kudirka, the Los Alamos scientist. Reitzman had immediately seen the information as one of those lucky, once-in-a-lifetime breaks, and had eventually approached both the Los Alamos directors and the A.D.A. There had been discreet discussions in northern New Mexico and suburban Maryland, augmented by Reitzman's own investigations into places as remote as the Colorado mountains, that had resulted in a working agreement bound by mutual interests and shared confidences. In a very real way, Andres Kudirka was the thin thread from which many diverse elements dangled precariously within a bubble of official secrecy.

"Tell me something," Reitzman said into the telephone, "*is* there anything for Pollack to find in Denver?

Because that was supposed to be your department, making sure there were no untidy loose ends lying around for someone to stumble over later on."

"What do I know about loose ends? I'm stuck here in this scientific greenhouse suffering acute diarrhea from the endless memos I'm forced to read."

"Justine, a rather nasty thought occurs to me: You didn't, by any chance, happen to mention Columbine Mining and Smelting to Pollack, did you?"

"I did, yes. For a very good reason. He asked about Kudirka's wife . . . I remember thinking that was rather odd. And he said there were gaps in your dossier on him, after Los Alamos and before Handley Pond. Which of course there would be—and incidentally, Simon, I think that was a mistake on your part, not fluffing out the details sufficiently during those years."

"Go on, Justine."

"Yes—well, Pollack wanted to know where Kudirka might have got his training for the nuclear plant job and I gave him a perfectly logical explanation which I'm sure he believed. We talked a bit about what else Kudirka might have been doing those eight or nine years unaccounted for, and I did mention Columbine in passing. I had to . . . that's why we invented it, remember?"

"Pollack's no fool," Reitzman said angrily, slicing off the end of a fresh small black cigar.

"It doesn't make any difference," Dr. Welles said. "I assure you, there are no traces in Denver."

"Aren't you forgetting Miss Eubanks?"

"Letty? No problem there—she's directly under Richardson's thumb at Rocky Mountain Power. That was one of my best tricks, I think—getting her set up in that job so we could keep a permanent eye on her."

"You'd better hope she's still in the bag, Justine old

girl," Reitzman said menacingly. "Deportation proceedings against undesirable aliens, particularly when the country concerned is a friendly one, like Britain, are such messy affairs. All sorts of people get hurt, love."

"You unconscionable bastard!" Dr. Welles said.

Reitzman smiled. "Keep in touch, won't you?"

8

AT STAPLETON INTERNATIONAL AIRPORT in Denver
the mobile boarding chute deposited Pollack inside the
busy terminal, where at the Economy Rent-A-Car
desk he inquired about ground transportation, preferably something sporty. As it happened, the sportiest
thing they had was a red Mustang II. "No Porsche?"
he asked the girl, who stared up at him through raised
eyebrows as if to say, Man, are *you* lost. "I'll take the
Mustang," he said, properly chastised.

From the airport he drove toward the downtown
area and cruised slowly down Broadway in the direction
of the Brown Palace Hotel. A few of the landmarks
were familiar, but not many; the last time he'd been
in Denver was in the early '50s when he had taken
some special Army training at Fort Carson in Colorado
Springs. The Brown Palace was still here and much
larger than before, having expanded into a second
building. Since his travel expenses from N.S.S. would
never allow that kind of luxury, he drove aimlessly
around most of the downtown area with its streets
set at a funny angle to the rest of the city, and finally
stopped at a tiny decrepit hotel on Broadway. He
hauled his own bags inside and, much against the
aging bellhop's wishes, all the way up to his third-
floor room where, he discovered, if he leaned out the
one window and cocked his head at an angle he could

see both a hazy outline of Mt. Evans and one of the less interesting corners of the Brown Palace.

He allowed the bellhop to bring him a bucket of ice and lay across the dusty, faded bedspread with a cold Pernod and water—surprisingly he had been able to pick up a one-tenth-pint bottle at the airport liquor store. He sipped the delicious cloudy yellow liquid and thought of all the things he could do. He could call George Davis, the Denver N.S.S. agent, except that there was no one in the world he less wanted to see or talk to at the moment. Or he could call someone at the Rocky Mountain Power Company, except that it was probably too late in the afternoon to make an appointment with anyone there. He could, of course, try to get in touch with Andres Kudirka himself, but that seemed a bit premature and was not the way Pollack preferred to work. Usually he left the crucial interview with his prime subject until after he had collected whatever information he could from other sources, because then it was easier to tell whether the subject was being evasive, or lying outright. Another alternative—really a last resort—would be to call back the scruffy, mean-looking bellhop and ask him where a stranger in town might find a mean, scruffy-looking girl to spend a few hours alone with. Except that he didn't trust the bellhop at all, and would probably always wonder whether the venereal disease he would no doubt contract had been a gift from the sly little man.

While Pollack was thinking about all these possibilities he drifted off to sleep, still holding the glass with two ice cubes in his hand. He awoke with a start, shortly after nine o'clock, unable at first to remember where he was. The glass had rolled beneath the bed and he didn't feel up to retrieving it. Instead he went into the bathroom to wash his face. While he was there the telephone rang. Wondering who it could be, he picked up the receiver and mumbled "Hello," fat beads of water dripping from his face and hands.

Although the connection was obviously still open, no one answered.

"Hello! Who's there?" he repeated, straining to hear any sound that might give him an idea of who was calling and from where. But there was nothing, just the faint crackling of an open line. He visualized a man standing in a dark room, his face hidden in shadows, holding a telephone and smiling to himself at the sound of Pollack's voice.

"Screw you, Charlie," Pollack said, and slammed down the receiver.

He grabbed the lined suede jacket he'd packed for the protection it would offer against the clear, cold Denver nights, left the room, and took the elevator down to the first floor. In the small lobby an old man was watching a color television set; the bellhop didn't seem to be around. Pollack stopped at the desk and asked the night clerk whether he had rung his room a moment ago.

"What's the number again?" the clerk asked him.

"Three-oh-six."

"No, sir, no calls from down here. Of course, somebody could have called you from outside and we'd just patch it through. Sometimes Shorty takes the switchboard if he's not busy."

Pollack nodded. "Shorty's the bellhop?"

"Yeah. He ain't around now, though. If you want I can have him get in touch with you when he comes back."

"Never mind," Pollack said, and walked out of the hotel in search of a café. He was hungry enough to eat whatever it was they'd probably serve him in a downtown diner at this time of night.

The next morning Pollack looked up the number of the administrative offices of the Rocky Mountain Power Company in the telephone book and discovered they were in the Equity Building, only four blocks away from his hotel. He moved the rented Mustang from its restricted parking spot on the street, left it in a nearby twenty-four-hour garage, and walked to the Equity Building.

In the lobby he stood in front of the personnel locator board and read every entry for Rocky Mountain Power before deciding on Mr. Henry Richardson, vice president in charge of the Nuclear Division. He took the elevator to the twenty-third floor and stepped out into a carpeted, plushly furnished reception area that would probably jibe with a Hollywood set designer's idea of a futuristic office. A beautiful girl with shoulder-length ash-blonde hair and green-tinged eyelashes almost that long smiled at him from behind a freely curving polished wood desk on which he saw no typewriter, no Dictaphone, no office equipment of any kind except a futuristic white plastic communication device with about twenty buttons. "May I help you, sir?" the beautiful girl asked him.

Pollack smiled back at her. "I hope so. I'm afraid I don't have an appointment but I'd like to see Mr. Richardson, if I may. It's a matter of some urgency. My name's Pollack, Yale Pollack, from the National Security Service."

He unfolded his ID card from his wallet and showed it to the girl, who seemed less than impressed. "I'll check for you, sir. Mr. Richardson may be in conference," she said, delicately pushing one of the twenty buttons on her instrument. Pollack saw that she had a tiny button speaker in her ear and an equally tiny mouthpiece curving out from beneath her hair on a slender wire stem. "Mr. Yale Pollack from National Security Service, Washington, D.C., to see Mr. Richardson," she whispered into the mouthpiece in sex-goddessy tones. "He says he doesn't have an appointment, Letty."

She looked up at Pollack and he smiled at her again, but his effort seemed to be wasted. He might as well have been an unwelcome toilet-brush salesman, he thought as he decided to conserve the energy it would take to charm this iceberg for some more worthy cause.

"Thank you, Letty," the girl addressed her mouthpiece, then said to Pollack, "Mr. Richardson will see you now—he's sending someone out for you."

The someone turned out to be a girl slightly older than the receptionist—in her late twenties, Pollack guessed—and not nearly so flamboyant. She was small and trim, with short dark hair and huge gray eyes. Her mouth appeared to smile in spite of itself.

"Well, here we are, Mr. Pollack," she said, extending her hand to him. "I'm Letty Eubanks, and I'm to take you to Mr. Richardson's office. If you'll follow me, please."

"Certainly," Pollack said, hurrying to catch up with her as she disappeared through a maze of connecting offices. "By the way, why do I need an escort?"

The girl turned around to look at him and suddenly her face became quite grave. "Officially it's because this is a confusing place and you might easily get lost without a guide."

"And unofficially?"

"Unofficially," she said, her eyes twinkling, "it's because they're all a bunch of paranoids around here and they hate to have strangers poking about."

"I see. Does that include you?"

"Oh, heavens no," she said brightly. "I like all sorts of things, including an occasional interesting-looking stranger from N.S.S."

Pollack laughed, thinking how much he liked this girl. "Do you happen to know what N.S.S. stands for?"

"National Security Service—the receptionist told me."

"Well, it doesn't matter, really. You just sounded as if you'd run into us before."

"I try to keep my ears open," she said. "In this job you have to."

"I'm sure you do, Miss . . . Eubanks?"

"Call me Letty—everybody does."

She led him into an outer office containing two desks and a row of chairs along one wall that were upholstered in a variety of brilliant colors. One of the desks was occupied by a girl busily typing a letter, and the other desk, unoccupied, had a small name-plate set on one corner that read "Miss Letty Eubanks." It appeared that Letty was more an administrative assistant than a secretary, and Pollack could not help feeling cheered by the "Miss" in front of her name.

"Let me just check quickly with Mr. Richardson again, Mr. Pollack. Have a seat if you wish."

"Thanks," he said, but when she knocked and entered another room, closing the door after her, Pollack remained standing and continued his inspection of the office. The first thing he noticed was a poster on the wall, showing a nuclear power plant in a serene pastoral setting with a small boy in the foreground holding a fishing pole—the same poster he had seen on the wall of Dr. Welles' office in Washington. There was no reason the poster shouldn't be in both places, of course, but he couldn't help feeling that Rocky

Mountain Power might be a branch office of A.D.A. Or the other way around.

The girl, Letty, reappeared and said that Mr. Richardson would see him now. "Just go on in," she told him with a smile, and Pollack did, closing the door behind him.

He and Richardson shook hands across a large, bare executive desk. "What can we do for you, Mr. Pollack?" Richardson said. "Letty tells me you're from the National Security Service. I do hope we haven't inadvertently violated any security regulations —we're very careful about that kind of thing, you know."

He spoke with a heavy Southern accent—Atlanta, or maybe Charleston, Pollack guessed. Richardson was bald except for a fringe of white hair above his ears, which stood out on both sides of his round, pink face like a child's afterthought toothpicked to a pumpkin. He could have been someone's sweet old grandfather, and possibly he was. Pollack got the immediate impression that behind the pleasant exterior was a man used to getting his own way and making things difficult for anyone who opposed him.

Ignoring Richardson's question about security violations, Pollack accepted the chair offered him, and said, "I'd like some information about one of your employees at the Handley Pond nuclear facility, Mr. Richardson. His name is Andres Kudirka. His A.D.A. operator's license is up for renewal and we're doing a routine check on his background and so forth. I imagine you keep files on your employees, don't you?"

"Well, not here—they'd have the files in Personnel." He punched a button on a small intercom. "Letty, run down to Personnel and pull the folder on a Mr. Kudirka, Andres Kudirka, would you please?"

He turned back to Pollack and studied him closely.

"Is it routine to send an investigator out from the Washington office on these license renewals? I would have thought that could be handled by a telephone call or two."

Pollack shrugged. "Sometimes it helps to be on the spot—there are things we can do in the field that can't very well be handled in the D.C. office."

Mr. Richardson nodded but kept his eyes on Pollack. "Well, sir, it's a nice time of year to be in Denver anyway. Will you be staying long, Mr. Pollack?"

"No longer than necessary, I'm afraid. Tell me about the plant, Mr. Richardson."

"Handley Pond? Surely . . . what would you like to know?"

"Everything."

"Well, now, that's a large order, Mr. Pollack. Perhaps we can arrange for you to join a tour of the facility while you're here. That way, you could ask your questions at the source, so to speak."

"Thanks, I'm not sure I'll have the time for that. Do you have any brochures I could look at? Providing, of course, they aren't too technical—my scientific knowledge stopped somewhere in the middle of high school chemistry."

Mr. Richardson swiveled in his chair, opened a paneled cabinet behind him, and extracted a handful of colorful booklets of various sizes. "There's something here for every level of interest, from grade school classes to college physics courses to the average housewife's passing interest. If I may say so, that's something Rocky Mountain Power has done an excellent job of —keeping the public informed about Handley Pond. Here, Mr. Pollack, read these over—I think they'll answer most of your questions."

Pollack opened a couple of the booklets at random, noting the clever drawings, the professional layout of the charts and statistics on safety records, levels of radiation monitored, economics of nuclear power plants and particularly breeder plants as compared with the standard old-fashioned coal-fired plants. It was all very convincing on a superficial level, and Pollack had no doubt that most people, after reading these brochures, would be convinced that the Handley Pond plant was one of the great wonders of the modern age.

"It's all there, Mr. Pollack. Nuclear reactor plants are safe, clean, reliable, and economical. And the *most* economical, of course, are the breeder reactors, because they actually breed more fuel than they use. Handley Pond is the first large-scale commercial liquid-metal fast breeder in the world, as you may already know. But by the year 2000 we expect to have more than four hundred breeders in operation. We're on the threshold of a new age in cheap, clean energy, Mr. Pollack, and the American people will be the direct beneficiaries."

Pollack smiled. "To say nothing of Rocky Mountain Power Company."

Some slight pain passed across Mr. Richardson's pleasant countenance. "Of course, Mr. Pollack, you understand we have a financial obligation to our stockholders. That's the difference between our free-marketplace capitalism in America and the socialistic or communistic systems in countries like Russia and China. After all, we're a publicly owned utility, you know."

"Yes, sir, I understand. But that's always seemed to me a slightly misleading term. 'Publicly owned' ought to mean owned by the public, shouldn't it? Not just a few people wealthy enough to be able to invest in the company's stock, which as far as I can see makes it a very private company indeed."

"Come, come, Mr. Pollack, we're arguing over semantics. 'Publicly owned' is the common and usual terminology for capital investment companies in which stock is issued and sold to the public. *You* can buy it, Mr. Pollack, *I* can buy it, *Letty* can buy it—"

"If we have the money."

"If you have the money, of course. We're not set up as a philanthropic organization. Do you have any idea how much it cost to build the Handley Pond plant, Mr. Pollack?"

Pollack shook his head and Richardson supplied the answer. "One billion eight hundred million dollars. We have a sizeable investment up there, one I think the Denver community can well be proud of. As a matter of fact, they *are* proud of it. We have excellent relations with the City of Denver and the State of Colorado. I think you'll find our community relations program is one of the finest in the country. We put on school programs, we talk to civic and social organizations, we maintain a speaker's bureau and a press and television bureau, we issue monthly reports about the operation of the plant, we give free guided tours to all sorts of people . . ."

"Free?"

"Of course."

"I believe you," Pollack said. "Besides, as I mentioned before, I don't know enough about the technical aspects of nuclear power to argue with you on any level. But I do read the newspapers—"

"Which are often biased, for their own reasons."

"That could be. But there are alternative energy sources, aren't there? Sources that are one-hundred-percent safe, like wind power and sun power, only nobody seems to be trying very hard to develop them, at least on any large scale."

"Mr. Pollack, I dislike repeating myself but I believe

we've already covered the dictum that a company—*any* company—has an obligation to provide a healthy degree of return to its investors. That's basic to our way of life in this country, to the profit motive, if you will."

"The American way, Mr. Richardson?"

Richardson ignored Pollack's obviously unpatriotic barb. "At this point in time we believe nuclear energy is the best solution to our energy needs and we've pursued that avenue vigorously. The Handley Pond plant is as safe as anything could be, Mr. Pollack. Why should we burden the people of Denver with a lot of theoretical nonsense about extreme possibilities, such as statistical laboratory figures about 'worst credible accidents'? We'd be doing them and us a terrible disservice. Scare-words the media have picked up, like 'scram,' 'criticality,' and 'nuclear excursion,' make our community relations programs just that much more difficult, and we certainly don't need any new mountains to climb."

Pollack was about to interject his own belief that the climbing of new mountains was what kept the human race going, but just then Letty knocked on the door and brought in the folder on Kudirka. "Sorry, it took longer than I thought," she said, handing it to Richardson. "Personnel didn't much like letting it out of their department, but I promised we'd take good care of it."

"Thank you, Letty."

While Miss Eubanks stood beside his desk, Richardson opened the folder and leafed through several sheets of paper that looked to Pollack like official forms. "Yes . . . Kudirka," Richardson said. "A fine employee, technically as capable and well qualified as anyone we've ever had on the engineering staff. Was there anything special you wanted to pursue?"

"Could I see the folder?" Pollack asked.

"I'm afraid not. Personnel records are confidential, you know."

"I have practically any clearance you could ask for, Mr. Richardson."

"So do we, Mr. Pollack. The answer is still no, without approval by higher authority. However, I'd be happy to answer any specific questions if I can."

Pollack sighed. The interview was turning into the worst sort of cat-and-mouse game, and he was probably at least partly to blame because of the way he'd antagonized Richardson, but he simply hadn't been able to help himself. "All right," he said, "what can you tell me about Mr. Kudirka's wife?"

"Let's see . . . The records show her name is Mariko—Japanese, I presume. She's at least ten years younger than her husband. They were married in 1954 at the chapel at Los Alamos, where Mr. Kudirka was working at the time. That's all I can tell you, I'm afraid."

"Better than nothing," Pollack said. "The other thing I'm interested in, just to complete our records, is where Kudirka was working the five years or so immediately preceding his employment by you at the Handley Pond plant."

"Well, that shouldn't be too difficult." Richardson flipped through several more pages in the folder. "Mr. Kudirka left Los Alamos in 1965 and took a post in the Nuclear Engineering Department at Stanford, where he apparently remained for the next five years, until 1970, when he left to travel and lecture at other colleges and universities across the country. He was quite in demand, apparently—his subject specialty was neutron bombardment and particle physics. We grabbed him off the lecture circuit with the chance to become

Chief Engineer at Handley Pond. He seemed pleased to come to work for us."

Pollack frowned. "That's it?"

A smile spreading across his cherubic face, Mr. Richardson closed the folder and handed it back to Letty. "That's it, Mr. Pollack. You know as much as we do now. I'm sorry we couldn't be more help . . . or were we?"

"What? Oh, yes, you were most helpful, Mr. Richardson," Pollack said, watching Letty leave the room with the personnel folder. "Well, I won't take up any more of your time. I'm just thinking, though—if it wouldn't be too much trouble I might like to take that tour of the plant after all, maybe talk to Kudirka while I'm there."

"Of course. Stop by the receptionist's desk at the front office. I'll call out and have her make up a special yellow pass. Do take care of it, Mr. Pollack— you'll be obliged to turn it in to the guard out at Handley Pond."

"Thanks, I will. Oh, by the way, there *was* one other thing: Have you ever heard of the Columbine Mining and Smelting Company?"

There was no perceptible change in Richardson's expression. "No, I can't say that I have. Any particular reason for asking?"

"Not really. It's supposed to be somewhere here in Colorado, and I thought if I had time I might look up a friend who works there."

"I see," Mr. Richardson said thoughtfully. "Well, sorry I can't help you. These little shoestring mining operations come and go every time some hillbilly gets two dollar bills to rub together. Some folks think there's still a gold rush going on out here in Colorado."

Pollack stood up and reached across the desk to shake hands with Richardson. A scrap of notepaper on the desk caught his eye. Somehow his own briefcase tipped under his arm toward the unzippered opening and several papers fell out across Richardson's desk. Richardson was obviously interested in seeing what the papers might reveal, and Pollack let him handle a couple of them while he concentrated on reading the upside-down handwriting on the scrap of paper. The top line spelled out the name of Dr. J. Welles, and directly under it was an even more familiar name—Yale Pollack.

"Thanks—I'm getting clumsy in my old age," Pollack said as they walked toward the door.

A curious coincidence about the note on Richardson's desk, he thought. Of course there could be any number of reasons for Richardson and Dr. Welles to be talking periodically on the phone, considering the nature of their respective jobs. And Richardson might have happened to scribble the name of his visitor today on the same pad. But eleven years of working at N.S.S. had made Pollack suspicious of *all* coincidences, because they usually turned out to be something else altogether.

He ran into Letty in the hallway, still carrying the personnel folder. "I don't suppose you'd let me take a quick peek into that?" he asked her.

She frowned at him, then smiled. "I'd lose my job, and probably my head. Are you coming back to visit us, Mr. Pollack?"

"That depends. Why?"

"I told you before, I like interesting strangers."

"I'll keep that in mind," Pollack said, watching the nice way she walked as she went off with the file on Andres Kudirka.

9

KUDIRKA STOOD FORLORNLY in the foyer of the plush, popular new downtown restaurant called The Bank. Ideally situated on Seventeenth Street in the heart of Denver's brokerage and banking district, its main attraction was that it had once actually been a commercial bank—the twenty-ton time-locked steel door was still on its hinges, and inside the former vault was a cozy eating room. Waiting, Kudirka watched the chic young men and women going and coming, laughing, talking, moving about with drinks in their hands and meeting their friends for a leisurely lunch. He wondered who they were, where they worked, what was the source of the income that allowed them to indulge themselves this way and be so completely blasé about it. He felt old, almost totally out of time and place.

The maître d' finally noticed him standing there and asked if there were something he could do for him. Kudirka cleared his throat. "I'm to meet a Mr. Henry Richardson for lunch but I do not know whether he has arrived."

The maître d' scanned his list thoughtfully, then brightened. "You're Mr. Kudirka? This way, please."

Richardson's table was not in the vault but just outside it, tucked into a tiny alcove where there was room for only one small table and two chairs. This secluded little table seemed almost serenely unaffected by the friendly commotion throughout the restaurant.

"Andres! Sit down, sit down," Richardson said, smiling and gesturing toward the empty chair across from him. "Would you like a drink? I've taken the liberty of ordering lunch for you. Seafood . . . crab Mornay. Delicious! And a bottle of domestic Chablis." His round cheeks were even rosier than usual in the subdued light from the room's small Tiffany lamps. "Isn't this a marvelous place? Nothing like this in Atlanta, I'll tell you . . . but of course you don't know Atlanta, do you?"

Kudirka sat rigidly uncomfortable in the chair, wondering what Richardson wanted or expected of him. When a bar waitress appeared he timidly ordered vodka, neat. "Do you have Wyborowa? It's . . . Polish." Seeing the waitress's puzzled expression, he shrugged and said, "No matter. Anything."

Richardson looked at Kudirka with interest. "Is that . . . whatever you said, Polish vodka, better than our American stuff?"

"Oh, I don't know. It is one hundred proof."

"Ah," said Richardson, sipping at his J. W. Dant Kentucky Sour Mash Bourbon, also one hundred proof. "Well, do you like the place? I take it you aren't a regular customer."

"No. I mean yes, it is very lively. No, I have not been here before. The sandwich machines at Neutron Two suit me, usually."

. "Yes," Richardson said. The kindly smile faded from his face as if someone had pulled the drapes across a sunlit window. "That's, ah, partly what I wanted to see you about, Andres. You really mustn't continue to call the Handley Pond plant by that pet name of yours. I realize, of course, that you mean no harm by it, but still . . . We've gone to a great deal of trouble to build an image in this community, Andres, an acceptable, decent image. And as our public relations department would say, the name *is* the image—first and foremost the name. So please, from now on, let's drop any further reference to Neutron Two, shall we? After all, that rather implies a Neutron One, doesn't it? Oh, here we are—I do hope you like my selection."

Another waitress set down two plates of steaming crab morsels covered with a light cheese sauce, while the bar waitress brought Kudirka's vodka and the luncheon wine. Kudirka watched Richardson scoop up a huge mouthful of the creamy crab; feeling somewhat nauseated, he tossed off the vodka in two quick gulps.

"You said partly, Mr. Richardson. What were the other reasons?"

Richardson held up his hand, putting Kudirka off while he continued to shovel forkfuls of crab into his mouth. "Delicious . . . absolutely heavenly! I'll bet I gain five pounds every time I eat here." He paused to wipe a trickle of Mornay sauce from his chin. "Andres, has anyone contacted you in the last few days, telephone or otherwise? Someone you didn't know, perhaps?"

Kudirka instantly thought of the visitor Mariko had been upset about—George Davis, an investigator for the National Security Service. Kudirka had learned of the organization when he had telephoned Davis that night.

"No, nothing like that," he lied to Richardson. "Why do you ask?"

"Because I've just had a telephone call *and* a visitor. The call was from Dr. Welles at A.D.A., warning me about a fellow named Pollack from the National Security Service—N.S.S. It's something like a cross between the F.B.I. and the C.I.A., I gather, except it isn't

84

nearly as well publicized. I doubt if you've even heard of them."

Kudirka shook his head. He poured wine into his glass, and then remembered to pour some into Richardson's glass too.

"The person who came to see me in my office was this same Mr. Pollack, and Dr. Welles was damned right to worry. Pollack seems to be poking around into *your* background, Andres."

"But I have done nothing," Kudirka protested, thinking how foolish that must sound to Richardson.

"He says it has to do with the renewal of your A.D.A. nuclear operator's license. But the fellow's rudely persistent, about things such as your wife's background, and particularly about the blank spot in your professional career. We don't know why, exactly. Of course there's always the possibility that N.S.S. or even A.D.A. has seen fit to purposely divert our attention—"

"Double-cross you. Is that the term?"

"Certainly not. I'm simply asking you to be especially careful if anyone, anyone at all, comes around asking questions, particularly about that period between 1971 and 1973."

"You say you're asking me," Kudirka said, sipping more wine although he felt light-headed already.

"This is hardly a joking matter, Andres. Listen to me—if anyone inquires, you're to tell them you were lecturing at several universities across the country, at seminars on particle physics, and so forth, but not on any regular basis. Weren't there a couple of Midwestern colleges where you actually did speak before you came with us?"

"Oh yes . . . Indiana, University of Chicago, Ohio State—"

"Good, good. Try to remember exactly when you

were at each location. Look up dates if you have to, because we want to give this Pollack fellow something concrete to chew on. Tell anyone who asks that you did a considerable amount of fishing during this time, and personal travel for relaxation, and perhaps just sitting and thinking on your front porch . . . Do you *have* a front porch, by the way?"

"No."

"Well, wherever. Those things they won't be able to check, no matter how much they'd like to."

Kudirka gripped the wineglass with bloodless fingers, realizing for the first time what an excellent Nazi Henry Richardson would have made. "I'm tired," he told Richardson, "tired of covering my tracks all these years, like some hunted, wounded animal who has nothing to go on any longer but instinct. And I do not like telling these lies! Do you realize, I no longer even know what I have told this person or that, what lie on what occasion. I do not even remember what my wife knows or does not know about me— It is ruining my *life!*"

Richardson put down his fork and reached across the table to place his hand on Kudirka's wrist. Kudirka found the pudgy fingers surprisingly strong, like steel talons.

"Do you think your life has been ruined before now? I'll tell you something, my fine Lithuanian friend —you can't even *imagine* the trouble you can easily be in if you fail to heed my words. Mariko is, I'm sure, a lovely woman, kind and thoughtful and intelligent. But your work is more important, do you understand that? Your wife is in this country illegally, always has been, and even after all these years she could be deported. And the employment record in our personnel files on Andres Kudirka is nothing but a tissue of lies, as you well know. Since Handley Pond

86

is licensed by A.D.A. your lies on all those forms constitute a federal offense, were you aware of that? You could go to prison for a long, long time, Andres, and your little wife would no longer even be waiting for you."

"You would do that to me?" Kudirka asked incredulously. "Destroy yourselves in order to destroy me?"

"My dear fellow, it isn't quite that way," Richardson said, relaxing into good humor once again. "Certainly you would be destroyed. As for us . . . a little bad publicity, a few letters to the editor of the *Denver Post* —but that's why we pay our community relations people those huge salaries. The public is notoriously fickle, you see. Today a scandal, but tomorrow some other scandal takes its place. What I'm saying is, if we're attacked, by this Pollack or anyone else, we'll simply have to fight back. And we're very good at it. I'm so afraid that you, Andres, would be that little skirmish's first and only real casualty.

"By the way," Richardson added, beaming angelically, "how was your lunch?"

Kudirka looked at his untouched plate and nearly retched. Here and there strings of cold crab poked up through the congealed mass of white sauce, like desolate victims of the next ice age.

10

As Pollack turned off Colfax Avenue he was delighted to see what kind of place Capitol Hill was. It reminded him of the less elegant parts of Georgetown —the rows of old houses, mostly red or gray stone and brick, ornate in a way that had signified wealth in late-nineteenth-century silver-rich Colorado. In some blocks nearly every house had its own imaginative cupolas and turrets mounted above the third or fourth floor, while below, near the sidewalk, the stone was chipped away in many places on the outside walls, exposing naked whitish areas where enterprising residents or passersby had scrawled obscenities in black crayon. These once-fine houses had long ago been subdivided into one-room apartments for people who either could afford no better or else preferred the easygoing ways and habitats of the mostly young, mostly long-haired residents of Capitol Hill.

On the fringes of Capitol Hill estate developers had torn down beautifully monstrous old houses by the dozens and constructed in their place gleaming new glass, metal, and plastic high-rise apartment bulidings, with underground parking for every occupant and massive security measures to protect them from the other inhabitants of the area. The apartments were mostly occupied by one kind of tenant—young, unmarried, well enough off to afford the good, swinging life without caring that this high-priced housing might crumble and crack apart the day after tomorrow. It was in such a building that George Davis lived.

Pollack spotted the address as he drove down High Street, and circled the block until he found a place to park. Once inside the deserted foyer of the building he searched the rows of mailbox buzzers until he found "G. Davis—1036." He pushed the button, wondering whether he should have called first; he had thought about doing that back at the hotel but hadn't, for some reason. It wouldn't surprise him to find George out at this time of the afternoon, but you never knew. He pushed the button again.

A girl in a blue ski sweater came into the foyer from the lobby inside the building. "Thanks," he said, courteously holding the door she had just opened. "How's the skiing?"

The girl stared at him as if he were one of those flatland crazies who think you can go skiing in Colorado in October, which of course he was. Holding the door open as he watched her leave the building, Pollack then walked into the inner lobby. This was one of his better days; sometimes he spent as long as an hour standing in a tiny apartment entrance waiting for someone to unwittingly let him in.

Pollack took the self-service elevator to the tenth floor and found number 1036 without difficulty. The floor had one long narrow hallway into which all the apartments opened—inconvenient for burglars or jealous boyfriends or anyone else lurking about, because that person would immediately be seen by anyone entering or leaving an apartment, or for that matter by anyone casually peering into the hall.

He took a set of burglar's picks from his pocket and glanced up and down the long open hall. George could have been visiting on another floor, or taking the garbage out, or engaged in any one of a number of pleasant or unpleasant activities when Pollack had buzzed him from downstairs. There was no one in sight now and no sound except the faint drone of a television set that might even have been on another floor. Pollack tapped lightly on the door—loud enough to rouse George if he were inside but not loud enough to disturb the neighbors. When nothing happened, he worked the picks in the lock for several minutes. The lock was new and tight, which meant it would take a while to pick unless he got lucky; lock companies count on the fact that people picking their locks don't have much time.

There was a noise down the hall that could have come from a door about to be opened. He began walking down the hallway away from the noise, beads of sweat dampening his hairline. Though he listened intently, he heard nothing more. He returned to 1036, thinking how little he wanted to stand out in the open all afternoon trying to pick George's lock.

While he laboriously worked the picks he began studying the door frame, and it was then he noticed the way the door jiggled a quarter of an inch or so within the lock when he touched it. He decided there might be an easier way after all. Lifting the collar of his shirt, he removed one of the celluloid stiffeners and slipped it around the side of the door at the point where the beveled edge of the lock's catch protruded into the metal clasp in the door frame. The little celluloid dagger slipped around the edge of the catch and held it in just enough so that when he shoved hard against the door it clicked open. Quickly he went inside and closed and locked the door behind him.

There was nothing very unusual about the apartment. The living room window afforded a magnificent panorama of the entire front range of the Rockies and, to one side, the downtown skyscrapers that must be something to see at night. Pollack was sure the handsome furnishings belonged to the building, since he credited George with almost no taste, or class, or even rudimentary acquaintance with a lot of things most civilized people would take for granted. It was a hugely biased view, Pollack realized, since if he were correct Simon Reitzman never would have hired Davis. Still, Pollack had little use for his fellow N.S.S. agent, considering him more of a large pain in the ass than anything else: bothersome in a way he couldn't define, and probably quite dangerous.

Methodically Pollack went through all of the cabinets and drawers and every piece of furniture in the living room, bedroom, kitchen, and bathroom, carefully feeling around the bottoms and back edges of drawers just as they had taught him in N.S.S. training. He felt more than a little foolish, knowing that George Davis must have had exactly the same training and thus would have had to be insane to hide anything in any of the places Pollack was looking. Just the same, he continued to search both the obvious and the not-so-obvious spots. After about twenty minutes of this he assured himself that there was no gun in the apartment, which meant that George had it with him. It was what Pollack would have guessed anyway—George was the kind of macho weapons freak who *always* had a gun with him. The regulation short-barreled .38, no doubt, and possibly something else a little special that he'd fixed up for himself, like a tiny palm pistol up his sleeve in a mechanism that would flip it down into his fingers the moment he twitched a particular forearm muscle. Pollack had seen those wicked little toys, and knew the kind of agents who felt a need to carry them.

In a green leather wastebasket beside a small desk in the living room, Pollack found a crumpled-up
91

Special Delivery envelope postmarked Washington, D.C., the previous day—the day Pollack had arrived in Denver. "George, George," Pollack said aloud, "you're getting sloppy living the high life in this altitude." Eventually he found the letter itself, also crumpled into a ball. It was, as he had somehow known it would be, from Reitzman, brief and to the point: "Davis—P. expected your area shortly. Give him all usual assistance. Keep me posted. S. Reitzman."

It was a strange note; strange because Reitzman would naturally expect this kind of cooperation from any area agent, and there would have been no need to alert George unless this was a special kind of code between them. Maybe I'm getting paranoid, Pollack thought. Maybe, in my eleven years as an investigative agent, I've become too dehumanized to ever again trust another person, no matter what the relationship. Maybe.

Carefully he recrumpled both the envelope and the letter and dropped them into the wastebasket in approximately their former positions. He continued to sit at the desk, staring at each individual article in the room and even at the moss-green walls, hoping something significant would jump out at him. There was a picture on the desk in a leather frame, a slightly out-of-focus photograph of a young man in his late twenties, healthy-looking, confident, ambitious, with anachronistically short blond hair, a carefully trimmed moustache that probably turned certain kinds of women on, and a noticeably athletic build. Good old George— that's what having been a Marine lieutenant during the height of Vietnam could do for you.

There was a girl standing beside George in the picture. About the same age as Davis, she seemed vaguely familiar to Pollack although he couldn't place her interesting, pretty face. She looked much too intelligent to be wasting her time with a boob like George, Pollack thought. He studied the photograph carefully for clues and found one—a Ferris wheel partly visible in the background, indicating the picture had been taken at an amusement park. But it didn't do him any good at all. He put the picture back into place and resumed his rational, unproductive thinking.

Something like a shadow moved briefly into the periphery of his left eye's field of vision. Since there was nowhere to go, he forced a smile and turned his head slightly without attempting to move from the chair. "Hello, George," he said, "I didn't hear you come in."

Looking every inch the stern ex-Marine officer, George Davis stood in the middle of the room for several seconds with his arms folded across his chest, staring at Pollack. Finally he said, "You weren't supposed to hear me. What the hell are you doing here, Yale?"

"You mean *here*?" Pollack indicated the apartment. "Just keeping in practice, George. Reitzman tells us not to let our cloak-and-dagger skills get rusty."

"Don't practice on *me*, buddy," George said menacingly, and then his movie-star face broke into a huge grin. "Hey, how 'bout a drink? I've been out on a tough case and I'm dried *out*, man!"

"Anything I ought to know about, old buddy?"

"No way. You know that ain't kosher, asking me that."

"I know. Like I say, just keeping in practice. I'll have a little Pernod and water on ice, if you have it."

"What the shit is Pernod? Scotch is what we have around here, buddy, and maybe there's bourbon if you've gone soft. Or I can make you a nice lemonade . . ."

"Scotch is fine, George, no water."

George went into the kitchen and Pollack stayed at the desk. It was slightly incriminating, being caught going through another man's personal belongings, but hardly worse than being in the apartment in the first place. On reflection, he found that he had no particular feeling about it one way or the other. "You must lead an interesting life, George," he called out toward the kitchen. "A bachelor like you with an eye for the women in a place like this—it must be heaven."

"Yeah, not bad at all, not at all. You oughta see some of the chicks that live in this building—building, hell, right on this floor. They'd knock those tired old eyes of yours right out of your fuzzy head. Here," he said, coming into the living room again and handing Pollack a drink. "You ever get permanently entangled with a woman, Yale?"

"Not permanently, no," Pollack said, feeling uncomfortable with George's personal questions. "Tell me more about how the wealthy young government-agent set lives in Denver, Colorado."

George's mouth curled into a half-smile. "Pretty much the same way you old-timers live, I reckon: we laugh a lot, drink a lot, screw anything that moves—what the hell kind of question is that?"

"Rude, I suppose. Tell me something, George, does it make any difference your being an N.S.S. agent, I mean in your private life?"

"Man, what've you been doing—sitting around here in my castle brooding about Life with a capital L or some goddamn thing? Of course it makes a difference—for one thing I've got to watch every word I say when I'm shacking with some broad, and that ain't easy, believe me. Sometimes they get the idea you're holding something back and then it's *really* tough. I use other names a lot, too, which kind of louses up your continuity if you know what I mean."

"They taught us not to do that, George, remember? Too hard to keep your stories straight if you can't even remember who you're supposed to be."

"It's all right if you don't get fucked up in your head."

"And you never do."

"I never do."

Pollack nodded; it would be exactly like George to take stupid, unnecessary chances, just to see if he could get away with them. "Tell me about the Kudirka thing, Superagent. Tell me about your interview with his wife and the neighbors."

"Not much to tell. The lady's a slant—or of Japanese origin, as they say in the manual. No looker, I'll tell you that. Her face is a lot more used up than the age we've got down for her. But then I guess living with the mad genius has taken its toll. She was scared shitless of my credentials—wanted to know what she'd done, what *he'd* done . . . you know the drill. If I had a dime for every interview subject who acted *so* surprised when we show up—"

"You'd be a wealthy man today. I know, I know . . . All of which has nothing to do with anything. A little bit of authority, particularly if it's mysterious authority like N.S.S., scares most people to death. Sometimes with good reason."

George laughed unpleasantly. "That ain't the way I play it, buddy. Pretty nearly everybody on earth has something to hide. If they act scared of me right off, I figure they're covering something and I really tear into them. Usually I'm right, as it happens."

"You must sleep well, with all that righteous indignation for a blanket."

"I sleep fine, thanks."

"I'll bet you do." Pollack picked up the photograph of George and the girl from the desk. "Who is she?"

"Letty Eubanks. Not that it's any of your business."

No wonder the girl had looked familiar and interesting, Pollack thought. "Sorry. I just thought it was kind of unusual for you to get soft enough to have a picture of yourself and a girl sitting around. What do you do when you bring your other girls over here and they see the picture?"

"It's one of your removable photos. Anyway, I've been sort of concentrating on Letty lately—she's really something special, buddy. Too bad you're not going to be around longer, or maybe you could meet her."

George was watching him carefully without appearing to be. Pollack shrugged and said, "Yeah, well, maybe some other time. Is she a local Denver product?"

"Now she is. Originally from a little mining town up in the mountains called Greenrock. Ever heard of it?"

"No."

"It's between Central City and Rollinsville. Ever heard of them?"

"No."

"Jesus, you Eastern dudes don't know nothin', do you? That was a big gold and silver mining area around 1890, I think it was."

"Did Miss Eubanks work in the mines, George?"

"Funny . . . *funny*. Her father did, though, before he died."

Pollack held the picture of Letty and George in his hand, remembering the conversation he had had with Dr. Welles in her office, especially the part about Andres Kudirka and the Columbine Mining and Smelting Company, which didn't exist.

"George, you ever hear of a mining company around here by the name of Columbine?"

George shook his head. "No, but it's not unlikely —sometimes Colorado's called the Columbine State.

Lots of things around here are called 'Columbine' something."

Pollack set the picture down. "Nice girl, George—nicer than you deserve, no doubt."

"Not *that* nice, buddy. She knows a lot about how to keep a man happy in bed."

"Sounds like your kind of girl, okay," Pollack said irritably, annoyed more than he should have been. "Listen, George, this is all very pleasant, chatting with you about your sordid sex life, but I really came here to do some work. Mrs. Kudirka didn't tell you anything about herself, I suppose?"

"Nothing that wasn't in the data sheet already."

"What about the neighbors?"

"Same thing. This Kudirka must lead a very quiet life. No complaints, no wild parties, no funny visitors late at night, nothing. The guy must be a hermit."

"Not necessarily. By the way, have you heard from our boss lately?"

George frowned, and though it was only a momentary flick of the eye Pollack knew he had glanced down at the wastebasket. "Yeah, Reitzman sent me a note to let me know you were coming—the old boy must be getting soft to treat us lowly field people so well. Why?"

"Just curious." Pollack checked his watch. "I'd better be going—have to earn my pay from Uncle somehow. You ought to see the roach parlor I'm staying in to keep Reitzman happy."

"Which hotel is it?"

"I don't know—I forget the name. It's down on Broadway, about a block from the Brown Palace. *Terrible* place—don't ever take a girl there, George."

"Not to worry, buddy."

"Incidentally, you didn't happen to call me there about nine o'clock last night, did you?"

97

"Call you? Hell, no. What's the matter—you letting something spook you?"

"I don't think so." George was such a beautiful liar —just no way to tell about him, ever. "Well, look," Pollack said, "I'll pick up this Kudirka thing and follow it on through . . . mostly a matter now of stitching up the loose ends and writing a report. Why don't you go ahead with whatever else you've been working on. That way we won't be falling over each other's heels."

George squinted at Pollack as if trying to ferret out hidden motives. "Okay, Yale, whatever you say. You're the boss."

That will be the day, Pollack thought. He stood up and walked over to the door of the apartment. When he turned the knob nothing happened.

"We playing games, George? What is it, a key-operated deadlock?"

George sat on the couch, laughing. "You picked your way in here, buddy, I guess you can pick your way out."

For a fraction of a second Pollack thought he might kill George. George was heavier and probably fought dirtier, but it would have been a pleasure to get in even one solid chop to that smug face under the blond god's-cap of hair. But he knew he couldn't afford the dramatics, so he took the set of burglar's picks from his pocket and tediously began working the slender metal rods into the keyhole. It was an excellent lock; he knew he was working more quickly than was prudent, hating the thought that he might fail entirely with George watching him.

After four or five minutes of concentrated effort he saw that it was simply no good. "George, will you come here a minute?" he said.

Grinning, George got up and came over beside Pollack. "Too tough for an old pro like you?"

"Lend me your knife a minute."

"That's cheating," George said. "You wouldn't lend *me* a knife." But then, reluctantly, he rolled up his shirt-sleeve and plucked something small and dagger-like from a leather holster strapped to his wrist. When he touched a button on its side a thin switchblade shot out from one end. He handed the knife to Pollack blade first.

"This thing government issue?" Pollack asked him.

"Don't worry about it. It's for emergencies only."

Pollack deftly inserted the blade beneath the pins of the door hinges which lifted out easily. He pried that edge of the door away from the wall enough to hook his fingers behind it, and bracing his foot against the wall he pulled at the edge of the door with all his strength. There was a satisfying cracking noise as the wooden door frame opposite the lock splintered. He lifted the door clear and leaned it at an angle against the wall.

"You'd better get that fixed pretty soon, George," he said. "I understand this is a high-crime area."

Smiling now at the way George's mouth hung open in imitation of the ruined door, Pollack stepped out into the hallway and walked briskly toward the elevator.

11

THEY WERE IN BED TOGETHER, sleeping without touching, as had been their habit for several years. Mariko, as always, slept soundly—as if drugged. But her husband's sleep was that of a restless man, a man gripped by thoughts that terrified him and caused his body to quiver, and often he woke up not knowing where he was—not even what country—and afraid to inhale for fear that the next breath might be his last.

Sometimes the potent laboratory alcohol soothed his nerves and sometimes it failed to have any noticeable effect at all. The pills he took were of so many different colors and types with so many noncompatible effects that he often didn't know whether he was asleep and dreaming or awake and hallucinating. It seemed to make little difference; the fabric of his life was gradually ripping apart at every seam and there was nothing he could do to stop it.

Now he slept, but fitfully, his dreams a tapestry woven by demons:

A city burning from sporadically exploding artillery shells, great mounds of rubble in the streets, fair-haired, blue-eyed citizens with unaccustomed expressions of fear and anxiety clouding their faces. Vilna? Perhaps. The year? Perhaps, again, 1942. The Germans were everywhere with their clicking boot heels and their total disdain for the Lithuanian people who only wished to be left alone to return to their farms, their small shops, their peaceful ways. One heard about the Jews, of course; but when one was suspected of *being* a Jew, or part-Jew, which amounted to the same thing in Nazi eyes, one became almost paralyzed with fear.

An eighteen-year-old boy in good health was valuable for many of the Occupation's work details; the back-breaking labor kept his mind numb, which was fortunate. A pretty and well-developed sixteen-year-old girl, like his sister Tinar, was another matter. Spoils of war, they called it. On a cloudy night Tinar failed to return home from her job cleaning a building used by the German headquarters staff. He went to find her, picking his way blindly through shattered bricks and splintered wooden beams, smoke from the newest fires stinging his eyes and nose. At the glass doors he halted and, peering through, did not believe what he saw: his sister, naked and laughing hysterically, stretched out on the stone floor beside a lantern, one German soldier just standing to button his trousers while another prepared to take his place. In a frenzy then, searching for a loose brick or board with which to break through the glass and confront her tormentors, he thought only of killing but would surely have been killed himself, as would Tinar. An explosion sent him reeling backward down the steps and tore away the entire front half of the building. Somehow only bruised and cut, he stumbled and shouted for a long time through clouds of dust and falling debris, but there was no answer, there would never be an answer from little Tinar.

The noxious clouds swirl in to envelop his mind, carrying him far away to another place of explosion and fire and death. Another time and another building, much later in his life . . . And again he survived,

101

by the fractional mercy of some unspeakable god who took away life at his pleasure. But slowly, now, as in some ritual awakening, he perceived the truth—that men were the agents of destruction, not gods; it was men who must be held accountable. He would speak out, he would destroy this conspiracy of silence that raged about him, paralyzing his mind.

"No! No! Not my fault!" he shouted, bolting upright in the dark bed, the sheets damp with his dreaming. "Too dangerous . . . I told them . . . I told them . . ."

"Breathe, Andres, breathe deep," Mariko soothed, holding him, kneading his rigid muscles. "Breathe, yes, that is good. Deep breaths, Andres. You are all right now, yes? I think you are all right."

He stared around the bedroom, shaking, trying to remember. "Where am I?" he pleaded. "Please, for God's sake, tell me where I am."

"You are in your own bed, Andres. In the city of Denver, state of Colorado, United States of America." She held him against her frail body until his trembling subsided. "Was it the bomb, Andres? Was it about Peliea?"

Kudirka shook his head slowly and looked at his wife, who for some foolish reason went on saving his life despite everything. "No, not about Peliea," he said thickly, but that was all he would tell her.

12

POLLACK CALLED Letty Eubanks twice the following day, but she was out of the office both times and he didn't leave his name or number, for several reasons. Finally, on the third try, she answered her extension.

"Hi," Pollack said. "You probably don't remember me—does the name 'interesting stranger' mean anything to you?"

"You sound like a weirdo, whoever you are," Letty said. "Come on over and we'll arm-wrestle."

Her offhand banter unnerved him. "It's Yale Pollack—National Security Service? Remember, I was in there yesterday poking around and asking questions, and you said something—"

"About interesting strangers. Sure, I remember. Did you think I'd ask just *anybody* to come over and arm-wrestle?"

Pollack chuckled. "Well, anyway, I find my terribly crowded schedule is suddenly bleak and bare all evening. The truth is, I'm lonely as hell in mile-high Denver town and the prospect of spending all night in some sleazy bar by myself is driving me to unheard-of heights of cheek. I thought maybe if you weren't all tied up I might meet you after work for a drink, or dinner if you know any good restaurants, whatever you say. The reason I'm picking on you is that you're the nicest person I've met in Denver."

"And I just happen to be the only *girl* you've met in Denver. Mr. Pollack, could I ask you a rather personal question?"

"Only if you don't call me Mr. Pollack."

"Okay, Yale—that's a funny name, Yale; remind me to ask you about it sometime. The question is, are you married?"

"I'm not married," Pollack said. "I was, a long time ago. Who knows, it may come up in our conversation."

"It doesn't have to. I'm sorry—I wasn't prying, really. It's just that I get awfully tired of discovering over and over again that what I thought was going to be a pleasant evening turns out to be some horny married man's big out-of-town fling. I don't need that."

"Nobody needs that."

"Right. Hey, you said something about dinner—you know what? Dinner is one of my favorite subjects. Why don't you come over to my place and let me cook for you? I don't get the chance all that often, because of one thing and another. *That* may come up in the conversation, too."

"It sounds like a traveling man's dream, even though I'm not actually a traveling man. What's your address, and what time?"

He wrote down what she told him, and after hanging up the telephone he looked up her street on a Denver city map he had bought at a service station. It turned out he wouldn't have much trouble finding her apartment, since it was only three or four blocks from George Davis's place in Capitol Hill. He couldn't decide whether or not this was another one of those coincidences, but it didn't bother him that much; he was simply doing a job on Letty Eubanks, and her relationship with George, while interesting, shouldn't interfere at all with what he had to do.

Restless, he sat in the cramped hotel room trying to read the *Denver Post* and getting nowhere with it —except for the front page the news all seemed to concern people and places unfamiliar to him. Finally it was a little after seven and he calculated that if he took his time going downstairs and claiming the car, and drove slowly, it might take him until almost seven-thirty, which was when she had told him to be there. He opened the door of his room and stared out into the dingy hall. For some reason he remembered the telephone caller who had refused to identify himself. Or herself.

He went back into the room and got the small suit-case out of the closet. From the elastic pocket at the back he took a little pouch of such useful things as straight pins, needles, a small spool of thread (black), and a roll of cellophane tape. He broke off two small pieces of tape and a ten-inch piece of thread, and put the other things away. He then taped one end of the thread to the bottom edge of the door, stepped into the empty hall and pulled the door shut, and attached the other end of the thread to the door frame just above the faded carpet. He shut the door all the way and heard it lock; the thread was totally invisible.

The rented red Mustang, though still running, was definitely lacking in pep. It sputtered and coughed on the way out of the parking garage and died twice in the street, confirming his suspicions that it had been born and bred in some different altitude and brought to Denver by an itinerant car thief. When a teen-aged boy with curly bangs raced his hijacked Chevy II engine beside Pollack at a stoplight, Pollack just laughed and watched the kid burn off enough rubber to make two new tires. He found the address Letty had given him without trouble and parked on the street, carefully marking down the mileage in the red expenses notebook. This time, he thought in passing, I will blow Reitzman's mind with my superb attention to detail.

Letty's apartment was arranged almost exactly like George's, except that she had obviously furnished it herself, and with a good deal more taste. It seemed warmer, *friendlier*—then he realized he was appraising Letty's velvet pants and frilly open-necked white blouse as much as he was the apartment, and she seemed to realize it too.

"My, my, Mr. Pollack, it can't be *that* long since you've seen a woman in her natural habitat," she laughed.

"You look . . . different, somehow," he said, genuinely impressed.

"That's called the working girl's metamorphosis. Want a drink before dinner? Name your poison, sir —keeping in mind there's a rare last-month's vintage rosé to go with the meat loaf."

"Oh, anything's fine."

"Well, what do you *like?*"

"Everything I see," he said, meaning it. "I'm a Pernod nut, actually, but I don't expect you've ever heard of it—nobody has. Scotch or something will be just fine."

While he was talking she had stooped to paw through a low cabinet and now stood triumphantly holding out to him the familiar green bottle, product of France. It appeared to be about three-quarters full.

"I don't believe it!" he said. "You mean you—"

"Never touch the stuff—to me it tastes like medicine. It's pure coincidence, that's all. I dated a Frenchman once, for about three weeks, until he got disgustingly French. He mentioned he liked Pernod, and being the pleasant sort I got this bottle for him. Since then no one else has had nerve enough to try it. Jacques —that was his name, Jacques—liked it with a little water and ice, as I remember. What about you?"

"Exactly the way I like it," Pollack said. "The French way."

She fixed a screwdriver for herself and they sat cozily on the small modern sofa and talked. Pollack felt relaxed, although he knew from past experience how dangerous that could be when he was working.

"I noticed," he said, "that you called me Mr. Pollack again. I thought I warned you about that."

"I'm sorry. *Yale*. How did you get that name?"

Pollack settled into the cushions. "It's a long story and it'll bore you silly, but you asked. My father was a doctor in the small town of Pine Lake, Virginia— *the* doctor, most of the time I was growing up. I hated everything about the medical profession—the instruments, the smell of antiseptic, even the poor sick people, for God's sake—and he knew it. One day I threw up all over the clinic. He just looked up at me from whatever wound he was dressing and said, 'So be a lawyer.' Not just *any* lawyer, mind you, but a lawyer with a diploma or whatever you get from Yale Law School. But it never happened."

Letty looked at him. "That happened when you were about ten years old?"

"I guess so."

"It's an interesting story. But how did you get the name Yale when you were born?"

"I don't know," he answered honestly. "They used to tell me that story and I was a gullible child."

"Unlike some of us," Letty said. "How old are you now?"

"Older than you, a lot older. I was one of the celebrated 'thirties Depression babies. I grew up and went to school in Pine Lake, but nothing special

107

happened. I guess I could have been a good student but I was bored, spent a lot of time looking out the window instead of at my arithmetic book. My mother died of cancer when I was thirteen—I don't think my father ever got over it. It changed him. I don't know, we never talked much after that, and when I got to be eighteen I was drafted and left Pine Lake for good. It's funny, you know, but there I am working in D.C. now and it's kind of sad to think that in forty-one years I've only come ninety-five miles from the place I was born. That's real progress."

Letty pushed a wayward lock of short dark hair out of her eyes. "That *is* sad—I mean your outlook is sad. You don't sound much like a go-get-'em secret agent to me. How'd you ever get into that line of work, anyway?"

"That's another long story," Pollack said, aware that he was talking too much. He swirled the glass around and watched the ice cubes dart through the cloudy Pernod. "You know why I like this stuff? I just figured it out—it's not because it's ninety proof and can zonk you in a hurry if that's what you want, and it's not even the flavor, although it's about the most refreshing thing I can think of. No, the *real* reason I like Pernod is the color—which, when you mix in a little water, becomes a mystical yellow-green cloud of pure wisdom. Do I sound drunk?"

"A little, maybe."

"Sorry. What about *your* life story, Miss Eubanks?"

"Oh, nothing much to tell. I was born ten or twelve years after you were, I guess. In Montana. My father was a hard-rock miner, always looking for the damn-all mother lode that would put us on easy street. We moved around a lot. Came to Colorado when I was just going into the sixth grade. We lived up in the mountains, in a little tiny town that probably didn't even have a Band-Aid, much less a doctor. When I graduated from high school in 1966 there was only enough money for a year at secretarial school and then I had to get a job. I worked for an oil man for a while, and then I was offered this job with Rocky Mountain Power Company at a big raise in salary, so here I am. Romantic, isn't it?"

"Yes," Pollack said. "Well, what I mean is, if you hadn't been working there yesterday I wouldn't have met you and you wouldn't have invited me to your apartment for dinner and—"

"You'd be in some sleazy bar drinking Pernod till it came out your ears, and loving it," she finished. "You hungry, by any chance?"

"Sure, anytime. We *could* just pour another drink, put our feet up, and forget all about dinner."

"No you can't, because I'm starved. And I just *love* my own meat loaf."

The table seemed made for two people who were at least very good friends. Pollack wondered as he watched her serving his plate across the flickering candles how many other men had sampled Letty Eubanks' meat loaf. It was an uncomfortable thought, made even more uncomfortable by his memory of the photograph in George's apartment. How could she ever have enjoyed herself with that overmuscled oaf?

"Wonderful meat loaf, Letty," he told her, and it was only a small lie. "Do you have any brothers or sisters?"

She glanced up sharply, then looked away. "I used to, a younger brother. Oliver and Corinne—my parents —sure loved that kid."

"Past tense?"

"They're all . . . dead now."

"I'm sorry, I shouldn't have been prying."

"No, it's all right. It was several years ago and I

ought to be over it by now. Besides, that's your job, isn't it? Prying, I mean?"

Pollack shook his head. "Do you think that's why I wanted to see you?"

"Probably."

"Okay, I suppose that's fair enough. Now that you've brought it up, *is* there any reason I should be investigating you?"

"None that I can think of. You seemed interested in this man Kudirka at the office. I don't know him— I've never even heard of him."

"I think I'm glad. Not that it would make any difference whether you knew him or not. He's just a routine part of a routine case, Letty. I've done hundreds like it and I'll probably do hundreds more before I die. Of boredom."

The telephone rang, sounding very loud in the small apartment. Letty cast a momentary quizzical glance at it before she excused herself and went to a little alcove outside the bedroom to answer it. She spoke in low tones to whomever it was, and at first Pollack couldn't glean anything from the conversation. But then the selective hearing that all good agents develop eventually filtered out the extraneous words and euphemisms and he began to pick out significant-sounding phrases: ". . . no, everything's fine. I told you . . . I'm sure he can't . . . because I'm way in *here,* that's why . . . a little after seven . . . I don't know, after a while . . . well, I'm not a professional like some people . . . don't use that kind of language . . . all right . . . yes, all right . . . told you I'd handle it . . . damn you, good-bye!"

She slammed down the receiver, came back to the table, and stared distractedly at her plate. "You want more meat loaf?" she asked Pollack, not looking at him. "There's plenty, and I don't want it left."

"Why not? You said you were your own best fan —you could warm it up and have another meat-loaf dinner some night."

"I don't eat here very much," she said noncommittally. She wiped her mouth with a paper napkin, simultaneously wiping away the tears that he had seen gathering in her eyes. "Well, let's have dessert in the comfortable chairs, shall we?" she said too brightly. "It's strawberry shortcake, and if you don't like it I'll kill you . . ." She stopped as if considering what she'd said and shook her head at him. "I didn't mean that. I say things I don't mean sometimes, okay? Everybody does, don't they?"

"Are you talking about Freudian slips, or just things in general?" Pollack asked her. "Because I didn't really think you had it in mind to do away with me, at least not until you'd charmed all those state secrets out of my deep subconscious. But I'll save you the trouble —I don't *know* any state secrets, and if I did I'd probably just tell them to you if you asked me. No broken glass up the penis or anything."

"Oh!" Letty shuddered. "How *horrible*—what a horrible imagination you must have."

"I didn't make that up," Pollack said. "In Korea they—it was a way of torturing uncooperative prisoners. They'd shove a hollow glass tube up into a man and then beat him until it shattered inside his body. You have no idea how effective it was psychologically."

Letty grimaced painfully. "The awful things human beings do to each other . . . Sometimes I think I'd like to be a cow, or a small, furry, uncomplicated animal with only the basic wants and needs."

"And you'd be slaughtered by your less sensitive neighbors."

"I suppose. What were you doing in Korea?"

"Fighting a war. Not really that dramatic, though. The Army sent me to ordnance disposal and demolition school, and you know something? I was scared all the time, every minute of every day, and I never got over it. I've never told that to anybody else—the machismo factor, I guess."

Letty shook her head. "You big, strong, silent warriors make me sick sometimes. You're like my father —he almost cut his leg off with an ax one time but he refused to let us take him to the doctor. He nearly died before we got the bleeding stopped."

"I agree," Pollack said. "I mean, that kind of stupid pride is a very expensive, worthless commodity. I guess the reason I don't talk about it much is that it doesn't sound like that much. It wasn't even wartime, technically—the truce had already been declared before I got over to Korea. Mostly we dug a lot of unexploded munitions out of schoolyards and rice paddies. Sometimes a guy on the team would spend two or three hours getting an artillery dud carefully pulled away from the dirt where it was buried, and then he'd be walking gently over toward the bomb truck with the thing cradled in his arms like a baby and it would go off—just *boom*—and there wouldn't be enough pieces of him left to pick up. I saw it happen once, to a friend of mine. I couldn't go out for two or three days after that, just stayed in my tent shaking and vomiting. They had to threaten me with a court-martial even then."

Letty sat biting her lip, having made no move to get the promised shortcake. "I don't think you should have told me all that, Yale," she said. "Somehow it's like putting strings around me, knowing all these things about your personal life."

"I'm sure you'll find some way to rise above it," he said, suddenly irritated. She frowned at him, then rose abruptly and went into the kitchen to prepare the dessert.

When they moved back into the living room for the shortcake Pollack took off his jacket and laid it across the back of the sofa. He was wearing a short-sleeved shirt, and he noticed Letty staring at the large grayish patch of scar tissue on his left arm. Seeing that it disturbed her, he attempted to cover the spot with his right hand. "Not very pretty, am I?" he said.

"Was it a bomb?"

"No, nothing like that. After the Army and college —U.C.L.A.—I went to work for the Forest Service in northern California, and I fought some fires, and eventually one of them fought back. Somehow I managed to let a blazing Douglas fir fall on my arm."

Letty reached over and ran her fingers gently across the old burn. Her hand felt cool and healing against his skin. He touched her, recognized compliance in her body, and kissed her for a long time. When they finally parted she tilted her head back and smiled up at him expectantly.

"Was that George on the phone a little while ago?" he asked her, purposely brutal.

Her smile froze and slowly disappeared, like a Popsicle in the blazing sun. "George who? Hey, are you sure you didn't jump the fence at some looney bin?"

"I *work* in a looney bin, Letty, but not the kind you mean. No, I just thought it might have been good old George Davis, the working girl's friend. You see, he told me all about you—*all* about you. And I saw the photograph from the amusement park."

"Elitch Gardens, last summer," she sighed. "My God, a girl can't have any secrets at all around here."

"What was it about? The phone call, I mean."

"That isn't really any of your business, is it? But

113

I guess maybe you can make anything your business, just by flashing that little card that says you N.S.S. types are exempt from all normal standards of decency. How's it feel to be an official bully?"

"Oh, hell, Letty, you're being childish." He considered a moment. "When I went to work for N.S.S. they promised me it would be mostly a desk job, a public contact job—'Asking questions and getting answers,' they told me, 'no rough stuff.' And that was exactly what I wanted. In certain respects, however, they lied."

"Don't tell me if you don't want to," Letty said, her tone softening.

"I wouldn't be telling you any of this if it mattered," Pollack said. "Actually, the first thing they did during training was to teach me about fourteen ways to kill a man with nothing more lethal than a ball-point pen. After that they taught me to lie, cheat, and steal, if necessary, for the good of the national security. Mostly the only lying I've found it necessary to do has been to my own superiors—to get around their asinine views of life and what's good for the country."

He studied Letty's face, wondering what she knew that she wasn't telling him and that might conceivably get him killed. "Now, back to George . . ."

Letty smiled thinly. "Yes, George. He's a very possessive person, did you know that?"

"No, I didn't. Do you like being possessed?"

"Not to that extent. Sometimes, I guess, like any other silly-headed romantic little girl, but not all the time. Sometimes it's just very nice being my own person."

"What about now—right this minute?"

"I'm giving that problem some serious thought," she said, smiling now as if she meant it.

He moved his hand slowly up her arm and across

the back of her neck, caressing her, stroking the soft white skin below her almost boyish black hair. Her eyes were closed, and he realized for the first time what an extraordinarily beautiful girl she was. Like a cat rubbing against warm skin, she arched her head back against his fingers. He bent to kiss her, but suddenly her body stiffened and lurched away from him and she opened her eyes as if waking from an unpleasant dream.

"Yale, no, please," she said. "It isn't that I don't want to, but I just mustn't get involved with you now. There are reasons . . ."

Pollack, nodding, removed his hand from her and struggled to his feet. "I think I understand, Letty. It's tough, isn't it, being a security-agent groupie—never knowing when a guy's making love to you whether you really turn him on or whether he's just setting you up for some fancy espionage work. I sympathize, believe me, and so, I'm sure, does George. And all the others, whoever they may have been."

She glared at him as if he were some amoebic mutation. "Am I to assume, then, that you got what you came for, and now you're leaving?"

"You bet."

She nodded slowly. "Go away, Yale Pollack, get the hell out of my life," she whispered. "You're a filthy-minded man without an ounce of human compassion in you. Who needs you to screw up my life any worse than it already is? Just go away."

He lifted his jacket from the sofa back and slung it over his shoulder. At the doorway of the apartment he turned back to her, and said, "Well, anyway, it was great meat loaf, Letty. I wouldn't have missed it for anything." His last view of her with huge tears rolling down her lovely cheeks caused him more distress than he dared to admit, even to himself.

115

13

_____

ON THE HIGHWAY north out of Denver Pollack had to
floor the accelerator of the sluggish Mustang to maintain the fifty-five-miles-per-hour limit. Ten miles or so
beyond the city limits he spotted, too late, a small
sign on the right-hand side of the road directing him
to make a sharp left to the Handley Pond Nuclear
Generating Station. He made a wide U-turn in the
highway and came back to the dirt road from the
opposite direction. Other tire marks in the dirt shoulder
indicated this was a fairly common mistake.

The dirt road crossed a cattle guard with loose
horizontal metal poles that nearly tore the car apart.
After the cattle guard it was just a pleasantly non-
descript country road—leading, apparently, nowhere—
until suddenly it dropped off and curved to the right
around a shallow lake. He could see then what he had
not been able to see from the highway; it sat gleaming
majestically in the sun, rising like a mirage out of what
appeared to be a field of lush green wheat.

Pollack guided the Mustang into the parking lot
beside a low, small building that served as a visitors'
center for the nuclear station. Open only during normal
weekday working hours, this preliminary building, Mr.
Richardson's secretary had explained, was as far as
most casual visitors ever got. Two hundred yards beyond the visitors' center was the nuclear plant itself,

enclosed in a cocoon of steel fencing topped with wicked-looking spirals of barbed wire.

Pollack got out of the car and stood gazing at the plant for a minute, wondering why it looked so familiar. And then he remembered: it was almost identical to the benign nuclear facility in the poster he had seen in both Henry Richardson's office and the A.D.A. office of Dr. Welles.

He took the special yellow pass from his pocket and walked into the visitors' center, where even with the pass there was a certain amount of stir about the fact that no one had informed them he was coming. Finally, after the man in charge made a quick call to the downtown offices of Rocky Mountain Power Company, they opened a door in the back wall of the station and the manager himself guided him along a path leading straight into the ominous-looking fence. Without the manager's visible help, a massive gate opened as they approached it; Pollack assumed it had been opened for them either by someone back in the visitors' center or by someone up ahead inside the plant.

"Security controls the gate from inside," the manager told him, almost as if he had read Pollack's mind. "Absolutely no one can get in or out without our knowledge."

"Why would anyone want to?" Pollack innocently asked. "What could they hope to gain?"

The manager shook his head and looked apprehensively at his unwelcome guest. "We live in perilous times, Mr. Pollack. Assassins are everywhere—madmen with bombs, the hippie element that hates anything to do with atomic energy, even some of the more radical environmentalists would like to see this place go up in a puff of smoke. We have to be very careful . . . very careful indeed."

"How do you sleep nights?" Pollack goaded him,

as they passed through the gate and walked toward a white concrete door set into the side of the main building. The door had a hemispherical top.

"We're being watched by Security right now," the manager said, pointing up to one of several small closed-circuit television cameras mounted high on the external walls which, rotating in their electric arcs, covered much of the ground between the perimeter fence and the plant. The manager took a plastic card from his pocket and fed it into a slot beside the door; there was a click and then a low hum as the door slid upward out of sight. The manager retrieved his card from the slot and they walked into a narrow metal tunnel fifteen feet long and barely high enough to stand in comfortably.

"This is the air lock, Mr. Pollack. It's the only way in or out of the plant. In a moment the door through which we just entered will close and seal automatically behind us, so tightly that not even a particle of dust can escape."

"Would that be radioactive dust?" Pollack asked.

"A particle of anything, Mr. Pollack. The air lock pressures down each time the outside door is opened, maintaining a slight negative air pressure inside as an additional safeguard."

Just as the manager had said it would, the outer door rumbled shut behind them on its greased tracks. Only then did Pollack notice the fluorescent lights spaced evenly along the sides of the tunnel. The enameled white metal shone depressingly in the pale blue light, enlivened only by an incongruously bright-red telephone protruding from the wall halfway through the tunnel. "That phone connects with the security desk inside," the manager explained to Pollack, "but it's simply a redundant safety precaution—no one's ever had to use it."

Mounted waist-high on the inner door was a wheel that reminded Pollack of those on submarine hatch covers he had seen in movies. A thick wire-grilled glass window was set into the door. Pollack tapped it with his fingernail and cupped his hand around his eye to peer through, but he could see nothing much on the other side. "Does someone have to come let us out of here?" he asked the manager. "It's a little spooky, to tell you the truth."

"Oh?" the manager said. "I thought you'd be used to this kind of thing." He looked almost as if he might smile. "Actually, we can go on through any time if you're getting nervous about it—I suppose sometimes I take my position as tour guide too seriously. The wheel on the door activates the air-pressure valve and maintains a tighter seal than would otherwise be possible. If you'd be so good as to turn it as far as possible to the left . . ."

Pollack attempted to turn the wheel but nothing happened; he tried again, straining until his neck muscles began to hurt.

"You see? Nothing, without this." The manager inserted his magnetic card into another slot beside the door and turned the wheel easily with one hand.

Pollack smiled crookedly. "You have fun making your little points, don't you?"

The door opened and they walked inside. Off to the left, a young man in white coveralls and white shoe covers and wearing a black holster containing a large revolver sat behind a desk marked "Security," his feet propped casually on the rim of a wastebasket.

The guard smiled when he saw the manager. "What brings you in here, Jim? You and this gentleman taking a tour of our little slaughterhouse?"

The manager blanched. "That's in very poor taste,

Wayne. This is Mr. Pollack from the National Security Service. He's here to see Andres Kudirka."

Wayne appraised Pollack a full minute or more before deciding to smile at him. "He'll have to sign in like everybody else, Jim."

"I know that," the manager said. "Get him some shoe covers, please."

After Pollack had signed the log book and pulled the shoe covers over his desert boots, the manager left him with Wayne and returned the way they had come. The security guard led Pollack through several doorways and up a corrugated metal ramp. Everything— the walls, the ceiling, the floor, the stairways and ramps and doors and pipes and various pieces of unidentified machinery—were all painted a glaring white. They passed through another door and entered a glass-enclosed room where a bearded man wearing a white smock sat at an oddly angled counter laid out around three sides of the room. Above the counter were more dials and switches and lights and meters than Pollack had ever seen in one place before. The man did not look up as they entered the room, and continued to turn a small screwdriver into the side of a metal box even after the guard called his name.

"Mr. Kudirka—there's someone here to see you!"
Kudirka finally glanced at Pollack. "You wish to see me?" He indicated a swivel chair beside his own at the control panel, but went on tinkering with the wires on the box gadget. "All right, Wayne, you may leave us," he said to the guard.

Pollack waited until the guard had left the area. Judging that an extended hand would be a waste of time, he simply said, "I'm Yale Pollack, from the National Security Service. We're doing a more or less routine background check on you—for your A.D.A.

120

license renewal, you know. There are a couple of small things we need to clear up."

Kudirka stared at him as if he hadn't been listening. "Have you seen the reactor yet, Mr. Pollack? Our expensive playtoy?"

"I'm not sure. Is that it up there?"

"Indeed it is."

Pollack tilted his head far back to peer up at where the control room ceiling should have been but was not. Empty space soared up so high that there seemed no end to it. In the middle of the space, rising about three-quarters of the distance to the top of the building, was a gigantic hexagonal concrete enclosure. Catwalks circled the structure at various levels; hoses and pipes entered and left the concrete through sealed portholes, cranelike machinery hovered around it, and at the topmost reaches grew a forest of metallic rods driven by motors and cables and electrical switches.

A nerve twitched angrily in Pollack's upper back. He rubbed his neck with his fingers and lowered his head to watch the console's blinking lights and fluctuating indicator needles responding to unseen forces controlled by no human hand. In a way the plant seemed to run itself, with only an amorphous humming and the cold swish of its fabricated air to indicate a life force of this eerie white monster that—who knew?— perhaps resented the interference of human beings. Pollack gazed up at the awesome reactor vessel again, drawn to it by a compulsive fear such as he had not known since the Korean nightmare. The sight of such a massive indoor construction diminished him to an insignificance he found truly disturbing.

"Christ, that's impressive!" he said in awe.

"Yes, it is," Kudirka agreed. "I have been here every day since the facility became operational and still I find myself sitting in this spot staring up for

121

many minutes at this incredible technological achievement. It is almost a religious experience for me, Mr. Pollack, do you comprehend that?"

Pollack nodded. "It's obvious you're a man devoted to his work, Mr. Kudirka. There aren't many of those around these days."

"Perhaps 'devoted' is not the proper terminology in this case. An analogy to early Egyptian slaves chained to the mill wheels seems more apropos."

Pollack considered the statement. "Still, no one holds a gun on you, forcing you to work here."

"Do they not indeed, Mr. Pollack? There is an entire arsenal of intangible weaponry available to employers these days."

"I guess that's one way to look at it. By the way, I'm sorry if one of our people frightened your wife. I understand he perhaps didn't completely identify himself."

"That would be Mr. George Davis, I take it?"

"Yes. He's a good man, I suppose. A bit impulsive for my tastes, but then he doesn't exactly work for me."

"He identified himself, Mr. Pollack. That was not the problem. The problem was that I have not done anything that ought to be investigated, and certainly Mariko has not. The two of us have led a rather quiet, secluded life in the scientific and academic communities of this country for a good many years. No scandals, no wife-swapping, no secrets smuggled out in the heels of our shoes to waiting agents of the Russians or the Chinese or whomever . . . I'm afraid you and Mr. Davis overestimate my importance, Mr. Pollack. I have no secrets to sell, even if I wished to become involved in such an odious pastime."

"Mr. Kudirka, no one suspects you of disloyalty to your adopted country. If that were the case, I assure you we would be proceeding somewhat differently. I

122

merely noted these curious holes in your background sheet, and when I'm dealing with something as potentially dangerous as nuclear security I don't like mysteries, even small ones. Even those that concern, say, your wife . . ."

"No mystery there. We met in southern California, at a conference of physicists at U.C.L.A. one summer while I was employed at Los Alamos."

"Oh? Then your wife is also a scientist?"

"Hardly. Mariko thinks science is largely expensive witchcraft. No, she was hired by the university to transcribe the conference discussions in shorthand. Since our marriage she has never worked, however; I am reasonably sure that if you asked her to produce a sentence in shorthand today she would be wholly unable to do so."

"I see," Pollack said, thinking how neatly that worked out. "The other thing that I'm concerned about is probably only a failure in our own data-collection system. I'm almost embarrassed to bring it up."

"Then remain silent." Kudirka smiled like a little boy with a big secret. "If *you* do not tell, *I* certainly will not; and your superiors will be none the wiser. Unless, of course, you are somehow recording our present conversation on one of those marvelously micro-miniaturized spy gadgets I have read about in *Scientific American*."

Pollack chuckled. "We don't work that way, Mr. Kudirka. Not usually, anyway. And I must say your idea of forgetting the whole thing is appealing in some ways. If I were doing this only because my superiors ordered it, I'd probably drop it right this minute. Unfortunately, perhaps, I'm one of those people who don't care for loose ends . . . I could never work a crossword puzzle down to the last three words and then abandon it, for instance."

Kudirka tapped the control counter with his index finger, in obvious agreement. "I believe we are alike in many ways, you and I, Mr. Pollack. Under other circumstances I believe we might even have become friends."

Pollack nodded. "Perhaps . . . who knows? Maybe we still will. In the meantime, I must ask you this: Between the time you left the Nuclear Engineering Department at Stanford in 1970 and the time you came to work as the chief operating engineer here at Handley Pond, what exactly were you doing? We need a detailed account of that period of time."

Kudirka stood and wandered aimlessly about the control room, now and then peering at a dial or adjusting a switch. "That is not very difficult, Mr. Pollack. A good deal of the time I was lecturing at various universities around the country."

"Could you be more specific?"

"I believe so." He paused. "University of Chicago, 1970, April or May. Ohio State University, the following October. The University of Indiana in January of 1971."

Pollack scribbled the names and dates in the same small red expenses notebook in which half an hour ago he had written down the exact distance from his hotel to Handley Pond—13.4 miles. "Those seem to be rather scattered dates, Mr. Kudirka. Would you be able to remember what you were doing between lectures, and more recently?"

Kudirka frowned. "Thinking, mostly. Considering the universe and the fullness thereof. Resting . . . I was very tired from my tutorial duties at Stanford. Oh yes—and fishing. I went fishing regularly."

"Oh? Where was that?"

"Why here, in Colorado. The mountain streams . . ."

"Your famous mountain trout, no doubt. I'm sorry I haven't had time to get in a little fishing on this trip. Could you tell me, by the way, what sort of line and bait you used?"

Kudirka glanced at Pollack and looked away. "Medium line . . . you understand, whatever was handy. I am not an expert fisherman."

"And the bait?"

"Worms?"

"I doubt it, Mr. Kudirka, I really doubt it."

Kudirka shrugged. "All right. It is true I did not spend much time fishing. And I suppose thinking does not sound like much, either."

Pollack laughed. "It probably isn't the most popular pastime, even if it ought to be. It complicates *my* job, of course—no way to check out when a man's thinking and when he isn't. I hope you understand these questions aren't just a form of harassment by N.S.S. or anyone else."

"I understand, Mr. Pollack. There are things that I cannot tell you, things I *will* not tell you. Some of it has to do with security and some does not, but no amount of questioning by you or Mr. Davis or anyone else will loosen my tongue. I dislike official prying, Mr. Pollack. If that attitude constitutes an uncooperative interview in your reports to your superiors, so be it."

Pollack put away his notebook and stood up. "No more personal questions, Mr. Kudirka. But I wonder . . . could I see something of the plant while I'm here?"

"Certainly . . . of course. I will take you myself. Smitty, my chief assistant, is around somewhere to watch the dials. As you can see we are not so busy now as we might be. This facility is to be shut down for a time. The company indicates two weeks, but I think longer—perhaps much longer. There have been

125

problems—things I perhaps should not even speak of, but you would no doubt hear them eventually in any case."

"What sort of problems?"

"Potentially dangerous ones . . . hairline cracks in the concrete containment structure, for example. At this point no one knows what to do about the problem, short of rebuilding the plant. I suspect they will think of something."

"You mean Rocky Mountain Power Company?"

"Yes—they and A.D.A. It seems highly unlikely they would let an almost two-billion-dollar investment be offered up for scrap. They will undoubtedly discover a solution, of sorts."

"Even if it doesn't make the plant safe to operate?"

"I did not say that, Mr. Pollack. Those concrete walls are almost five feet thick and are reinforced with steel plates. Naturally, if there were to be an excursion . . ."

"What's an excursion? I hate to sound so ignorant."

"A nuclear runaway chain reaction that breaches the containment structure. There are all sorts of safety features built into the operation of the plant to prevent that, of course. Do you see those electrohydraulic drives at the top of the reactor up there?"

He pointed up above the control room to a mass of machinery atop the rods leading down into the reactor. "Those drive mechanisms operate the fuel rods and the scram system—the poison rods that can shut the entire reactor down quickly. 'Poison' is a figure of speech, of course; they are made of boron carbide, a substance with a great capacity to absorb free neutrons. When someone at the controls, or any one of several automatic systems based on temperature and pressure gauges, allows those rods to descend into the reactor core, they stop the nuclear reaction. They can be controlled very precisely so our little fire is burning in the manner we wish it to be."

It sounded simple enough the way Kudirka explained it—simple, and extremely dangerous. "What happens if those rods are raised too high?" Pollack asked him.

"Very bad things happen. The temperatures in the core may jump instantly from a few thousand degrees to tens of thousands, which puts a very great strain on the sodium cooling system. If that system proves to be inadequate, the core of the reactor begins to melt, and we run the risk of throwing at least some of the plutonium fuel together in what is called a 'prompt critical' position."

Pollack shook his head. "That's bad, right?"

"Only if you consider a nuclear explosion bad. Oh, chances are that it would not be nearly so spectacular as an atomic bomb explosion, for instance, which is what the power company people mean when they say no nuclear plant is capable of exploding like a bomb. That is a technical distinction only a fool would take seriously. It is, I'm afraid, meant to take people's minds off the real problems, just as the official laughter over the 'China syndrome' was supposed to do."

"What on earth is the China syndrome?"

"Simply the theory that once a large reactor core got entirely out of control the fire would become so intense and would feed on itself to such an extent that nothing on earth could contain it—the bottom of the reactor would melt, and then the concrete foundations of the plant itself, and the molten ball of almost pure destructive energy would start burning its way through our planet straight down to China. No one has yet proved or disproved the theory satisfactorily, at least not to my satisfaction."

"I can see why people laugh at it, though," Pollack

said. "It sounds so ridiculous. But if the plant can't actually explode like a bomb, what really would be the worst possible thing that could happen?"

"The eternal pessimist, Mr. Pollack? It is an interesting question. If the containment structure ruptured and the plant walls were breached—not an unthinkable postulate by any means—any sort of explosion and fire would propel so much radioactive plutonium into the air that if there were the right kind of slow, steady breeze and the right weather conditions—"

"Right, *how?*"

"Oh, perhaps a temperature inversion where a layer of warm upper air keeps a layer of cooler air stagnant close to ground level—a condition that exists fairly often here east of the mountains, by the way. The plutonium dust particles would be carried down to Denver and spread over the city like a lethal blanket. A large part of Denver's population could be dead in a week's time."

Pollack stared at the engineer incredulously. "That's a lot of people, Mr. Kudirka. If this is true, why was the plant built only twelve miles from a major population center like Denver in the first place?"

"Economics, Mr. Pollack. The economics of electrical power transmission, no matter what the fuel used to create it initially, are such that long-distance transmission simply is not feasible—it costs too much to make construction of plants in remote, sparsely populated areas worthwhile. So the power companies gamble that their safety features will actually work in an emergency, and build their plants as close to the cities they serve as the public will tolerate. The uninformed public, I might add."

Kudirka led Pollack out of the control room to begin their tour of the building. On a section of the containment wall itself Pollack pointed out a bit of graffiti to Kudirka, who smiled at the message scrawled in what looked like green crayon:

DON'T FUCK WITH MOTHER NATURE'S NEUTRONS

"I'm rather surprised to see that kind of thing in this pristine, ultracontrolled atmosphere," Pollack told Kudirka.

Kudirka shook his head. "Why? Neutron Two is not a concentration camp, after all."

"I thought the name of this place was Handley Pond."

"It is," Kudirka said, walking on ahead.

They passed a wall sign explaining in detail the in-plant alarm system of bells and sirens and who to notify in case of accident: health physics, the local sheriff, the Colorado State Patrol. "Would any of that do any good in a real emergency, like the kind you were telling me about?" Pollack asked.

Kudirka shook his head again. "Almost none. Think about it—how would you notify all the people of Denver in a few minutes' time? Where would they go? Who in his right mind would stay behind to prevent looting and protect property, knowing his chances of survival would be minimal at best? That sign is total nonsense, Mr. Pollack."

As they began to climb the gleaming white ramps leading to the upper catwalks Pollack looked up and again experienced the awesomeness of all that vast, soaring space enclosing unseen engines of indescribable power. Everywhere were the white metal forms, pulsating, vibrating just below the level of human consciousness. Hesitantly he reached out his hand and touched the nearest wall, expecting it to exude the warmth of a live, functioning being, but it was deathly cold. He laughed nervously.

"All this amuses you, Mr. Pollack?"

"No, no . . . I was just remembering a science-fiction story I once read, about a Martian who invaded the body of a porcelain bathtub and later devoured a man during his morning shower. This plant reminds me of that bathtub, somehow."

"Yes." Kudirka nodded. "One should not underestimate this particular bathtub, I think."

They passed a humming generator of some kind and Pollack asked Kudirka about the electrical supply for the plant—what would happen if somehow the power to operate the control rods and other safety devices failed?

"We have auxiliary power sources," Kudirka said. "They switch on automatically if anything happens to the main lines. Believe me, there is more redundancy built into the coolant lines and the power lines and every other major system than you would imagine possible. It is the only way we know to protect ourselves."

Pollack was thoughtful as they climbed toward the top of the reactor. "From what you've said, it seems to me that about the only way the plant could really be jeopardized is if someone deliberately sabotaged it. Is that possible, do you think?"

Kudirka, leading the way up the ramp, turned sharply and stared down at Pollack. "Only a madman would contemplate such a thing, Mr. Pollack."

Pollack had to agree it was unthinkable.

14 _____

"MAY I HELP YOU, SIR?"

The small nameplate over her plump right breast identified her as Mrs. Elise Forester, Bureau of Land Management. Pollack consulted the notes he had jotted down during a telephone conversation with someone in their information office. "Is this the Engineering and Survey Records Office?" he asked her.

"Yes, sir, it is."

"Then I guess you can help me. I'd like to dig through some old mining claim records but I'm afraid I don't have much to go on. Just a name—Eubanks, Oliver Eubanks."

"Are you Mr. Eubanks?"

"No," Pollack said, "he's my father-in-law. My wife and I are trying to locate some mining property that's been in her family for years."

Mrs. Forester looked slightly skeptical. "Well, sir, we have no way of running a locator by name. Mining patents aren't filed alphabetically. Perhaps if you have the section, range, and township . . ."

"No, I'm sorry—I see I should have come better prepared. The only thing besides the name that I'm sure of is the approximate location, somewhere north of Central City in the direction of Rollinsville."

"Oh, that should be a help," Mrs. Forester said. She went to a filing cabinet and brought back a large-scale platted map showing all the townships in the area he had mentioned. "These ought to do it," she said, jotting down the numbers on a slip of paper. From under the counter she brought a huge book that contained a chronological listing of the mines patented in the particular geographic area he had asked about.

"I'm afraid this may be quite a job," she apologized. "You're welcome to look through the book for your father-in-law's name—what was it, Eubanks?—but of course you realize only the original claimants, the person or persons filing the original patent on the discovery of the lode, will be shown. Some of these old mines have been bought, sold, traded, and subdivided ten or fifteen times since the original ownership."

"That's fine. Thanks for your help," Pollack said, and took the book to a table off in a corner of the room reserved for just such laborious research.

When he returned the book to Mrs. Forester almost two hours later he had managed to find four different mines in the Central City area originally staked out by Oliver Eubanks; two of them were filed under "Oliver and Corinne Eubanks" and one of these was named "Letitia #1." Letty, he concluded. He had written down the exact location of each mine, down to the quarter-section. Now what he needed were some good topographic maps of the general area, and the place for those was the U.S. Geological Survey.

On the way downtown to the Federal Building in the red Mustang he realized that he felt good; it even seemed possible that he might be getting some answers soon. It bothered him, though, that there were so many people involved in what should have been a simple, straightforward case—Reitzman, Dr. Welles, Henry Richardson, George, Letty, Andres Kudirka and his wife. All of them were linked together in a way that Pollack did not yet understand fully, but he somehow felt sure that it had something to do with an event that had taken place up in the mountains west of Denver several years ago. Columbine . . .

Pollack glanced out the car window toward the west where, under clear blue skies, the back range of mountains was capped by the delicate white of the year's first significant snow. That view alone, he thought, would be enough to convince half the population of the East Coast to relocate here.

At the U.S.G.S. Public Inquiry Office he bought the topographic maps of four different quadrangles, each at a scale of 1:24000, for fifty cents apiece. The maps, as the sales clerk had been pleased to point out, contained sufficient detail that even individual houses were shown as little black squares. Pollack took the maps back to his hotel room and, spreading them out on the dusty bedspread, began correlating the mine locations with the actual topographic features shown on the maps and their proximity to towns, roads, and rivers. When he had the four mines plotted he circled the area they encompassed with a red pencil. The circle touched the northern edge of the town of Central City and was generally in the region lying between there and Rollinsville.

The telephone rang, startling him. He was surprised to hear Letty's voice on the other end.

"I'm apologizing for the other night," she said, "whether it was my fault or not. And I don't want to hear any more about it, ever."

"Okay."

"See how liberated I am?"

He wasn't sure whether she was laughing at herself or at him, but he realized he didn't care. "I'm glad you called," he said. "Really."

"Good. Because I have a kind of favor to ask you. I mean, since tomorrow's Saturday and I don't have to work, I thought maybe you might take me shopping in your luxurious rented automobile."

Pollack laughed. "It isn't luxurious—it isn't even mechanically decent, but who knows? *You* may like it. One question, though—do you *have* to go shopping?"

"Make me a better offer, Mr. Pollack. Shopping I can do anytime."

"Okay. I looked over at the mountains today, really looked at them for the first time since I've been here, and you know something? They're gorgeous. I'd like to drive up and see them at close range, if you wouldn't mind being my tour guide. We flatlanders get lost pretty easily."

There was a moment of silence. "It's a deal. Pick me up whenever you're ready—I rise with the sun."

"That makes one of us," he said. "In a nice sort of way, Letty, you're crazy."

He hung up the phone and went back to studying the maps. In almost the exact center of the area he had circled, the area dotted by Oliver Eubanks' former mining properties, was the town of Greenrock.

15 _____

When he picked Letty up on Saturday morning, Pollack thought that the Mustang was bucking more than usual. They hadn't gone more than a block when she noticed it too. "Are you sure this thing can make it up our hills?" she asked him, though she appeared to be teasing rather than genuinely worried. Pollack threw up his hands. "I don't know—for two cents I'd take it back to the rental company and make them eat it."

"We're certainly feeling brutal this morning, aren't we?"

He looked across at Letty—girlishly bright in a misty print blouse and soft denim jeans, with sunglasses as large as two saucers—and he smiled broadly. "I'm glad you came with me," he said, meaning it.

On the way she asked him to stop at her bank, which was on Colfax Avenue and close to where she lived. "Are banks open on Saturdays?" he asked her, surprised.

"Mine is. That's one of the reasons I go there, for the extra service they provide the working girl."

"Wonderful. Today supermarkets and banks—tomorrow maybe even doctors' offices, though I doubt it."

It was her turn to smile. "Obstetricians, maybe. When a girl needs one of those she needs him in a hurry."

"Oh? Speaking from experience, by any chance?"

"No, sir. Not that it's any of your business." She glanced at him over the top of her sunglasses. "My experiences may have been broad and varied, but that doesn't happen to have been one of them, thank God."

"I must get you to tell me all about your experiences sometime."

"So you can put it all down in your little red notebook? Fat chance, security man." But the corners of her mouth were smiling when she said it.

The bank had a drive-in lane, but Letty said she preferred to go inside. Pollack went with her. He stayed discreetly behind when she went to one of the glass-topped tables in the lobby, and it was only by accident that he happened to see her reach into her purse and take out a white envelope from which she extracted three one-hundred-dollar bills. She crumpled up the envelope and dropped it into a wastepaper receptacle on the table, after which she wrote something in her checkbook. Like a Mafia payoff, Pollack thought; who else sends hundred-dollar bills through the mail?

When she went to the teller's cage with her deposit slip and the money Pollack drifted over to the table and casually retrieved the envelope. It was stamped, with no return address, and was addressed by typewriter to Letty at her apartment. The postmark was so faint that only the state—Colorado—was legible. He slipped the envelope into his jacket pocket and wandered away from the table before Letty could become suspicious.

At Letty's direction they took Highway 6 out of Denver toward Central City, but from there on he drove according to a map he had picked up earlier at a gas station. "Where are we going?" she asked him once, not as if it really mattered but just that she was curious. Pollack wouldn't tell her, claiming that it was a surprise.

At Central City they stopped and wandered through some of the touristy stores selling polished rocks and crystalline geodes and arrowheads and trinkets made of silver and turquoise, though no genuine turquoise at all was found around the area. At other shops displaying antique mining implements Letty demonstrated her knowledgeability by explaining their functions to Pollack. "My father was a miner, did I tell you that?" she said. "Up until the time I was ten years old my doll carriage was a broken ore cart on a little piece of track. My baby brother and I used to play doctor with a carbide lantern hooked onto a hard hat, and I could break rocks with a hand pick as well as my father."

Pollack took Letty to the Golden Nugget for a lunch of Polish sausage sandwiches and huge steins of dark beer. The jukebox played endless rounds of country and western songs, all of which sounded alike to Pollack. "I can tell you're not a Nashville fan," Letty said, laughing at the way he grimaced at a particularly nasal singer's lament.

"I don't have anything against the *town* of Nashville, just the music they produce. Though come to think of it, Nashville isn't such a great place either, particularly in the summertime."

"And what kind of music *do* you like, master?"

He saw that she was goading him and smiled, wondering how to answer her without calling attention to the fact that he was no longer all that young. The truth was, he knew nothing at all about the music popular with people under thirty, like Letty. "When Stan Kenton stopped recording," he finally told her, "I kind of lost interest."

"Oh, boy!" Letty hooted. "I can see I'm going to

have to spend some time educating you, just so your ears don't atrophy."

It sounded like a proposition of sorts. Pollack paid the check and took Letty's hand as they walked back to the rented Mustang.

Without consulting Letty he took a secondary county road north out of Central City. The grade was fairly steep and the Mustang's engine labored mightily to get them over the crest of each successive hill. His foot often pressing the accelerator pedal flat against the floor, Pollack felt that he was actually pushing the car up into the mountains with his own leg muscles. Having thoroughly cursed Economy Rent-A-Car already, he was about to start in on the Ford Motor Company when they passed a few lonely-looking houses and then abruptly found themselves in the center of a typical little mountain town. Even though they had passed no signs along the road, Pollack knew, without quite knowing how he knew, that they had reached the epicenter of the area he had circled earlier on the U.S.G.S. topographic map, and that this was undoubtedly the town of Greenrock.

"Funny little town," he said to Letty. "I wonder what it is?"

He watched for her reaction but it betrayed nothing; she seemed to be interested in the buildings and the people, but no more than any tourist would be. Lady, you are one hell of an actress, he thought to himself. The question was, Why?

He glanced at the gas gauge, and although it indicated the tank was only about half empty he pulled the car into a service station and told the attendant to fill it up. He got out and went inside to pay for the gas so that he could casually ask the attendant a few questions—about a man named Oliver Eubanks and a company named Columbine Mining and Smelting.

"I'm sorry, mister," the man said, "I only been up here six months, since my wife's mother died. Ain't never heard of either one of them names."

Pollack nodded. "I'd sure like to find out where that company used to be, and where old man Eubanks lived."

"Well, you might try asking some of the old-timers in town here. Don't be too surprised if they ain't very friendly, though—folks around here don't much like any kind of strangers, and strangers that ask a lot of questions aren't likely to feel very welcome."

Pollack nodded again and accepted his change from a ten-dollar bill. "Have a nice day," the attendant said, smiling and waving as Pollack climbed back into the car and drove off up the street.

They passed a drugstore and Pollack, braking quickly, turned in toward the curb. "I'll only be a minute," he said to Letty. "I need something for my lips— they're so chapped they're about to fall off." It sounded plausible even to him, because in fact his lips had been cracked and peeling for days in the low humidity of Colorado. A resident of Washington, D.C., would probably never live long enough to get accustomed to it.

The druggist, it turned out, was no more helpful than the gas station attendant. But an old man who had been standing beside the glass cases staring be-musedly at a rack of pipes with rainbow-colored bowls must have heard Pollack's question because he squinted up and said, "Would that be old Oliver Eubanks, the miner?" Pollack said yes, that was indeed who he was talking about.

"Dead now," the old man said. He had a scraggly beard and eyes so pale that Pollack wondered whether they might be glass. "His place was destroyed two-three years ago when the plant blowed up. Wife and son gone, too. I always liked old Oliver, even though most folks thought he was a hard-minded sumbitch."

Pollack wondered now how much he could trust the eighty-year-old mind of this man but knew that he had no choice. "What about the plant?" he asked him. "What kind of plant was it?"

The old man stared at his hands, as if all his memories might be stored in them. "Gone now. Abandoned. They just come up here one day, not long after the accident, and hauled all the usable equipment and stuff down the mountain in big vans. It was all kind of secretive-like. They was in and out so fast nobody had a chance to find out what they was doing."

"What was on the vans, do you remember? Any company name?"

"Nope . . . as near as I can remember there wasn't nothing on 'em. Just plain white vans, *big* things, big enough to haul off the whole town of Greenrock if they'd wanted to, I reckon. It *was* kinda funny there being no markings on 'em, now as I think about it."

"Was Oliver Eubanks' daughter killed too?"

" 'Course not. She was workin' down to Denver then —only thing that saved her. Even the boy's dog got killed."

Pollack got the general directions to the plant from the old man and went back out to the car. "I just looked in the mirror and I think I could use some of that Chap Stick myself," Letty said.

"Oh . . . they didn't have any," Pollack mumbled, "they were out."

They drove west out of the little town on a gravel road the old man had mentioned. "Where are we going, Yale?" Letty asked him. Her mood seemed to have changed, but she still wasn't giving anything away by her expression. Pollack continued to drive in silence. The air was getting colder now and the sun seemed to

140

have been replaced by waves of dark-edged clouds. Absently he pulled his jacket collar up around his neck to keep off the chill.

Around a bend in the road they suddenly came upon the ruins of a building, an ominous, deserted hulk with a heavy chain-link fence surrounding it. Parts of the structure had obviously burned, while other parts looked as if they might have been ripped apart intentionally by wrecking cranes. The building was perched on a hill of its own, so that Pollack, looking up from the road, saw dark clouds scudding eerily across the horizon as a backdrop to the somber ruins. It was like the garish cover of some paperback Gothic novel. If somewhere in the distance a wolf had howled just then it wouldn't have surprised him at all.

He stopped the engine, got out of the car, and walked up close to the fence to take a better look. Rusting scrap metal and wooden debris lay everywhere around the remains of the building, as if a war might have been fought here years ago. Weeds and delicate mountain wildflowers grew up through jagged holes in abandoned pieces of equipment. A rusting sign on the fence proclaimed that the area had been posted by the county sheriff and that trespassers would be fined heavily and jailed. Close to the fence Pollack noticed a charred board lying partly buried in the dirt. Curious, he turned it over and saw the faint outlines of lettering:

C L BIN M NG AN ME

The right side of the board was broken off, but there was no doubt in his mind that it had once been a sign hanging over the plant's entrance, and that it had spelled out COLUMBINE MINING AND SMELTING COMPANY.

When he returned to the car Letty was wiping her eyes with a Kleenex. "You've been crying, haven't you?" he said.

She shook her head. "I know you must think I'm ridiculous. It's just something about the day . . . the deserted building. It depresses me."

Without commenting, he swung the car back out onto the gravel road and continued slowly in the direction they had been traveling earlier. The road banked steeply off to the left and headed into a grove of scarred and leafless trees. It was only the end of October and many trees, even at this altitude, still had as much as half their leaves, Pollack realized. The trees in the grove ahead had to be dead—it was the only explanation. Now that he thought of it, they had passed no sizable plant life of any kind since a good distance before they had reached the ruined plant. The possible explanations scraped at the edges of Pollack's mind.

By the side of the road past the dead trees, Pollack saw the unmistakable outlines of the foundation of a small house or cabin; part of a rock fireplace was still standing up out of the weeds. "Stop the car!" Letty suddenly yelled, flinging open the door and leaping out while they were still moving.

He cut the ignition and got out himself, coming up behind her where she stood staring down at the crumbling ground, tears streaming down her face. She must have heard him because her body jerked as if he had punched her. "Why, Yale? Why did you bring me up here?" she sobbed.

He exhaled slowly, hating the times his job required him to be a bastard. "This is where your family lived, isn't it?" he said. "I had to know, Letty, please believe me. I'm going to have to ask you more questions about what happened to them."

She wiped ineffectually at her tears with the back of her hand. "I should have known what you were after—stupid me, I thought maybe just possibly you might be enjoying my company and that we might be

142

able to have a nice uncomplicated ride in the mountains. If I'd known where you were taking me I never would have come."

"I know that," he said. "That's why there was no other way. Please, Letty, you're not making it any easier. Will you tell me what happened?"

She looked at him as if he were a menacing stranger. "You probably know as much as I do about it already. My family died here, all of them—my father, my mother, my kid brother Billy, even his scruffy little white dog. On a lovely sunny afternoon, people said. Pop loved this little house—he still talked about finding the mother lode in these hills, the king of them all, so I wouldn't have to work anymore and could come back here to live with them. He never could understand that I *liked* living in the city, *liked* my job as secretary to an important oil man. My father didn't have much use for civilization, no use at all for the fancy technological marvels of our time, and he was right, too, wasn't he? Because it was one of those technological marvels that killed him . . ."

Pollack took her arm gently. "Letty, I'm very sorry about your family and I'm sorry to be asking these questions, but I think you understand I have to. What else can you tell me about the accident—or whatever it was?"

She shook her head. "Nothing . . . that's it. The building blew up, or burned, or spewed out poison, I don't know. It took away my family, isn't that enough? What else do you want from me—color photographs of the bodies?"

He decided to let up for now, even though he knew there was more. There had to be. Sooner or later she'd tell him, and if she didn't he'd get his information some other way. There was always more than one solution to any problem—at least there always had been up until now. They got into the car and drove back down to Greenrock in silence. It was easy enough to find the sheriff's office—a one-story brick building with a star on the glass door and a single police car with red lights and sirens parked outside. Letty wanted to come inside with him and Pollack thought it might be a good idea—just hearing someone else talk about the plant and the accident might help her decide to speak more freely. Or maybe it wouldn't, but that was a chance he'd have to take.

The sheriff was a big, raw-boned part-time rancher with a shock of red hair and hands like scarred red hams. He was pleasant enough, even after Pollack showed him his N.S.S. identification, but seemed to think Pollack and all employees of the federal government must be crazy. "The left hand of Uncle Sam doesn't know what the right hand's doing, Mr. Pollack. It was federal people that came up here and built the plant in the first place, except of course they didn't *tell* anybody they was federal people. Columbine Mining and Smelting Company is what they called it. 'Course, people around here know a little something about mining—most of 'em figured out there was something funny about the plant right off. Don't know how come you don't know all this already—it was federal people that came and hauled the stuff away in big vans after the accident."

"What stuff was that, Sheriff?"

"I don't know. Could've been atom bombs, for all anybody around here knows. They got a writ of some kind from the governor, telling me to put up signs and keep everybody out."

"For how long?"

The sheriff chortled. "Till they tell me different, I reckon. If I live that long."

144

16 _____

THE TWO MEN had been talking quietly together in the
front window booth of the Lazy Hour Café for nearly
an hour, stirring only when the older one needed to
visit the men's room or when they periodically sig-
naled the waitress over to refill their coffee cups.
From where they sat they could see the entire main
street of Greenrock from one end to the other. Except
for them, the café had no customers.

They watched silently through the window as a
somewhat battered red Mustang entered the town and
pulled up to park outside the sheriff's office. After a
while Yale Pollack and Letty Eubanks got out of the
car and went inside the building.

"There they are," the older man said. "I was beginning to think we'd missed them somehow."

The young man nodded. "Mr. Richardson, why do
you think they're talking to the sheriff?"

"Oh, I suppose we both know that, don't we,
George? Pollack must have seen the sign posted up
at the plant. It's only natural he'd want to talk with
the good sheriff."

"How much do you think the sheriff knows?"

"Not much. But then it really doesn't matter, does
it? I believe you have a job to do, George—you'd
better get on it."

"Don't order me around, Mr. Richardson, I don't

like it." He toyed with the handle of his coffee cup. "Besides, nobody told me this would have to include Letty."

The older man smiled pinkly. "Well, now you've been told. It's really quite simple: she would have had to be disposed of sooner or later anyway. Don't look so disturbed, George—it isn't as if you were seriously in love with the lady."

"She thinks I am."

"That's good. That served a particular purpose and you did your job very well. But now it's over. There's no need for you to be charming any longer, there's only a need for you to be efficient with the tools of your trade."

"Okay . . . *okay!* Reitzman approved it, that much I know. But are you sure she has to be part of it?"

"Quite sure, George. Oh, and don't bother coming back here to the café—I don't think we should be seen together again. You *will* call me with the news, I assume?"

The young man nodded and stood up. "I'll tell you one thing seriously, Mr. Richardson," he said, "I just hope I never miss a payment on my light bill."

The older man smiled agreeably and settled back in the booth as his companion walked out into the street. Big muddy raindrops began to spatter against the window and a bolt of lightning zigzagged above the mountains. The rain was an unexpected bonus.

17 _____

THE ROAD DOWN THE MOUNTAIN from Greenrock to Central City was mostly curves at first, then gradually straightened to short dips that quickly leveled out again. Pollack was enjoying himself, pretending to be a Grand Prix driver to impress Letty, and while the Mustang did nothing going uphill it managed to maintain a certain style going down. Using a complicated cross-hand technique, he would ease into a curve around to the left, aware that on the right only a foot or so of loose gravel separated the paved surface from sheer drops hundreds of feet down to the valley floor. At the precise point at which he knew that he could make it safely, he would push into the accelerator just enough to feel, or think he could feel, the rear end begin to skid out.

"You amaze me," Letty said breathlessly. "I didn't think you were exactly the daredevil type."

Pollack laughed. "I'm showing off for my girlfriend. Does it bother you?"

"Not as long as you can handle it." She clutched the window crank as they took another curve a little faster than she felt comfortable with. "Was the sheriff back there any help, Yale?"

"Not much. I seem to be shooting blanks today— everyone who ought to be able to clear things up for me turns out to be just as ignorant as I am, or else they're holding out." He looked over at Letty with what he hoped was a significant expression, but she was watching the road.

They came onto a long sloping downgrade and he automatically shifted into Drive 2, applying additional engine torque to help brake the car's forward movement. But when he saw that the hill got steeper and tailed off into a right-hand curve he slammed down rather hard on the brake pedal. The car slowed enough to make it around the turn but in that fraction of a second he felt a mushiness under his foot and, glancing down between his knees, saw the pedal descend rapidly all the way to the floor.

"Jesus!" he whispered under his breath. His stomach turned over one full revolution as he felt the car involuntarily begin to pick up speed. His lurch toward the emergency brake was pure reflex action; he yanked it three times in rapid succession before the fact penetrated his brain that the emergency brake cable was not attached to anything beneath the car. "No brakes, Letty!" he yelled, already searching the road ahead for likely possibilities. "We're going to crash!"

When he glanced over at her she appeared petrified, her eyes and mouth open wide. But then she seemed to shake herself into alertness, and leaned forward in her seat to peer through the windshield in search of something that might be to their advantage.

"I know this road!" she shouted. "Let me think—please God, please God, let me remember! . . . There's another curve coming up, to the left—I don't think it's too bad . . ."

He saw the curve and braced himself for it, hitting his horn at the same time because there was no way he could make it without crossing over the yellow line into the left lane and no way to see if anything was coming toward them. As they roared across the road, tires screaming, the driver of an oncoming Jeep saw them in just enough time to jerk his vehicle over into the side of the cliff and let them pass. Pollack was grateful for the Jeep driver's quick reflexes, but that wouldn't help now because they were on a long downhill slope of roadway, straight but increasingly steep, and the momentum toward the bottom would almost certainly carry them out of control. The road seemed much narrower than it was, a tiny concrete thread between a sheer drop on the right and a rock and dirt wall on the left. Pollack began wondering what it would be like to die, and remembered those times in the Army when he had thought about dying, sometimes thought about nothing else for days at a time. But previous experience in contemplating death, when you got right down to it, was no help at all.

"I'm going to try to scrape the bank," he told Letty. "It's our only chance—and it may flip us right across the road and over the edge. Tuck your head into your arms—here we go!"

Praying that their luck with light traffic would hold a few seconds longer, he edged the car across the road and off the other side so that the left wheels were spinning in gravel while the right side remained on the pavement. He pulled himself as far over in the seat toward Letty as he could, and cut in against the bank. A high-pitched screech of shearing metal assaulted his eardrums as a projection of rock ripped a great jagged chunk from the left front fender, and the screech continued as other rock points scraped bare metal along the door and left rear fender. Sweat poured down Pollack's face as he tried to hold the caroming Mustang steady under the terrific impact of the piercing boulders. It was impossible to tell whether they had slowed or not, and he knew now that it didn't make any difference; the car, and they, would shortly be torn apart and scattered along hundreds of feet of asphalt.

Through the film of sweat over his eyes he saw a car heading up the hill straight toward them. There was no time to consider this last incredible piece of bad luck rationally, he simply held the wheel where it was and watched the other car wobble indecisively and then slide sideways, its rear wheels dropping off the right side of the road as Pollack and Letty screamed by on the left. Poor bastard, Pollack thought, though the other car was now safely stopped on the edge of the road, its rear wheels spinning over empty space.

Letty raised her head to see if they were still alive. "Yale, listen," she shouted, "there's another left curve up ahead but there's a field off to the right and I don't think the drop on the right side is bad there. Do you think . . . ?"

"I think," he said. "Get down!"

She had called it correctly, except that when she said the drop-off wasn't bad she must have meant for a goat with four-wheel drive. They slammed into the first gully off the road and both of them went crashing upward into the overhead upholstery despite their seat belts. The steering wheel had been wrenched out of his hands by the jolt but somehow he caught it again and strained every muscle in his body to keep the front wheels pointed straight into the field over each successive ridge and gully. He spotted a massive hay mound and aimed for it, closing his eyes at the last moment because he realized, too late, that he actually had no idea what a hay mound looked like, that they might be plowing full-tilt into a mound of clay or rock or hardened cow manure. He thought that somehow he would prefer being splattered against rock to being buried alive in dung.

The mound turned out to be hay, and the hurtling

150

Mustang burrowed a neat round ten-foot hole halfway through it. Nobody's head crashed through the windshield, and after a minute or two, when their nerves had stopped jumping, they found that they were in relatively good shape. The doors, of course, refused to open, and although the windows did open the hay was packed so tightly against the car that it would have taken them hours to dig their way through it. Pollack spent a frustrating five minutes hacking away at the back window with a screwdriver from the glove box, until Letty, studying their predicament, asked him why he didn't restart the engine and simply back out through the tunnel the car had undoubtedly left behind them, Pollack put the screwdriver down and stared at her. And then stared for a while at the thin coating of hay against the rear window. Frowning, he crawled over the seat and turned on the ignition. "I don't know how I've managed without you all these years and years," he said. "Tying my own shoes, *feeding* myself . . ."

"Keep that in mind next time you try to kill me," she said.

When they emerged from the haystack they saw a black line of cars already stopped along the edge of the highway to gawk at them. "Wave at them or something to keep them happy for a few minutes," Pollack said, cutting the engine again. He slipped off his jacket and crawled beneath the car, seeing exactly what he expected to see: first, that the screws meant to hold the emergency brake cable in its bracket had been removed; and second, that both brake lines had been cut almost all the way through at the point of most pressure, close to a bend, so that the fluid would continue to flow normally until a sudden harsh strain— such as when he had slammed on the brakes on the steep decline—would rupture the lines completely. The job had been done by an expert—an expert assassin.

He crawled out from under the car and stood up, brushing the hay and dirt from his sleeves. "It was done on purpose, Letty, by someone who knew exactly what he was doing."

Letty looked puzzled. "But how could you possibly know?"

"Because that's my business, remember? I could do the same kind of job—I've been trained for it."

"Have you ever done . . . this kind of job, Yale?"

"I wouldn't tell you if I had. Come on, let's get back up to the road."

They walked slowly, Pollack helping Letty negotiate the rough terrain. Once back at the road they managed to get a ride down into Central City, where Pollack arranged with a local garage to send a wrecker out for the Mustang. "It belongs to Economy Rent-A-Car in Denver," he told the garageman. "You can fix it, scrap it, do anything you want with it as long as you send them the bill. Personally, I never want to see it again."

He and Letty walked out to the highway leading back into Denver, where for half an hour they watched cars pass his outstretched thumb as if the drivers couldn't imagine what he wanted. The wind came up, blowing dirt and litter along the side of the road, and it began to drizzle lightly. When Letty started to shiver in her summerish clothes, Pollack pulled his jacket gently around her shoulders.

She smiled at him. "Some days are rougher than others in the secret-agent business, right?"

He nodded and shrugged. After a while he said, "Letty, listen to me. Someone tried to kill both of us this afternoon. They were too professional for it to have been a mistake—they wanted you dead as well as me. Don't you think it's time you told me everything you know about this business?"

Letty stared at the rain glistening on the road. "All

152

right—I guess I have to trust somebody. That Columbine plant wasn't connected with mining or smelting at all—I suppose you know that. It was some kind of secret government project."

"What was its purpose?"

"I don't *know*, Yale—I'm telling the truth. After the accident some people from Washington got in touch with me and told me it was a top-secret military weapons project, that it involved the security and defense of the entire country, and that no word must ever get out about the explosion. I was pretty naive then, I guess I would have believed anything they told me. They seemed very sympathetic about my family. There was a generous insurance settlement check in the mail to me almost immediately, but of course that couldn't bring them back—I felt almost guilty about accepting it. And apparently there's some kind of arrangement for continuing payments, because every month I get money through the mail, in a plain envelope."

Pollack knew that wasn't the way any federal agency operated but he saw no need to tell her. "Do you know anything else about the explosion—what caused it or anything?"

"No, nothing. Except that it killed some of their own people, too. One of the men from Washington told me that."

"What about Andres Kudirka, the man I was asking about in Richardson's office the other day? Do you know him, or know anything about him?"

"No, other than the fact that he runs our Handley Pond nuclear plant. I don't think he ever comes into the office."

"Okay, one more question—and it's important, Letty. Who knew you were coming up here to the mountains with me today?"

"No one," she said. Too quickly, it seemed to Pollack.

"You're sure? Letty, I don't know what kind of loyalties you have to other people, but this could mean a great deal to me and maybe to both of us. It could mean the difference between living and dying."

She wrapped herself in his jacket and looked away from him, down the dark road. "All right. I didn't want you to know because I was afraid you'd be jealous, that you'd—what you told me that time about being a security groupie, that you'd think it was true after all." She peered sideways at him. "I talked to George Davis on the phone yesterday, after you called, and he wanted me to have dinner with him tonight. He called *me*, Yale, honestly. So I told him where I'd be today. And who with."

Frowning, Pollack thought over what she'd said, considering the ramifications.

"But that's silly, Yale. Surely you don't think he . . . oh my God, you *do!*"

A bearded older man driving an almost-new Cadillac finally stopped to pick them up and took them all the way into Denver. Claiming it was not far out of his way, he dropped them off at the front door of Letty's apartment building. They both thanked him, and when he drove off Letty asked Pollack to stay for dinner, which he saw no reason not to do. While she was in the kitchen preparing a beautiful ham omelet large enough for a regiment, Pollack tried to call Kudirka at home but no one answered. Their discussion would have to wait until tomorrow—Sunday— when presumably the scientist would not be working.

Pollack ate heartily but Letty only played with her food, her mind seeming to be somewhere else. "I guess you think I'm pretty stupid," she said after a while, "and I guess you're right. Oh, I wasn't really in

154

love with George, but it *was* exciting being around him, never knowing when he'd get a telephone call and have to go off somewhere in the middle of the night, all buckled up with guns and things. He liked me, Yale, I *know* he did. How could he have wanted to kill me? Is that something they teach you in those security-agent training courses? I mean, I think I have a right to know—because here you are and here *I* am . . ."

"That's not standard training for anybody that I know of, Letty. Some guys are just bastards, that's all. And some are more dangerous than others."

"I guess so. Even my boss, sweet old Mr. Richardson, must have been fooled—he used to tell me George sounded like the answer to a maiden's prayers."

"Yeah." He cocked his head at Letty. "You're going to think I'm insane, but I don't think you ought to risk going back to work until this is cleared up. I have more than a hunch that Henry Richardson is in on some part of it—to what extent I don't know, but I don't want you taking any chances."

"Yes, sir, Mr. Pollack. Gee, you security people are sure masterful when you want to be."

"You bet," he said.

After dinner Pollack sampled more of the Pernod from the bottle he was beginning to consider his own private stock. When he saw how late it was getting and started to leave, wondering how he would get back to the hotel without wheels, Letty told him he didn't have to go if he didn't want to. She put a stack of slow, quiet records on the stereo and they danced sedately in the living room for a while, and finally, touched by each other's shyness, they undressed and lay side by side on Letty's water bed. They made love for a long time, until Pollack, aching from the day's activities, fell asleep suddenly, like a child without a care.

18

MARTHA RICHARDSON had always been a pretty woman, quick to smile, a fine and thoughtful hostess at the many social affairs her husband's position required, and anything but a subscriber to women's liberation. She had grown up in Atlanta in a large white house less than three blocks from the similar large white house where Henry Richardson had spent his childhood. They had attended the same schools, and she had been directly responsible for his passing high school English, having written more than one term paper for him. But there was a *quid pro quo* involved —he escorted her to fall dances and spring dances, bobbed for apples with her at Christmas parties given by their well-to-do white middle-class friends, and it had been more or less taken for granted by everyone they knew that they would marry eventually.

Since neither Martha nor Henry was the kind of person to disappoint friends and relatives, they did indeed marry, immediately following their graduation from college. From time to time they had mentioned children, but somehow there had been none. When things started becoming racially tense in mid-'50s Georgia they had looked for a part of the country where the atmosphere was less volatile. Georgia Power and Light was sorry to lose Henry, but of course provided him with an excellent letter of recommendation to the Rocky Mountain Power Company, where he had done well and eventually been made vice president of the rapidly expanding nuclear division. He had seen early that the nuclear division of almost any metropolitan power company in the nation was the place to be, and now that he was running things in Denver Martha was quite proud of him.

Tonight, however, she was not happy with her Henry. She had wanted him to take her to an afternoon concert at Phipps Auditorium, but instead he had disappeared early in the morning with some cock-and-bull story about having to go to the mountains on business—on Saturday, if you please—and by the time he had returned it was after dark and she had not planned dinner. In fact, she had put her kempt gray hair up in curlers—as she had every night of their married life—and gone to bed. Now she stood at the door of his den, watching him as he toyed with the telephone on his desk under the single leather-shaded lamp. She pulled her elegant chiffon robe tighter about her pleasantly spreading body and glared at him.

"Have you eaten, Henry?"

He looked up, momentarily startled, and shook his head. "I'm not hungry, dear—we had a sandwich earlier. Go on back to bed. I have a few things to attend to here, a telephone call to make . . ."

"At this hour? Who could you possibly be going to call this late?"

"Washington, dear. A.D.A."

She looked at her jeweled watch. "Lord, Henry, it's two hours later back there, do you realize that? Can't it wait till morning?"

"No, it cannot. Martha, I'm rather tired and I'm simply not up to a lot of explanations tonight. Run along, dear, I'll be there shortly."

"It doesn't really matter, Henry. Stay up all night

if you wish, calling people long distance around the country to chat. You seem to have time for nearly everything except me these days, do you realize that? I'm getting pretty sick of playing second fiddle to Rocky Mountain Power, Henry."

Henry nodded. "Go to bed, Martha," he said, thinking, Menopause was sure no bed of roses for the husband either. When she had left the den he dialed Dr. Welles' home number in Washington and listened to the various electronic clicks that preceded completion of the connection. As her number rang he wondered, as he often had, what sort of home life a woman like Dr. Welles could possibly have. Mannish in looks and personality, Dr. Welles refuted his lifelong conception of what a woman ideally should be. In comparison, Martha with all her nagging was a paragon of womanly virtues.

"Yes?" It was unmistakably Dr. Welles' voice.

"Henry Richardson here, Doctor. Sorry to bother you this late, but I thought you'd want to know that the, ah, project has been taken care of. Davis was going to give me a final report but I haven't heard from him. Still, I think you can safely assume we've accomplished our objective. He's a good man and obviously knows what he's doing, though I can't say I'd be willing to trust him with my daughter."

"You haven't *got* a daughter, Henry. Save those tears for the other crocodiles."

"Just making conversation, Doctor. Incidentally, I really don't believe there's any need to tell Reitzman —he might get a trifle upset since it *was* one of his people."

"Simon agreed in principle—"

"Yes, I know—he agrees to *lots* of things when he thinks it might be to his advantage, but afterward you never know how he'll react. He's a devious, devious man, and more than a little unstable if you ask me."

"I'm sure no one asked you, Henry. Was there anything else?"

The conversation was not going so well that he would have chosen to bring it up right now, but perhaps it would be more natural this way. "Yes, one other thing," he said. "As soon as we've shut down Handley Pond completely and run the tests, and then power up again, I'd like to boost the megawatt rating to at least eighteen hundred and eventually target for a maximum two thousand. The stockholders are complaining again about the low profit margin—I do believe they expected miracles, overnight wealth and so forth."

"No, Henry, absolutely not. The design parameters were based on a maximum throughput of fifteen hundred megawatts, and even then we stretched things a bit, as I believe you're aware. Bloody hard to do, too, with those environmental groups looking over our shoulder the entire time. All that saved us was that we knew more polysyllabic technical words than they did."

Henry sighed audibly. "Doctor, I think you should reconsider. It's the only way we can show a large profit quickly enough to satisfy the investors, and I don't believe I need to remind you of the kind of influence these people have, both here and in Washington. Our jobs are definitely on the line in this case. Definitely."

"Don't threaten me, Henry Richardson. I said no, and that's the end of it. I don't want any more Columbines on my hands—or have you forgotten so soon?"

"You worry too much," Richardson said. "We'll talk about this again at a later date, Doctor. I suggest you have some nice hot tea and milk—excellent for the stomach, the English stomach anyway."

"Right enough, Henry. And do enjoy your—what do they call it?—fatback, fish roe, and grits. But of course they've never heard of those things in Denver, Colorado, have they?"

"Good night," Richardson said, and quietly cradled the telephone receiver. In the semidarkness he felt his face glowing a deep, angry pink. *Transvestite bitch,* he was thinking, when the telephone rang beneath his hand. He snatched it up quickly.

"Mr. Richardson?"

"Yes, George."

"They got out—both of them. I don't understand it but they did."

Richardson tapped his finger against the polished surface of the desk. "That's too bad, George. You came highly recommended, your work was supposed to be excellent."

"There was nothing wrong with my *work!*"

"All right, George. You realize this puts me in a rather embarrassing position. "We'll just have to think of something else, won't we?"

"Sure. You want me to try his hotel?"

"Not now—perhaps later, though. Above all we must remain calm."

"I always remain calm, Mr. Richardson. That's my job, remember?"

"Apparently Mr. Pollack feels the same way about *his* job. Goodnight, George—oh, and George, let's keep in touch, shall we?"

19

It was the middle of Sunday afternoon before Pollack got away from Letty's apartment. He had meant to leave much earlier, but she was so nice to be with that he couldn't tear himself away. "You make me feel like a sex-crazed juvenile involved in his first love affair," he told her. "You're just incredible, you know that? If you turn out to be some kind of illusion, or somebody's practical joke, I'll join the spirit union and haunt you to your dying day."

She pulled his head down and playfully bit his neck. "Somehow I just can't picture you in ghostly robes, floating around my apartment scaring other guys away. You want to take a shower with me?"

He laughed, surprised. "What?"

"Shower. You know—you turn the little handle and the water squirts down on you? Come on, Yale, loosen up a little. You might even enjoy it."

The warm water steam-coated the mirror in the pinkly feminine bathroom. Gravely he applied soap to her firm young body, working in large slippery circles until his hands tingled.

"That's a marvelous technique you have," he said when it was his turn to be soaped.

Her eyes lowered, she replied demurely, "Of course —what did you expect from a professional?"

Laughing, they dried each other's bodies and rubbed

their skins with a fragrant oil that Letty said made you very, very sexy, and afterward they made love again on her pleasantly gurgling water bed.

When, finally, he had to go she watched him dress as if it were the most fascinating process she had ever witnessed. "You look nice in your clothes," she told him, and Pollack, never having been complimented that way before, didn't know what to say. "You also look nice without them," she added, which prompted him to cross the room and kiss her upturned face one last time.

"Don't go out," he told her. "Don't even answer the phone if you don't have to. The bad guys have most of the aces right now, and until we can get a few of them back I don't want you taking any chances."

He waved to her from the door of her apartment, liking the way she stood leaning beautifully and un-self-consciously naked against the wall. "Be careful, Yale," she all but whispered, and he knew that if he didn't leave then he never would.

Stranded without a car, he walked up to Colfax Avenue hoping to find a taxi. For some time he stood on the sidewalk opposite photography studios with their live nude models and triple-X-rated movie houses and, funniest of all, a topless shoeshine parlor ("See them swinging while they work, folks!"). Eventually an illegally cruising taxi picked him up and took him to a car rental agency where he had to settle for either a Lincoln Continental at twenty-five dollars a day plus fifteen cents a mile or a pea-green Volkswagen bug. He signed for the Volkswagen, hating the way he had to fold up his legs, accordion-style, to get inside. Still, it managed to take him across town without any major unpleasant incidents—which, for the moment, was enough.

*   *   *

Andres Kudirka's house in the suburbs southeast of Denver was about as he had pictured it from George Davis's description, right down to the dilapidated Oldsmobile parked in the driveway. Kudirka himself let Pollack in and seemed only mildly surprised to see him. "This is my wife Mariko, Mr. Pollack," he said, introducing a tiny woman dressed in a long yellow robe that Pollack took to be not ethnic-Japanese but of some religious significance, possibly Buddhist.

"Ah, yes," Pollack said, extending his hand to her. "This is the lovely young secretary you met at U.C.L.A. one summer at that physicists' conference."

Mariko cocked her head at him. "Oh, no, sir, you must be mistaken . . ." She glanced at her husband and halted in midsentence.

Pollack patted her hand. "It's all right, Mrs. Kudirka, we're all friends here."

"That depends," Kudirka said, not smiling. "What is it you want?"

Pollack squinted at him. "What every man wants, Mr. Kudirka—happiness, security, the love of a good woman . . ."

"But specifically," Kudirka said.

"Right. Is there somewhere we can talk privately?"

"Of course. Mariko was just on her way to the outpatient clinic at the hospital for more tests. They don't usually give them on Sundays, but they seemed to want to make an exception in her case."

"I'm sorry," Pollack said. "I hope it's nothing serious."

"We all do, Mr. Pollack. So far, despite a number of doctors who have taken an interest in her and innumerable and sometimes painful tests, there is still no accurate diagnosis. But in due time, presumably . . ." He pressed Mariko's hand, his attention trailing off into unspoken thoughts.

Kudirka led Pollack to a flowered sofa, then sat himself in a swivel chair drawn up to a desk. Pollack took out the red notebook and thumbed through it, as if to refresh his memory of recent events. In fact, he had already committed to memory almost every scrap of information in the little notebook. "Mr. Kudirka," he began, "I believe you to be an honorable man, an honest man, a person who dislikes sham and hypocrisy. Am I correct?"

"Essentially."

"Yes. You also admire straightforwardness, I believe, which is why I intend being blunt. Mr. Kudirka, I want you to tell me everything you know about the Columbine Mining and Smelting Company and your connection with it."

Kudirka glanced away quickly, studying something invisible on the beige stucco wall beside the desk. "I suppose I have no choice?"

"You do, certainly. You can remain silent now, until I swear out a federal warrant for your arrest, on a probable charge of conspiracy to commit espionage. Or murder."

He watched Kudirka closely. "Which shall it be?"

Kudirka faced him again, nodding as if, having been caught with the evidence in his hands, he was now anxious to tell everything he knew about his heinous crimes. "You know there was no espionage—I assume you fabricated that part to frighten me. Also, there was no murder, at least in the usual sense of the word. Moral murder, perhaps—certainly not legal murder."

"You're perfectly correct, Mr. Kudirka. Once in a while I forget myself and begin acting like a policeman of the state, trying to frighten people into confessing crimes of which they may or may not be guilty. It's an old tactic, one not worthy of human beings. Un-

164

fortunately, as we all know, it works only too well. Now please, go on with your story."

"Where would you like me to begin?"

"This Columbine plant, well hidden in the mountains by its very inaccessibility, was actually an experimental nuclear reactor of some kind, wasn't it?"

"Yes—a full-scale prototype breeder reactor."

"And let me guess—it was officially called Neutron One?"

"Exactly. Neutron One was the name appearing in the official correspondence between the Atomic Development Agency and Rocky Mountain Power Company. The name 'Columbine' was one they invented as an identity cover for the general public. Mountain people in Colorado are very protective about their lands, and almost surely they never would have allowed the plant to be built if they had known what it was. Everyone thought it would be easier if we camouflaged its true nature, since it was only for research and was never intended to produce actual consumable power. Away from public view, we could run tests at our leisure."

"And you were in on it from the beginning?"

"Almost from the beginning, yes. A.D.A. was asked to recommend someone to do preliminary engineering feasibility studies as far back as . . . oh, 1962 or so, while I was still at Los Alamos. I continued with the studies after I left to teach at Stanford—even the university was kept ignorant of the plant's planned existence and was allowed to believe I was merely doing theoretical investigations. Once the plant was built, I was asked to operate it, though 'asked' is perhaps not the proper word."

"You mean the corporate shotgun you mentioned earlier?"

Kudirka nodded gravely. "Of course there are personal considerations I have not told you about, and probably I shall remain silent on these matters. Believe me or not, Mr. Pollack, I have not enjoyed one decent night's sleep since the accident, and that was three years ago."

"Tell me about the accident. What happened, exactly?"

"Even now I find it difficult to discuss," Kudirka said. He got up from the desk and began pacing about the small living room. His wife Mariko came from the back part of the house and passed them in the tiny hallway on her way to the front door. Kudirka looked up but said nothing, and Mariko opened the door and closed it after her as silently as a mouse—or a boarder who only rented space in the scientist's house.

"The explosion ruptured both the reactor vessel and the containment structure, though at first I was only aware that the reactor was disintegrating—"

"Explosion!" Pollack interrupted. "I thought you told me before, out at Handley Pond, that nuclear generating plants couldn't explode."

Kudirka shook his head. "*I* didn't tell you that, Mr. Pollack. Rocky Mountain Power Company hires a good many people to say such things for publication. By and large I suppose they've been quite effective. It wasn't the radioactive plutonium fuel in the reactor core that exploded, but rather the sodium that is used as a coolant. Sodium is highly volatile and produces extreme reactions with all sorts of substances, including common water—H_2O. Unfortunately it is also the best high-speed, high-volume coolant we know of, which was why the plant's design specifications called for its use."

"But surely liquid sodium doesn't just spontaneously erupt?"

"That is correct. One of Neutron One's main water

lines ruptured—developed a longitudinal split some eight feet long, as we later discoverd, though of course we never knew how—and water mixed explosively with the superheated sodium. Poom!" He jerked his hands in the air to suggest the resulting explosion. "Then, because the coolant was gone and the explosion had ruined the scram or fast shut-down control mechanism, the reactor core instantly overheated, melted, and became supercritical, spewing out radioactive plutonium particles through the breach in the containment wall. These microscopic particles drifted almost a mile downwind. Fortunately for the people who lived in the town—"

"That would be Greenrock?"

"Greenrock, yes. Fortunately, there was almost no wind and no temperature inversion conditions to hold the particles close to the earth instead of allowing them to dissipate in the atmosphere. Under such conditions there could have been a massacre. Unfortunately, the particles drifted directly toward an occupied cabin on a hillside below the plant. The owner, a Mr. Eubanks, his wife, his son, and a family pet all died almost immediately of massive fibrosis of the lungs."

"What's that, exactly?"

"Fibrosis? It is a kind of scar tissue that develops sometimes after surgery. Plutonium breathed into the lungs produces the same effect—the lungs harden, breathing stops, the organism dies. It is an unpleasant death, Mr. Pollack. Two of the plant's operators died inside the building of direct radiation burns, also an unpleasant death. I escaped with my life only because I was outside at the time, on the upwind side, checking the radiation-monitoring system. I sometimes wish I too had been inside."

Pollack scribbled in the red notebook his own shorthand version of what Kudirka had been telling him. "And what happened after the accident?"

"That truly is the worst part, Mr. Pollack, worse even than the tragic deaths of the Eubanks family. Instead of admitting to the authorities that a nuclear accident had occurred at a secret experimental facility, A.D.A. and Rocky Mountain Power kept all of it entirely secret. Too much was destroyed to rebuild the plant, so they sent up huge unmarked vans to salvage what they could of the equipment. Having failed to convince anyone that we ought to come forward honestly with the facts, I began filing official detailed reports of everything I knew about the plant design and what might have led to the accident. In fact I strongly suggested that the entire breeder-reactor program be stopped because of the inherently unsafe conditions under which they must operate. But my reports were always put aside, or destroyed, and never reached anyone who had the power to redirect the program into safer, more useful channels. A.D.A. and every power company in the country had too much invested, too much at stake, to risk losing it all because one of their employees suddenly decided he had done enough damage to other human beings for one lifetime and wished no more part in it."

"But you still work for them, Mr. Kudirka. That's a little hard to explain, even to your own conscience, isn't it?"

"That is between my conscience and myself, Mr. Pollack. There are things you do not understand about me, about my life. If it makes it any easier for you, I will admit that I have had to live with a crushing burden of guilt since those peole died as the result of an imperfect technology in which I, Andres Kudirka, played an admittedly large part."

Pollack nodded. "That raises another question in

my mind, about other energy sources besides petroleum and nuclear power. Are you at all interested in *that* kind of technology?"

"Indeed I am," Kudirka said. "We have known about alternative power sources for years, and in some cases for centuries, but only small groups of thoughtful people, who are considered lunatics by the officials, are even discussing these things seriously. Some experimental technologies—such as magnetohydrodynamics or M.H.D., which is simply hot gases moving through a magnetic field to create electric current—are so abstruse that the public loses interest before they can be made to understand them. But others are as common as the wind and the sun. In fact, solar power and wind power complement each other beautifully, since most wind occurs during times of little or no sun. As a result of studies in New Mexico we know that geothermal power is a viable alternative energy source, at least in the Western United States where actions of the tectonic plates in the earth's crust are beginning to be understood. Remarkably efficient fuel cells exist today, Mr. Pollack. Tidal water power projects are feasible along our coastlines. And for the population which does not live in the West or along a coast, technologies for reprocessing garbage and refuse to produce fuel *do* exist and *do* work."

Kudirka had become so emotionally involved in his subject that beads of sweat appeared on his forehead and glistened in the hairs of his beard. "The Congress implies that action will be taken someday, but that is like saying never. Our small planet is running out of time, Mr. Pollack, and the fools will not listen."

Pollack slipped the red notebook back into his pocket and looked around him at the small dark room, convinced now that Kudirka had probably led exactly the kind of dreary life that George Davis had imagined for him. "Do you have a typewriter here?" he asked the scientist.

Puzzled, Kudirka said, "Yes, I do—do you wish to use it?" He opened a small closet, took a portable machine off a shelf, set it on the desk. "It does not work very well, I'm afraid. It is very old."

Pollack opened his wallet and pulled out the slightly crumpled envelope Letty Eubanks had discarded in the bank. He rolled it into the typewriter and pecked out several words on it beside the address already there. "As I believe you can see, Mr. Kudirka," he pointed out, "there's a break in the lower-case L in exactly the same place—which indicates, of course, that this envelope was originally addressed on this machine. Are you, in fact, the one who sends Letty Eubanks three hundred dollars every month through the mail?"

Kudirka pressed his hands wearily against his face, his fingertips rubbing circular patterns on his closed eyelids. Then he looked up and smiled helplessly at Pollack. "Is that foolish of me, Mr. Pollack, the foolishness of an old and guilty man? Yes, *yes!* I send the money anonymously each month, since the accident that killed every other member of her family. I suppose you would call it blood money, an outward expression of my inward guilt."

"Hardly. I'm not, after all, a psychiatrist."

"Please, Mr. Pollack, do not tell her. Miss Eubanks seems to be quite independent, and even though she undoubtedly needs the money I believe if she were to know where it comes from, and why, she would refuse to accept it. She may think it has something to do with the supersecret defense plant, which is how they explained Neutron One, and that the money somehow comes from the government. That three hundred dollars is not nearly enough to make up for her suffering. You may find this difficult to believe—especially since I detect a note of cynicism in your personality—but I have grown to think of Miss Eubanks as my own daughter, as the child that, for reasons of genetics, Mariko and I will never have."

"I understand that quite readily, Mr. Kudirka, cynicism or not. By the way, do you remember a man named George Davis? An N.S.S. agent, like me, who came to your house and spoke with your wife several days ago?"

"I do indeed. Though I have never met the man I believe him to be capable of great evil."

"Then you're a good judge of character, because Mr. Davis tried to kill Letty and me yesterday afternoon on a mountain not far from where Neutron One used to be."

"Kill Letty?" A deep frown creased Kudirka's forehead, and suddenly he leaped into the center of the room like a madman, cursing in a language Pollack could only guess was Lithuanian. "I will execute him! I *will!*" Kudirka shouted in English. "He is a beast and must be destroyed, as the power companies must be destroyed by their own greed and corruption! It is time we acted, Mr. Pollack—it is growing late and there are only a few of us left who can stop them!"

"Easy, Kudirka," Pollack said, alarmed by the wild look in the scientist's eyes. "Letty and I are both all right, no one was hurt. And in any case, nothing would be gained by taking matters into your own hands. In this country we have laws, mostly good laws, and mostly they work if you give them a chance. If I didn't believe that I couldn't be in this business, Mr. Kudirka. That's the truth."

The crazed look seemed to waver a moment and then slide away from Kudirka's too-bright eyes. "You are correct, of course . . . I have been under much strain lately, with Mariko's health problems and other things." He smiled suddenly, as if the past few minutes had not existed. "May I bring you something to drink?"

"All right," Pollack said, and watched Kudirka go toward the kitchen. He wandered aimlessly around the small room, looking at the few somber paintings on the walls and at the small shrine that must have been Mariko's, wondering what kind of life they had together.

"Mr. Pollack," Kudirka called out from the kitchen, "now that you know about Neutron One . . . what will happen to me, do you suppose?"

Pollack thought about the possibilities. "I can't say, Mr. Kudirka, it depends on so many things. I expect whatever happens you can count on losing your job, but I'm sure you knew that already. If Richardson or someone at A.D.A. is convicted of a criminal act— withholding information about a multiple homicide or something of the sort—you could conceivably be fined and maybe even imprisoned as an accessory. A lot would depend on your defense tactics in court, and of course on what the jury believed."

Kudirka said no more. Pollack wandered over to the desk and bent down to look at a small framed photograph of three young men, one of them obviously Kudirka, standing beside a pre–World War II car. Pollack wasn't sure of the make but guessed it could be a Plymouth. As he held the frame up closer for a better look, he saw, reflected in the glass, Kudirka standing behind him holding something in a hand raised high over his head. Pollack started to turn when a searing pain ripped through the back of his skull. *Suckered by an amateur,* he had time to think, before the unbearable pain slid quietly and easily into a soothing ocean of blackness.

20

KUDIRKA DROVE with the exaggerated caution of a man who knows he is drunk and is terrified that the police will stop him. By now he was certainly drunk, according to the most lenient of legal measuring devices; since leaving his house he had consumed the contents of one laboratory bottle of alcohol as well as a handful of amphetamines, and was now drinking from another bottle with one hand while steering deliberately with the other. But it was more than just the alcohol and the pills that terrified Kudirka, for on the seat beside him, in plain view should anyone happen to stop the car and glance inside, was a loaded single-barreled shotgun of German manufacture that he had fired perhaps a dozen times in the past five years. Now, at a few minutes before eight o'clock on a Sunday evening, he was going hunting.

He parked the aging Oldsmobile sedan on the street in front of the building and sat rigid behind the wheel, watching the well-lighted but deserted doorway. He tipped the tiny bottle against his lips again, his hands shaking so badly that more than half of what remained spilled down his chin. I must be insane, he thought. However, even in insanity there were rules, there was logic and illogic, there was retribution for evil.

He got out of the car and went around to the trunk, opened it with a key, and took out several sheets of newspaper which he carried to the front seat. Carefully he wrapped many layers of newspaper around the shotgun, both stock and barrel, until the weapon took on the appearance of a child's toy bundled for Christmas. With even more newspaper he padded out here and filled in there until the object was unrecognizable as a gun.

Carefully locking the car, he tucked the package securely under his arm and carried it up the steps and through the outer door of the building. The name tags beneath the bank of numbered mailboxes were confusing in their variety but he finally found the right one. He settled into a corner of the small foyer to wait. Eventually a man in his forties came up the outside steps into the foyer and, glancing at Kudirka suspiciously, busied himself opening one of the mail slots. Kudirka could see that it was empty.

The man faced Kudirka and smiled pleasantly. "Are you waiting for someone?"

"Yes," Kudirka replied. "My friend will be along shortly."

"Oh," the man said. "That's a pity. It's such a lonely night— I thought I detected your soul crying out for companionship. I have liqueurs in my room—"

"No, thank you," Kudirka said.

"Drambuie, Benedictine, Chartreuse . . . We could toast this bitch metropolis, we could sing the wild poets, we could dance—ah, but I see you're a man with other things on his mind. Excuse me, sir, for bothering you."

He extended his hand to Kudirka, who reluctantly shook it. The man's grip was surprisingly strong; with Kudirka's fingers clutched firmly in his own he pulled Kudirka's hand quickly against the front of his pants, rubbing hard just below the zipper. Kudirka jerked his hand away and let out such a deep-voiced growl

174

that the man, frightened, backed away and, producing a key from his pocket, opened the inner door and hurried through. Quietly Kudirka advanced and slipped his foot across the terrazzo floor until it rested an inch or so inside the doorway. The heavy door was gradually pulled shut by the mechanical closer, until it came to rest against Kudirka's shoe.

When the man had disappeared into an elevator, Kudirka walked through the door and, not wanting to wait for the elevator's return, found the stairway and began slowly climbing the bare concrete steps. It was harder climbing than he had though it would be—too long out of practice, too long without any real exercise, he supposed. Still, the stairway was a good idea, since no one at all was likely to see him here.

By the time he reached the right floor his heart was pounding loudly in his ears and he swayed dangerously, clutching at the railing for support. For a while he thought he might faint, and then the swimming in his head produced a similar motion in his stomach and he nearly vomited. Not now, he thought, not yet; there are things I still must do.

He squatted on the cold gray concrete floor and unwrapped his parcel, leaving the paper where it fell. From his coat pocket he took a pair of black driving gloves and pulled them over his fingers. Using his pocket handkerchief, he thoroughly wiped every inch of the shotgun. Then he opened the door onto the floor and poked his head around the corner. There was no one in sight in either direction of the long hallway. Carrying the shotgun in his right hand by the trigger guard, the barrel slung down beside his right leg, he walked slowly up the hall, his eye on the apartment numbers. Finally he stopped before the door marked 1036 and put his ear close to the wood; there was no sound from within. He rapped hard against the door with the gloved knuckles of his left hand.

A woman in a tan raincoat came out of an apartment several doors down the hall on the left. Kudirka kept the gun down by his right side and watched her intently, but she hardly seemed to notice him. In a moment she had reached the elevator and was pushing the button, but at that moment the door to apartment 1036 opened and George Davis, bare-legged under a maroon robe, said, "What do you want?"

Kudirka stared at the man. "You are Mr. George Davis?"

Davis saw the gun and could not take his eyes from it. "That depends—who are you?"

Kudirka shook off the question. "You are an evil man, Mr. Davis. You attempted to kill Letty Eubanks and a Mr. Pollack who, I understand, works for the same organization you do. Is that correct?"

Davis moved his head from side to side, his eyes still on the gun. "You're crazy, buddy, I don't know what you're talking about."

"The inadequacy of the law, Mr. Davis, is what I am talking about. The swiftness of evil and the stagnation of justice. But there are remedies, Mr. Davis."

The elevator doors at the end of the hall opened and the woman stepped inside, the doors closing behind her. Kudirka raised the shotgun with his right hand and cradled the barrel in his left so that it pointed straight at Davis's chest. "You will never bother Miss Eubanks again," Kudirka said, his voice barely audible.

Davis lunged for the heavy door but was not fast enough—the shotgun roared and he was thrown back into the room, his upper torso burst open like a ripe, spurting melon. A nude blonde girl with loose flowing

176

hair suddenly appeared from a back room and, hardly glancing at Kudirka, stared wide-eyed at Davis's blood-spattered body on the floor. "Georgie?" she whimpered, her hand trembling at her mouth. Then she began screaming.

Jolted into action, Kudirka threw the shotgun into the room beside the body and closed the door. He walked calmly but quickly toward the stairway, descended to the ninth floor, and again entered the hallway where he walked to the elevator. It was slow in coming but he imagined, correctly, that there was little chance of his being caught here. When the doors finally opened he stepped inside and pushed the ground floor button, relieved that he was alone. He kept his finger on the button marked CLOSE DOOR, hoping this would keep anyone else from stopping the elevator although he wasn't sure it would. The phrase from the Old Testament that he had found several nights ago was suddenly burning inside his head: *"Vengeance is mine, saith the Lord . . . vengeance is mine."*

It was only after he had left the building without incident that he began to shake violently. With no remorse, with a feeling of something like satisfaction in the bold and honorable thing he had accomplished, he started the engine of the Oldsmobile and drove away, confident he had not been seen.

21

His hearing was the first of his senses to return; something rustled beside his ear, like crumpled silk, and he tried to turn his head to discover the source of the sound. But nothing else worked. He was sure his eyes were open but everything was so dark he could not determine what was directly in front of him, or even which way was up and which down. Worst of all, at first he could not remember where he was.

"Mr. Pollack, wake up . . . are you hearing me? This is Mariko, the wife of Andres. Can you raise your head, Mr. Pollack?"

It seemed unlikely. Pollack tried very hard and found that his position was indeed changing, that he seemed to be lying on the floor, a bristly rug beneath him, and that now his head, supported by an arm from underneath, was assuming a more or less perpendicular relationship to the floor. He could see Mariko's worried face in the dim light, and he remembered that he was in Kudirka's house, and that something had happened to him, something unpleasant. The back of his head ached and hummed and roared as though being stung by a million bees during an earthquake.

"How long have I been here?" he asked her.

"I do not know—I have been out, and now when

I return I find you here like this. What happened. Mr. Pollack?"

"Ohhh, Mariko, I wish I knew," Pollack groaned, gently feeling the lump on the back of his head. "I suspect your husband hit me with something pretty heavy, though I can't imagine why. Can you?"

Mariko, on her knees beside him, pressed a cool wet towel against the wound. "Rest, please, Mr. Pollack. No, I do not know why he would strike you. There are many things I do not understand about Andres these days. He is . . ."

"Not the same man you married?"

"He does not talk to me for several years. He is worried most terribly, I think. Also, his mind is . . . sometimes not right. He forgets things that he should not forget. He has great anger sometimes, for no reason. I have tried to understand, to help him, but he does not wish help. And so I no longer try. The world is full of sorrows, Mr. Pollack. Not all of them belong to my husband."

Pollack sat very still with Mariko's soothing hand at the back of his neck, his brain gradually slowing down in its revolutions until it finally stopped spinning altogether. Why had Kudirka hit him? It didn't seem to have accomplished anything very much, and yet there must have been a reason. Something he felt he had to do, maybe, and didn't want Pollack around to witness. Something quite possibly violent, given his willingness to thump a federal agent.

Pollack felt in his pocket for the little red notebook, but it wasn't there. A bad sign—there were quite a few things in it that he'd just as soon Kudirka didn't see. Some of the things were about Kudirka, though nothing incriminating; but of course Kudirka wouldn't know that. Names and dates, locations (of the town of Greenrock, of the Eubanks cabin, of the phony Columbine Mining and Smelting plant), partial transcriptions of conversations he had had with Kudirka, Richardson, Letty, and George Davis.

Davis! That had to be it—they had been talking about how it was undoubtedly Davis who had tried to kill Letty and him in the car on the mountainside. Kudirka, filled with guilt and paternally protective of Letty, would want to destroy anything that could harm her. Which meant George Davis, almost certainly.

Pollack attempted to stand without Mariko's assistance, but found that his legs had turned to loose rubber. "You should rest," Mariko told him. He sank down into the chair at Kudirka's desk and thought about calling Davis's apartment, but there wasn't much to say, actually. And he still had a large score to settle with Davis about his doing the handyman routine on the Mustang. Besides, he wanted very much to find out who besides Davis would like to see him out of the way. No, he had to face Davis in person; there was no other alternative.

He struggled to his feet again, noticing how every other part of his body ached as badly as his head. "Thank you, Mariko, you've been very kind," he said, "but I really must go earn my pitifully inadequate salary."

Mariko shrugged sadly. "You are as bad as Andres," she said. "Men are stupid to hurt themselves with their affairs. You will want to see Andres?"

"Yes, I will. I must go now, but please—if your husband comes back, try to keep him here until I can contact him, will you?"

Mariko shook her head. "I cannot make him do anything, Mr. Pollack. If he is in trouble he is the only one who can help himself. I am . . . not able to help anyone, now."

She went to her little shrine in the corner of the

room. "What do you mean?" Pollack asked her, but she was already staring at a small burning candle and did not answer him. Her shoulders shook from behind, as if she might be weeping.

He opened the front door himself and walked out of the house, acutely aware of the difference between real people and those cardboard secret agents on television who were always getting beaten within an inch of their lives and hopping up minutes later to do battle with thirty or forty aikido experts. Somehow, despite Reitzman's loyalty to all the world's fictional superheroes, most of them weren't even remotely believable. Real people bleed. Pollack wanted to tell him, and eventually real people even die.

22

THE HOUSE WAS DARK except for the flickering yellow
light of Mariko's shrine candle. Puzzled, Kudirka stared
at it, and realized that something was wrong—Mariko
never left the candle burning after her devotions.

"Mariko!" he called out. There was no answer.

He wondered where Mr. Pollack had gone. He
rummaged in the bottom drawer of the desk where he
kept his secret cache of bottles filled with laboratory
alcohol. His shaking fingers closed around the last
remaining bottle, which he brought slowly, reverently
to his lips, only to discover that somehow the cork
must have worked loose and all but a crystalline drop
or two had evaporated. Enraged, he flung the bottle
across the room to shatter against the wall. A small
supply of liquor for their rare visitors was kept in the
kitchen in a cabinet beside the soap powders and scrub-
bing cloths, and it was here that he found a bottle of
vodka and began to drink from it in large, hungry
gulps. This should do it, he thought, any minute now
a mighty warmth will overtake my body and render
me capable of, if not reason, at least peaceful sleep. I
pray to God . . .

Still holding the bottle by its neck, he roamed the
house as if it were unfamiliar to him, at last emerging
into the bedroom where, dimly lighted from the open
door of the bathroom, the familiar form of his wife lay

stretched across the bed. Stealthily he moved beside her and bent down to peer close at her shadowed face. With a start he saw that her eyes were open wide, staring at him.

"Mariko! Why didn't you answer me before?"

The dark eyes blinked, but otherwise there was no change in her expression.

"Mariko, I don't understand you," he said. He tilted the bottle once again and moved away from the bed. "A man . . . a man needs reassurances, Mariko—particularly a man in need of an understanding ear and heart. There are times—you must realize—times to forget your own petty wishes and frivolous desires, times to rally to the support of your husband who, whether you realize it or not, needs you. Yes—I, Andres Kudirka, need you very badly because, you see, things have not been going well lately and certain events have occurred— Oh, I do not really expect you to understand, but you might show a grain of sympathy, Mariko. After all, it is not as if there were nothing being offered in return. I feed you, as much as you will eat, which is nothing; I clothe you, not that it matters what dresses I bring you because for a long time now you have chosen to spend your waking hours in those hopeless gray peasant rags. And, although I do not like to mention this, I single-handedly brought you from the island of Peliea and effectively saved your life, and married you, and have provided for you ever since. That you had no children can scarcely be blamed on me, and though your life may not have been all that you could have wished for, it has certainly been better than many. Don't you think, Mariko, that I deserve *some* consideration?"

She stared at him with glazed eyes, her hands folded across her chest in an attitude of death. Suddenly she inhaled, trembled, and sighed. "If there is such a place

183

as hell," she whispered, her voice laced with venom, "then I will not be a stranger there."

Frowning, Kudirka said, "What do you mean? I don't understand you." He shook his head; she no longer even sounded like Mariko. He drank deeply from the vodka bottle. "How did things go at the clinic today?"

Her dark eyes slowly filled with tears. "There is something in my blood, Andres. The doctor said . . . that it will not go away, and that it will get worse, much worse. There is medicine, for cases not so far along. He gave some to me—he is a good man but he has no hope, I could tell by his voice and the way he looked at me. In a few months, maybe one year . . . I am to die in pieces from the radiation, Andres, from your beautiful, evil bomb. Should I be laughing?"

Kudirka put the bottle down by the bed and knelt on the floor beside Mariko, taking her face gently in his hands. "Oh God, my poor Mariko! Are you certain of what the doctor said? Sometimes . . . sometimes you do not get the English words exactly right—it is not your fault but you may have made a mistake, a tiny mistake this time."

"No mistake," she said, pulling her head away from him. "I have known for a long time before the doctor told me, that I am dying from the sickness you and the other animals, the scientists, put on my island."

Suddenly she sprang upright in the bed and lashed out at Kudirka, beating at his face with her small fists, raking the flesh with her nails while he was still too stunned to back away. "You killed my family!" she shouted. "Assassin! Now you have killed me also. I wish you had never brought me from the island—I wish you had let me die there with my own people! I hate you, Kudirka, you are evil evil *evil!*"

Suddenly, she slumped back down onto the bed, seeming also to collapse inwardly. Kudirka felt the small pathetic body twist away from his touch. He remained where he had knelt, not daring to make a sound, until her breathing finally became a regular series of deep, attenuated sighs. Then, finding an extra blanket in the closet, he wrapped himself in its warmth and shambled drunkenly into the living room to the couch, where he sat drinking, until there was no more vodka. Then, slowly, he toppled into a horizontal position and closed his burning eyes.

The blanket had slipped away from his shoulders and he shivered from the cold. The small desk lamp was still on as he had left it, casting an unfriendly glare on the sparse furnishings in the room. His clothes stuck to his body with cold sweat; he had been dreaming again, the same old nightmares of the plant exploding through tongues of orange flame and him unable to do anything about it or to save its victims. But this time Mariko had somehow been involved . . .

He went quietly into the darkened bedroom and stared at the lump of Mariko's body silhouetted against the brilliant moonlight streaming in through the open window. When he bent closer to the bed he saw that she was lying on her back, which was unusual, and that her arms were bent at the elbows and her hands clasped at her neck, almost as if she were praying to a Christian god in which she had never believed. And then he saw that her eyes were half open.

"Mariko," he whispered, "I wish to apologize for my behavior earlier. It was inexcusable and you had every right to be angry with me. Please, can you forgive me?"

She did not answer. He took her right hand and tried to pull it away from her face, but her fingers were entwined together. He bent closer, staring through

185

a haze of alcohol-induced weariness. A mounting terror caused him to switch on the lamp beside the bed. Mariko's fingers were laced tightly around the handle of a short, serrated knife she customarily used to peel vegetables. The blade, all of it, had disappeared into the soft hollow at the base of her throat. A thin river of blood had spilled down one side of her neck and collected in a pool beneath her left ear.

He touched the carotid artery, knowing even as he did so that it had been some time since her heart had pumped its last. Her skin was cold and waxy. Tears beginning to stream down his face, he quickly drew his hand away and turned toward the open window. "God damn you!" he shouted, looking out toward the glacial stars. "What pain has she ever caused *you?* She had only the poor luck to be born . . ."

The moonlight glinted brightly off a silvery surface on the dresser—the top of a bottle of perfume he had bought her and which she had cherished but had never worn because she dreaded the thought of using it up. He rushed at the dresser and swept his hand hard across the top, sending the perfume bottle and several china figurines and a brass vase and various vials and jars crashing violently across the room. The mirror above the dresser offended him, too, with its mocking image of a drunken, bearded murderer; he ripped it from the wall and threw it to the floor where it shattered. His shoes crushing slivers of glass, he raged convulsively into the living room and began overturning furniture, hurling chairs and lamps and footstools against the walls with such force that the plasterboard gave way in spots, leaving gaping holes. He spied her candles and the little shrine with the Buddha-like figure in the corner of the room, and rushed to destroy it with his bare hands, to show his contempt for such a puny god who would allow his Mariko to suffer so.

186

He stopped before the shrine, his hand raised, but instead of striking out at her things he began to beat himself across the chest and belly with tightly clenched fists. His strength seemed to drain suddenly; sobbing, he fell to his knees and then crumpled on the floor, saying her name over and over, as if some magic incantation might bring her back.

After a while his tears dried into hard crusts on his unshaven cheeks. He crawled over to the desk on his hands and knees and found a book of matches in a drawer, then crawled back to Mariko's shrine where he lit a single blue candle. He stared at the flame a long time, dry-eyed and bitter, thinking about what he was going to do. So much death and destruction, and all connected with his precious science of atoms and neutrons and curies of radiation. There had to be a sign, a sign to the people that such destruction must stop forever, and that those responsible must be punished. But alone, what sign could he make?

He went to a window and parted the drapes so that the moonlight streamed into the living room. He stared out at the night, imagining that if he could see far enough across the roofs of houses and the trees and highways he would be able to catch a glimpse of Neutron Two, stolidly perched on its hill north of the city, guarded by only one or two guards now that it had been shut down for maintenance, silent and obese, the plant as well as the guard, and both of them useless.

And then it came to him, like one of those blinding flashes of insight that Einstein was said to have had. Violence is what people understand, violence and horror so unthinkable it cannot be ignored even by the ignorant. And if I am strong, he thought, and do not waver from my purpose, such violence is within my capabilities. And God will help me.

From all over the house and the garage he began

to collect the materials he thought he would need: a straight wooden ladder, two thick rubber kitchen mats, wirecutters, pliers, a screwdriver, and a metal reel of insulated wire. In a drawer of the little desk he found a sturdy wooden slingshot and a sack of marbles, which he had learned to use skillfully the previous summer to scare off the ugly starlings that disturbed the peacefulness of his backyard feeder. He searched hurriedly through his basement workshop for suitable voltage and resistance meters and a measuring tape, and from an old tube-type radio he clipped out the lead wires and removed the step-down power transformer—not large enough for the job, probably, but it would have to do.

He piled all these things in the middle of the living room and went looking for a sack. When at last he found a duffel-type laundry bag he threw the equipment into it and stood looking around the room, trying to think of anything he might have forgotten. Someone would discover Mariko eventually; there was no use worrying about that now. But there was something else that had to be done, though whether it would ever be accepted as legal notification of his intentions he could not guess.

He sat at the desk with a sheet of paper and methodically began writing out instructions that, in the event of his death, everything he owned was to go to Miss Letty Eubanks. He signed and dated the piece of paper, folded it twice, and slipped it into an envelope which he licked and sealed. He wrote her name in large letters across the envelope, which he then propped against a green leatherette pencil holder in the middle of the desk. Almost done, he thought, but not quite yet.

He looked up her name in the telephone book and dialed the number, glancing at his watch as the telephone rang repeatedly. It was ten minutes to three—no reason why she should answer at all. But after the twelfth ring the line clicked and a sleepy voice said, "Yes?"

"Miss Eubanks," Kudirka said, "I have very little time. You do not know me—"

"Listen, whoever you are, I don't talk to strangers at whatever ungodly time it must be now— Is it anything important?"

"Yes," Kudirka said. "There is so much that I should explain but . . . oh God, this is too stupid, there is no time." His throat closed on the words, choking him. "My name is Andres Kudirka, which I am sure means nothing to anyone. But soon it will—it will, I promise you."

"You said this was important."

"It is. I want you to know two things. ~~The first is~~ that George Davis is dead. Quite dead. He will no longer be a problem to you. The second is that in a few days you should be hearing from my attorney—or in any case, *someone*—with rather interesting news for you. I am sorry to have troubled you, Miss Eubanks. I am sorry about . . . everything."

He hung up the telephone and sat staring at the letter on the desk, knowing that it could never make up for her losses, her sorrows. But it was the best he could do—a great deal better, in fact, than he had ever been able to do for Mariko. Poor displaced Micronesian; he wished there were some way he could fly her back to her beloved island of Peliea and there scatter her ashes in the wind and ocean spray. Pointless to think about that now, though; there would be no more trips for either of them.

He gathered the neck of the laundry bag together and hoisted it onto his shoulder, picked up the ladder under his other arm, and ran blindly out the door to his car.

23

SIMON REITZMAN sat with his legs draped over an arm of a huge black glove-leather easy chair in the library of his posh Chevy Chase home, wearing Tibetan raw silk lounging pajamas under a casually elegant rust-colored velvet robe. It was not unusual that his lights should be on at five o'clock in the morning; Reitzman was often restless or bored at odd hours and, fortunately, seemed to function well on far less sleep than most of the agents who worked for him. At the moment he was reading aloud from the unbearably romantic and unscannable verses of Walt Whitman's *Leaves of Grass*:

> ". . . and the beautiful day pass'd well,
> And the next came with equal joy, and with the
>   next at evening came my friend,
> And that night while all was still I heard the
>   waters roll slowly continually up the shores,
> I heard the hissing rustle of the liquid and sands
>   as directed to me whispering to congratulate
>   me,
> For the one I love most lay sleeping by me under
>   the same cover in the cool night,
> In the stillness in the autumn moonbeams his face
>   was inclined toward me,
> And his arm lay lightly around my breast—and
>   that night I was happy."

"Mon petit chou," Reitzman murmured, staring down at the open sleepy face of the young man who lived with him. "Poor Roger . . . you'd much rather be sleeping peacefully than listening to your Simon drone on about some poor old fag's yearnings, wouldn't you?" And Reitzman, smiling indulgently, let his fingers trail absently through the thick sandy curls of the young man's hair as he resumed reading aloud.

The telephone rang, sounding very loud in the still room. Annoyed because the jangling had broken his mood, Reitzman reached over the young man's head to the coffee table and picked up the receiver—a bone-and-gold turn-of-the-century French instrument that had cost him six thousand francs in a Paris antique shop and almost that much to have installed by Potomac Bell Telephone.

It was Baker, the duty officer at N.S.S. headquarters. "There's a call for you from Denver, Colorado, sir —he sounds urgent. Shall I patch him through?"

"Yes, Baker. On the secure line, if you would."

The connection was barely passable. "Sorry to bother you at this hour, Reitzman—what is it out there, five o'clock? Anyway, it couldn't be helped."

Reitzman frowned. "Who is this?"

"What? Oh, sorry—I thought your man identified me. Browning. Special agent in charge of the Denver regional office, F.B.I. We were the ones cooperated with your people on that suspected East German courier thing a few months back."

"Yes, yes, I remember."

"Listen, Reitzman, one of your agents just got zapped here. Why the hell don't you keep me informed when you're pulling some tricky operation in my territory?"

"There's no 'tricky' operation in Denver that I know of, Browning. Tell me, who was it that was killed?"

191

"Who *was* it? Jesus Christ, man, have you got an army operating out of my city?"

"It's much too early in the day for humor, Browning. Who was the agent?"

"Uh . . . let's see, here it is. Davis, George L."

Reitzman shifted the receiver to his other ear. "I assume you've verified that."

"Yes, sir. Blond, Caucasian, five feet eleven, weight one eighty-five, scar on upper-left forearm . . . How much do you want?"

"That's enough. Method?"

"What's that?"

"How did Mr. Davis buy the farm, as you Westerners so colorfully put it?"

"Oh, that. Blasted with a shotgun, close range. He was pretty well splattered around."

Reitzman sighed heavily; the conversation was beginning to depress him. "All right, Browning, keep him on ice. Someone from our office will contact you later today about disposition of the body. By the way, any idea who might have done it?"

"No, none at all. Of course we really aren't on the case yet since we don't have automatic jurisdiction. The Denver chief of police called us in right away because of the federal-agent angle. I called *you* because I thought you'd want to know as soon as possible—I know *I* sure as hell would if it was one of my men."

"Yes. Thank you, Browning, we'll keep in touch."

Reitzman picked up the poetry book again but held it unopened in his lap. Roger had gone to sleep, his head tilted over against the side of Reitzman's chair in an uncomfortable-looking position. Reitzman sighed ruefully. "Sometimes I wonder why I put up with you," he said aloud, knowing the answer before he asked the question.

Strange about George Davis out in Denver, and such

a waste. George had been a beautiful boy, all muscles and white teeth and glowing good health. And not a bad agent, either . . . Unimaginative, perhaps, and rather too impetuous for his own good, but still he followed orders unquestioningly and *that* was a quality you didn't find every day. Now someone in Denver, Colorado, had done him in—splattered him around, as the F.B.I. man had said. It would mean trouble for Reitzman, questions from the Director, perhaps a discreet departmental investigation. They always took a death on the staff harder than Reitzman thought necessary; after all, they were all aware they were in a business where an occasional violent killing was just another operational tool, like double-entry accounting, or keypunching investigative data for the computer. All it really meant was that his division would be one agent undermanned for a shorter or longer period, depending on how long it would take to secure a replacement.

The telephone rang again and Reitzman snatched up the receiver. "What *is* it, Baker?"

A female voice on the other end said, "This is Operator 201 in Denver. I have a collect long-distance call from a Mr. Yale Pollack for Simon Reitzman— will you accept the charges?"

"Oh my God! Yes, put him through, operator."

"Hello, Simon? This is Pollack. I have some information I think you should know about."

"Pollack, don't you know better than to call me direct at my home phone? What do you think we have a twenty-four-hour duty officer for? And how did you know I would accept the charges?"

"Just a lucky hunch."

"Save your humor for someone who appreciates low burlesque."

"I don't know anybody like that. Simon, George

193

Davis was killed about three hours ago. I was just over there talking to the local cops."

"I know about that already."

"How?"

"You're not the only person running around Denver playing junior G-man. Browning from the F.B.I. called me."

"Okay. Did he tell you Davis had a girl in his apartment at the time? She might be able to make a statement someday, but not right away. Davis got it at close range with a shotgun, and I guess his blonde lady friend took one look at the pieces and something snapped in her head—the hospital says she doesn't even remember her own name."

"Do you know who she is?"

"No. She didn't have anything to do with it, though."

"Suppose you tell me how you know that."

"Simon, I think I know who killed Davis and why. Things are getting god-awfully sticky here. I don't really have time to explain, but if everything goes right I may be back in D.C. in a few days."

Reitzman tapped the receiver with his knuckle. "Pollack, listen carefully because I don't intend to repeat myself: Drop the case and get back to Washington on the first plane, bus, or streetcar out of Denver, preferably within the next hour or so. The alternative is that you can kiss your seniority good-bye, *and* your job, *and* any possibility of ever seeing a nickel of your federal pension."

"I don't believe you're serious," Pollack said. "You know you couldn't make that kind of one-sided decision stick."

"You're trying my patience, Pollack. I meant every word I said, and you know I can make it stick. This is a division chief speaking to an investigative agent, with all the backing that N.S.S. management can provide. It will be handled by the book, and I guarantee that you'll be hanged by the book. And Pollack . . . just in case you have some idea you can beat me before a commission or in court, I promise you I'll use my considerable influence to see that you won't even be able to get a job on a D.C. sanitation truck if you don't do exactly as I say. You've known me for eleven years, Pollack—you know that I'm not above fighting dirty to win. As a matter of fact, I *enjoy* fighting dirty."

"I believe you. Which is why I had the uncommonly good sense to call you on an open line, hoping you'd accept the call, because I'm sitting here in my dingy little hotel room tape-recording every incriminating word you're saying. It won't be acceptable in a court of law, but we both know it will never get that far. Don't we, Simon?"

Reitzman switched the receiver to his other hand and rubbed his smoothly shaven cheek with the back of his hand, mulling over the possibility that Pollack might be telling the truth. "Let's be reasonable, Pollack," he said evenly. "You've been working under a strain lately—we've all noticed it, as a matter of fact I've documented my thoughts on that very subject in several memos that I've dated and filed away . . . just in case. My reason for recalling you from the field will be obvious. I believe you are no longer capable of functioning properly as an investigative agent, since your presence in Denver did nothing but get one of our top agents killed. I had no choice but to reluctantly recall you to Washington for a period of observation and, if necessary, proper psychiatric care. Do you understand what I'm saying, Pollack?"

There was a pause at the other end of the line. "I understand that you're a son of a bitch, Reitzman. I also understand a lot of other things that've been bothering me lately. Poor Kudirka . . . he was nothing but a pawn."

"What's that, Pollack? Were you saying something to me?"

"No, not really. I was just thinking aloud about how I never really wanted a job on a sanitation truck anyway. Good night, Simon—sorry I bothered you."

Pollack replaced the telephone on its cradle and sat staring at it as if it might suddenly and maliciously attack him. Letty, sitting beside him on the unmade bed, rubbed the back of his neck with her cool, capable hand. "He's angry with you, isn't he?" she asked him.

"Yes, but it doesn't matter."

"Why did you tell him you were recording the conversation when you weren't?"

"Oh, I don't know—I guess I thought it might shake him up a bit. But of course I was forgetting that nothing ever shakes Simon Reitzman. He told me himself how much he enjoys playing dirty. Compared to him I'm nothing but a rank amateur. Letty, tell me again what you're doing in my hotel room at three in the morning."

She raised her eyebrows, then laughed. "I thought you people usually used a rubber hose in these interrogation sessions."

"Just tell me, Letty. My brain's not functioning well —even Reitzman noticed that."

"All right. Mr. Kudirka called me. He sounded a little wild, or maybe incoherent is a better word. At first I couldn't figure out who he was or what he wanted. He told me George Davis was dead, and I remember thinking I ought to feel something deep or sad, but I just didn't, Yale. Was that awful of me?"

"No, of course not. Under the circumstances."

"Then he said something else about a letter for me

196

but I didn't understand that part. When he hung up I tried to call you but your line was busy. I didn't know what else to do but I knew I ought to do something, so I just got in my car and came over here."

"You're crazy," Pollack said.

"I am?"

"Yes. God help me, I think it's what I like about you." He took her face between his hands and kissed her gently on the lips. "Listen, I have to go back to Kudirka's house—it's the only place I can think of that he'd be. You'd better get out of here and get some sleep."

Letty put her arm around his waist and held on tight. "You've very cruel, Mr. Pollack. I've never been kicked out of a man's hotel room at this time in the morning in my whole professional career. Don't you care anything at all about my reputation?"

"No," he said, and kissed her again. "You know I'd like nothing better than to slowly undress you right this minute and do several unspeakable things to your lovely body. But I can't, Letty—not until I've settled this thing with Kudirka."

"Then I'm coming with you," Letty pouted. "And if you say no . . ."

"Letty . . ."

"I'll start screaming as loud as I can and you'll have an awful time explaining your way out of *that* to the other occupants of this hotel. They might even put you in jail."

"All right," he said, after he saw that she meant it. "You're involved in this too, so I suppose you have some rights. Besides, I don't need a rape charge right now— Would you really do that to me, Letty?"

She stuck her tongue out at him. "Want to try me?"

"Later," he said. "Right now there's work to do."

24

LETTY OFFERED to let him drive her car, which pleased Pollack for several reasons—not the least of which was that he could leave the pea-green rented Volkswagen parked around the corner from the hotel where, he fervently hoped, someone would steal it. He drove straight to Kudirka's house through deserted streets, often hitting seventy-five and eighty.

There were lights on inside the house. They stood on the small front porch ringing the musical-chime doorbell repeatedly, but no one came to open the door. "Just my luck," Pollack said, thinking he was going to have to slip the lock or dive through a window or something else spectacular out of the agents' manual. But then almost accidentally he turned the handle and the heavy door miraculously swung inward by itself.

"You see how easy it is when you know how?" he said, grinning at her. Cautiously he led the way into the living room, where they stood surrounded by signs of a terrible struggle or a maniac on the loose. Letty sucked in her breath, her eyes widening as she surveyed the almost totally destroyed room.

"Anybody home?" Pollack called out. "Kudirka . . . you here?"

There was no answer. He told Letty to stay where she was while he searched the rest of the house. The second room he tried was the master bedroom; as soon as he switched on the overhead light he saw Kudirka's wife Mariko in bed and knew that she was dead. He bent over the still, small figure and attempted to find a pulse, but his mind was already racing ahead to explore possible motives, the likelihood of witnesses, whether or not it could have been made to look like suicide but wasn't. Kudirka had loved this woman in some special way of his own—Pollack had sensed that even through their apparent indifference to each other. Now it made sense to him that Kudirka had found her like this, lost his mind, and begun ransacking the house, but been stopped by something—only the two rooms were torn apart. What emotion could have been power-ful enough to stop him, and more important, where was he now?

Pollack quickly looked through the rest of the house, certain that Kudirka was not there. When he returned to the living room Letty was standing with her back to him, staring at something on the desk. "What is it?" he asked her, and she reached down and picked up an envelope with her name on it and handed it to him.

"What do you suppose it is, Yale? Do you think I ought to open it?"

Pollack tapped the envelope against his hand. "No, better not, I think the police will want everything just the way it was. I suspect this is something like a will, which means it should be opened by the proper author-ities."

"But why is it addressed to me?"

"Letty, Kudirka thought a great deal of you, and he also had a heavy burden of guilt to haul around with him. I suspect in his own slightly twisted way he was trying to take the place of your father, because he . . . because he felt responsible for your father's death."

Letty looked at him uncomprehendingly. "Yale? What are you *saying?*"

He saw the clouds of confusion in her eyes and knew that he owed her an explanation. "I haven't told you before because I still wasn't sure who I could trust or where any of this was leading me, Letty. Andres Kudirka was the design engineer at that secret plant up above Greenrock, and he knew it was unsafe but he couldn't do anything about it. Then one day something happened—it exploded and killed five people, including three members of your family. I'm sorry to keep opening up old wounds, Letty, but that's what this envelope is all about, and that's what the money you get anonymously every month is all about. The misdirected, overpowering guilt of a man driven virtually insane by the consequences of a technology that he himself was largely responsible for."

"Oh, how horrible!" Letty said, her fist pressed against her mouth. She shook her head at the white envelope with her name scrawled across it. "Didn't he *know* I wouldn't have wanted to take money from him under those circumstances?"

"Probably. That's why he never told you about it . . . until now."

Something clicked in Pollack's mind as he considered the oddity of what he had just said. Why should Kudirka, after all this time of secrecy, suddenly decide to confess everything in a public way? "Letty," he said, "why does someone all of a sudden disclose a carefully guarded secret?"

"I don't know—because the secret no longer matters, I guess."

"Right! And the reason it no longer matters to Mr. Kudirka is because— Letty, where do you suppose they keep the telephone book?"

They found the book in a desk drawer. Hurriedly Pollack looked up the number of the regional F.B.I. office and dialed, trying to remember the name Reitzman had mentioned earlier on the telephone. *Browning,* that was it.

"Hello, Mr. Browning, please," he told the girl who answered, hoping there was only one Browning in that office and that they were used to getting calls at three-thirty in the morning.

"This is Browning," a clipped Midwestern voice said.

"Mr. Browning, my name's Pollack—I work for Simon Reitzman, whom I believe you talked to earlier this evening in Washington. I think you should know that Andres Kudirka, the nuclear scientist, is missing and his wife has apparently committed suicide at their home—I'm calling from there now."

"What?" Letty yelled. "You didn't say anything about someone being dead!"

"Shh!" Pollack said. "One other thing . . . I'm certain I know where Kudirka went, and we've got to stop him. He's a little crazy now, I believe—no, what I actually mean is that he's more than likely completely out of his mind with fear and guilt and a lot of other things, but I don't have time to explain. Trust me, Browning. Call Henry Richardson at home or wherever you have to—he's in charge of the nuclear division at Rocky Mountain Power Company. Whatever else he is, he's a practical man and I believe he'll do everything in his power to save the Handley Pond Nuclear Generating Station. That's where I think Kudirka went. Have Richardson call the guards at the plant and alert them that Kudirka may try to—I don't know, destroy something. Tell him to hold him no matter what, but not to hurt him if they can help it. I think you'd better get some state patrol or local police

201

muscle out there too, just in case—whoever you think might be useful. I'm going after Kudirka myself."

"Look, Pollack or whatever your name is—what I want you to do is just to let us handle it. You're way out of your territory, friend, and I don't want you getting in my way. I'm sure Mr. Reitzman would agree with me."

"Shit!" Pollack said, disgusted by this kind of bureaucratic run-around with which he was so familiar. "This is no time for a jurisdictional dispute, Browning. The man's out of his head, he could do anything. And I'm sorry but it's partly my mess too, and I usually try to take care of my own messes. It's one of my big hang-ups."

"Pollack—"

He slammed down the receiver, and after a last quick look around Kudirka's house for some clue that probably didn't exist, he propelled Letty outside toward her car. "Wouldn't you rather wait here for the police?" he asked her, but she just glared at him without answering and he gave up.

They drove north toward the plant, and once they had left the lights of the city behind them they could see that it was a nearly starless night. "The air's so heavy," Letty said, "it feels as if it must weigh a ton. I can hardly breathe. Do you feel it, too?"

Pollack nodded. "The smog or something is bad— the headlights are bouncing right back in my face. There's a breeze but it's not blowing the smog away very fast."

Letty smiled. "You Easterners don't know anything about weather, do you? That's one of our famous temperature inversions—the weatherman talks about them all the time."

Pollack remembered that someone else had mentioned temperature inversions recently, but he couldn't think who or in what connection. The hair on the back of his neck ruffled in the turbid air coming through the open window as they drove north.

25 _____

THE WIND WHISTLED SHRILLY through the car window and the damp air collected in little rivers at the corners of the windshield. Kudirka had turned the car radio on to a newscast but paid scant attention; those things most people talked and worried about, all those events of earth-shaking importance, scarcely penetrated his consciousness. The single-mindedness about which he had sometimes been chided by less dedicated co-workers screened out whatever was currently troubling the Shah of Iran or the small Southeast Asian countries or what remained of the Kennedy family. But when the announcer said, "And now for the Denver weather picture," Kudirka unhooked his mind from his own immediate concerns and listened:

"As you may have suspected if you're outside any-where in the metropolitan area, Denver is presently experiencing what the weather bureau calls a tem-perature inversion—which is simply a layer of warm air trapped in the upper atmosphere holding a pocket of colder air close to the surface. The temperature aloft, in fact, is some thirty degrees warmer than it is right now out at Stapleton Airport. And there is a steady breeze from the north at twenty-six miles per hour, which is just not quite enough to push Denver's cold air pocket out onto the plains and disperse what some of you may have already identified as our increasing smog problem. The Colorado Department of Health measuring station at Twenty-first Street and Broadway reports a concentration of carbon monoxide and particulates just two points under the emergency level. Older citizens and those with chronic respiratory diseases are urged to remain indoors until further notice . . ."

Kudirka turned into the road leading to the plant and switched off the radio and the headlights, hoping he would still be able to see well enough. It was likely there was only a single guard inside the building, but that could be good or bad depending on which guard it was. He drove carefully into the parking lot and stopped beyond a single parked car. One car, one guard. Perhaps.

He got out of the car and stood beside it for a moment, looking back the way he had come, toward Denver. He could just make out the twinkling lights of the sprawling city twelve miles to the south. Remembering what the weather report had said, he calculated that the breeze just now leaving the spot where he stood would reach the center of the city in less than thirty minutes.

Neutron Two sat behind him like a giant slumbering dragon, its angular outlines silhouetted brightly against the somber night sky by powerful sodium vapor floodlights attached high up on the exterior walls of the main building. Kudirka himself had specified sodium vapor rather than the more common mercury vapor because of the candlepower needed for the closed-circuit sweep television cameras mounted in niches beneath the floodlights. Too efficient for my own good, he thought wryly, but since the lighting and camera system scanned only a small area beyond the main entrance corridor he would have time later to worry about that.

The first, and potentially most serious, problem was how to evade the perimeter alarm system, which was activated by ground vibration. He knew all about that system, because he had helped install it and had even dug most of the holes for the buried sensors himself, lest a laborer hired for the job knowingly or unknowingly come into possession of vital information. He lifted the laundry bag full of tools and equipment from the back seat and carried it to a point well outside the electrified barbed-wire fence. There, buried four inches underground and some three feet apart in an invisible line five feet out from the fence, were the delicate pressure and vibration sensors that completely encircled Neutron Two. Wonderful gadgets, right off the shelf from a company in Trenton, New Jersey, and set by Kudirka himself to a sensitivity level such that anything moving between the security line and the fence would set off an alarm inside the building and simultaneously alert the county sheriff's office. Kudirka smiled to himself, remembering the time shortly after the system was installed when a stray jackrabbit had set off the alarm. By the time they had got outside to see what was happening the rabbit had hit the electrified fence and was hanging there in midair, a brown stinking mess of fried fur and skin.

If you plan to breach a security system, Kudirka mused, there are certain advantages to having designed it yourself. The scientist remembered that, as he had gone about the task of designing a burglar-proof system for the plant, he'd wondered how he himself could overcome the very obstacles he was building. In the case of the ground tremblor system, he calculated that only a person who knew precisely where the sensors were buried would stand a chance of evading them. And Kudirka knew. Approximately. Which was why he hesitated now, nervously studying the five-foot no-man's-land between the imaginary line and the fence.

He remembered working out a rough plan to bury the sensors every three feet around the building. But where had he started? Logical to start at the closest point to the main walkway by the gate, but he was sure he *hadn't* started there. Gently he put down the laundry bag and walked over to the gate, being careful to stay well outside the five-foot line. And then he remembered —he was sure he had started at the first upright fence support left of the gate, continuing clockwise around the building. From his pocket he took a steel measuring tape and began marking off three-foot intervals around to the left. When he reached the place where he had decided he would try to breach the system he stopped, carefully marking the spot on the ground with the closed tape measure. Though he worried that he'd been inexact in his measurements, he got down on his hands and knees beside the marker, took a deep breath, and gingerly began inching his way forward toward the fence.

After a while he stopped and extended the tape-measure as far as it would go. Sliding the flexible steel across the ground until the far tip just missed touching the fence, he extended his arm so that his fingers rested above the five-foot mark. With his left hand he retracted the tape and replaced it in his pocket; his right hand gradually came to rest on the ground below the spot where it had been extended. Somewhere just below his fingers was a small steel button encased in plastic, one inch in diameter, with three hairlike wires radiating from it at 120-degree angles. Lift one of these wires and the alarm went off; depress one of these wires and the same thing happened; even *look* at the sensor too closely and suddenly it would be all over.

Carefully he began gouging out small clumps of dirt with his fingers, repeating the process over and over until there was a shallow depression under his hand about three inches deep. Now he moved the sandy dirt almost grain by grain between thumb and forefinger; sweat poured from his hairline down across his face and into his eyes, clouding his vision. He lay almost full-length on the ground, his right arm stretched out before him so that the weight of his body would not be close enough to the sensor to activate the alarm. It was an uncomfortable position, one that prevented him from clearly seeing what he was doing, and the ground was cold; his muscles were beginning to ache and his arms and fingers felt as if they might go numb at any moment. But he continued to search in the cold dirt for the elusive button, trying not to think about the consequences if his finger, or even a fingernail, should bring up with the next few grains of dirt one of the sensor's delicate, nervous arms.

Two more scoops, he told himself, no more—it was all his nerves would bear. But when two scoops produced nothing he took a third scoop and then a fourth, almost certain now that he was digging in the wrong spot. And then, on the fifth scoop, his fingertips brushed something more solid than dirt. A rock, perhaps; it was possible. With the delicacy of an eye surgeon, he felt around the edge of the smooth hard thing until he came to the base of a wire and he knew he had found it.

There was no question in his mind now—he knew his heart would never be able to stand the strain if he attempted to follow his original plan to dig up the sensor intact. Now the only possibility was to find the wire connecting this sensor to the next one in the chain three feet away. He began to dig just to the left of the uncovered sensor, this time with somewhat more confidence, until his fingers came in contact with the connecting wire. It would have been a simple matter then to cut the wire, but the system had anticipated this; any interruption in the flow of current activated the alarm just as quickly as a disturbed sensor. Fully aware of this fail-safe feature, Kudirka had picked this particular segment of the fence because the next sensor to the left was the one connected by underground wires to the alarm system inside the building.

Kudirka dug more dirt away from the connecting wire until a six-inch length of it lay free in a hollow trench. He took a folding knife from his pocket and carefully began scraping away the insulation. When he had two sufficiently bare spots of wire he cautiously backed away from the place where he had been lying and stood up to stretch. The pain in his back and shoulder muscles was so intense that he nearly cried out. I'm too old for this kind of commando exercise, he thought, but after another minute or two of stretching he felt better. He went over to where he had left the laundry bag and felt around inside for the transformer from the radio and a roll of electrical tape.

Again he stretched out his body full-length on the cold earth. Quickly attaching the lead wires from the high side of the transformer to one of the bare spots on the connecting wire, he methodically wrapped the splice with electrical tape, taking no chances that halfway through this operation the two wires might suddenly pull apart. To the other bare spot—the one closest to the sensor connected to the building—he attached the wires from the low side of the transformer and again wrapped the connection tightly. The transformer was now fully connected to the sensor wire in two places about five inches apart, though the current still flowed as before through the connecting wire because of its lower resistance. All that remained was for Kudirka to cut the connecting wire between the two splices; the current would then flow into one side of the transformer normally and out the other side almost normally, but not quite, for then the current would be only about one-fourth as strong.

The idea was good. The voltage at the system monitor inside the building would be too low to activate the alarm but still high enough to register normally on the current monitor. Or so he hoped, because in fact he had long ago forgotten the system tolerances printed in the alarm company's specification sheets. He glanced up at the nearest side of the building, some thirty yards away, the building which had been his spiritual home since before it was constructed. Strange, he thought, how there were some things that could be controlled and some, equally ordinary, that could not. The sequence of events during the next few minutes of his life would, no matter what happened, be largely uncontrollable and therefore immensely frightening. But he had been frightened before. He took a deep breath and exhaled slowly, then pressed the wire cutters in toward the trench and with one quick squeeze snipped the connecting wire in two.

Miraculously, nothing happened. No brief flash at the connecting wires, indicating an unforeseen short circuit; no alarm bell from inside the plant, though it was probable he would not have been able to hear it anyway; and best of all, no guard with drawn gun rushing outside to see what had set off the sensitive system. He waited another second or two, then searched the ground behind him until he found a rock about the size of a baseball. Standing just behind the exposed connecting wire between the two sensors, he tossed the rock directly into the center of the three-foot-wide pathway he had left himself, and watched and listened intently as it hit the ground with a small thud.

Again, nothing happened.

Kudirka put his hand over his heart and felt its wild beating. Was it normal? Abnormal? How ironic it would be to have come this far and then, in sight of success, suddenly drop dead from a heart seizure! "Please, God," he whispered, "what I am doing is important. It would be unfair of you to stop me now."

When his breathing had settled somewhat he went back to the car and took the wooden extension ladder from the rear seat. He took the rubber kitchen mats out of the laundry bag, then slung the bag over his shoulder by the ropes to facilitate carrying it. He placed the two thick rubber mats carefully on the ground in the deactivated area about four feet from the electrified fence; the distance between the two pieces of rubber was exactly the width of the ladder. Carrying the ladder into the area he stepped as lightly as possible, knowing there was some chance that even if the sensors had been effectively nullified for normal vibrations a heavy ground jolt might still set off the alarm. He placed the legs of the ladder precisely on the two patches of rubber and slowly moved the upper end toward the top of the fence, aware that if the ladder accidently brushed the fence while he was still touching the ground even the low conductivity of the wood might not be enough to save him from a fatal charge. When the ladder was within an inch or two of the fence he let go with both hands at once, allowing it to bounce down against the rolls of barbed wire at the top. After checking to see that he had all of his equipment, he began climbing the bobbing ladder rung by painful rung, pausing only briefly at the top before stepping carefully over the charged wire and half-dropping, half-falling to the ground.

Now his commitment was irrevocable—there was no way for him to get back over the fence. Strangely, this knowledge elated him and seemed to infuse his tired body with new strength. Quickly he searched for the television cameras which, moving in their perpetual arcs, guarded the immediate approaches to the building. They had been designed to pick up no more than a twenty-foot radius and it was in this area that the lighting was concentrated. In a sense the cameras were highly artificial eyes, and without the powerful floodlights they would oscillate in total blindness. The lights, like all lights, burned out eventually and had to be replaced. When a light quit working an indicator lamp on a control panel inside the building glowed, with the same color and intensity as hundreds of other malfunction indicators. No bells rang, no alarms sounded; it was something that might not be noticed for a while —until the next regularly scheduled check, at least— and by then it might be too late.

He lifted the laundry bag off his shoulder and felt in it for the slingshot and the small sack of marbles. Fitting one of the glass balls into the leather pouch and feeling a little like David fighting Goliath, he pulled back the elastic string, aimed at the floodlight nearest the entrance corridor, and let go. The missile hit the concrete just below the light and ricocheted off with a loud twang. Quickly he fitted another marble into the pouch and fired it off at a slightly higher angle. When it struck, the pressurized light exploded with a brilliant flash, then quietly died in a wisp of smoke, plunging the area where Kudirka stood into sudden darkness.

He grabbed the laundry bag by its ropes and ran with it to the outside door. It was so dark here that he had to feel the wall with circular motions of his fingertips in order to locate the slot for his coded magnetic card. Keeping one finger in the slot so he wouldn't lose it, he dug the card out of his pocket and inserted the magnetic edge into the slot. There was the usual loud click as the electronic locking mechanism released and the foot-thick steel-reinforced concrete door rumbled up into its own concealed space. As soon as Kudirka stepped into the gleaming white corridor of the air lock the door began to come down behind him and snapped quickly back into place, sealing him in. But of course that was the point; that was the way Kudirka had designed it.

The fluorescent lights along the glaring walls blinded him momentarily. He passed the red emergency telephone and went directly to the other end of the tunnel. Peering through the thick wire-reinforced window set into the inside door just above the air-pressure valve wheel, he could just make out, off to the left, the young guard Wayne sitting at the security desk reading a magazine. Kudirka's heart began to pound heavily against his ribs as he realized he had failed to plan this part of his mission very carefully. From here on in he would have only his instincts to guide him.

He rested the tool bag on the floor and pressed his magnetic card into the slot beside the inner door, but nothing happened—no click, no hum, nothing. He tried the valve wheel, knowing even as he did so that it was no use, the whole entry mechanism had obviously been locked from the inside. He walked back down the tunnel to the midway point, dragging the tool bag after him, and lifted the red telephone receiver off its hook.

"Wayne," he said when the guard had responded, "this is Andres Kudirka. Could you please let me in?"

"I'm sorry, Mr. Kudirka," Wayne said, "but I have orders from Mr. Richardson not to let anyone into the plant, for any reason."

Kudirka wiped his mouth with the back of his hand, felt the dryness of his lips. "Yes, yes, Wayne, I am sure you are just doing your job. But I have foolishly

213

hurt myself and I need medical attention right away. You can look through the glass porthole and see for yourself."

He wasn't going to like this part of the operation, but there was no other alternative now. He reached into the tool bag and clutched a small-pointed screwdriver with his right hand. Quickly rolling up his left shirt-sleeve, he placed the point of the screwdriver on the skin of his forearm and pressed down hard, making a gash three inches long and deep enough to damage several secondary veins. The blood squirted to the surface of his arm and began pouring down over the back of his hand. Closing his eyes for a moment to steady himself, he dropped the screwdriver back into the bag just as Wayne's face appeared at the porthole. When he saw the blood dripping onto the spotless white floor he looked worriedly at Kudirka for a moment and then pressed the release switch that operated the pressure valve from inside. The massive inner door, a twin to the outer door except for its porthole, rumbled upward and Kudirka, smiling, dragged his bag through into the plant. The door closed behind him.

"I must look the fool, Wayne, don't I? Such a nuisance to be old and clumsy."

"For God's sake, what happened to you?" Wayne said, frowning. "Hey, Mr. Kudirka, I'm still not supposed to let you in here, you know? I have strict orders from Mr. Richardson . . ."

"I'm sure you do, Wayne. But in fact you know me a great deal better than you know Mr. Richardson, do you not? You have seen me here almost every day for several years now. We are co-workers, so to speak, on this magnificent project—oh, could you possibly get me a bandage?"

214

"Sure—there's a first-aid kit over at my desk. But I still don't understand how you got into the air lock without my knowing it. I could swear all the systems were working A-OK."

"I will explain it to you in a moment, Wayne, but I seem to be bleeding to death. If you could find that bandage for me . . ."

"Oh, yeah. Here, I'll just get this kit—"

As he turned and bent over one of the desk drawers Kudirka slipped his hand inside the tool bag, extracted the large wrench, and swung it with all his strength at the back of Wayne's head. The guard crumpled and fell without a sound.

Still carrying the bag of equipment, Kudirka raced to the control room and flicked on the lights throughout the plant, most of which had been turned off at night since the maintenance shift had begun. With no wasted motion he began pulling switches and punching buttons across the width of the massive control panel, until a decided hum vibrated throughout the vaulting spaces above him in which nestled the slumbering reactor core. A particularly stirring symphony to his ears, the hum was caused partly by the building's automatic air-filtration system but, most important, by distant servo-motors lifting the control rods that in a matter of minutes would light the atomic fires in the belly of the reactor.

Neutron Two is going critical! he wanted to shout to the flawed containment walls. Looking upward through the maze of catwalks and machinery, he began to roar and shake his fists. "You fools!" he bellowed. "Neutron Two *is* going critical!" His voice, greatly distorted, banged off the gleaming white surfaces of the building like a billion steel marbles set loose in some colossal, endless rainpipe.

215

26 _____

POLLACK GUIDED Letty's car cautiously into the parking lot and stopped a few feet from Kudirka's Oldsmobile. "He's here, okay," he said to Letty. "I was hoping I'd be wrong, but no such luck."

They both sat staring at the eerily lighted, silent building. "Do you think the guards would have let him in?" Letty asked.

"That depends on whether our good friend Henry Richardson got the word and warned them in time. I have the feeling that Kudirka is a very resourceful fellow, though. I'm pretty sure he's inside right now, one way or another."

Pollack got out of the car and quietly shut the door. Ducking low, he crept over to Kudirka's car and peered in the windows, but there was nothing at all unusual inside. The trunk lid was locked, as trunk lids always are. He crept back to Letty's car and poked his head in the open passenger-side window.

"I'm going to try to get inside the plant," he told her. "If Kudirka could do it, I can too. I want you to stay put here in the car like a good girl, understand? Someone will be along shortly—maybe the entire Colorado State Police force."

"That's fine, Yale, that's wonderful . . . I'm glad you have everything so well organized. But I'm coming with you."

"No, you're not."

Letty stared at him through the window with her luminous gray eyes as if to say, Are you for real? And then suddenly she flipped the latch and shoved the door open hard with her foot, banging it into Pollack broadside and nearly knocking him down.

"Move it out of the way, sonny, if you can't do anything useful," she said. "You may think I'm going to sit out here by myself in the dark and wait for some maniac to come up and strangle me or blow up my gas tank or something, but let me tell you, I'm not *entirely* crazy. If you're going inside, then so am I. Although, truthfully, it seems ever so much more practical to wait until the police get here."

He gripped her arm hard and started to say something angry, which was the way he felt, but instead he shrugged and released her. "I can't make you stay, I guess. But I think I ought to tell you, this place may be booby-trapped from hell to Christmas. Kudirka's mind is all messed up—I'm really convinced of that now. He's crazy enough to do almost anything, and that might even include killing a few people if he thinks they're getting in his way. I just don't want you to be one of the casualties."

"Haven't you heard?" Letty said. "I'm already one of the casualties." There was no self-pity in her voice, just the tone of a schoolteacher reciting hard facts.

Pollack nodded. "All right. We'll have to be very quiet and very, very careful. Let's try the front gate first—it's so obvious it may not even be locked."

But he was wrong. The gate appeared to be solidly closed and was secured by a manually operated cypher lock attached to the gatepost. "He may have come this way but I doubt it," Pollack whispered. "Anytime this gate opens I imagine something lights up at the guard station inside. Don't touch the gate—I want to try something."

He unfastened his belt and pulled it out through the waist loops of his pants. Standing back about three feet, he grasped the belt by its leather tip and swung its heavy metal buckle against the wire grating, causing it to crackle and spit little streaks of high-voltage lightning. "That's what would have happened to *us*," he told Letty, putting the belt on again. "Come on, let's see what's around the other side of the building. The whole fence is electrified—don't even get close to it."

"Don't worry—I plan to stay one step behind you," Letty whispered. "If you blow us up I'll never forgive you."

Together they walked counterclockwise around the outside of the plant following the contours of the fence and straining their eyes in the dim light. The ground inside the fence seemed to be well lighted everywhere except at the front of the building by the gate, which struck Pollack as strange enough to be significant. Up ahead he spotted an object leaning against the fence and hurried to check it out, leaving Letty behind. It was a ladder resting on what looked like two rubber mats, its upper end dangling over the top strands of electrified barbed wire.

"What is it?" Letty whispered, catching up with him. She saw the ladder and moved closer to inspect it.

"Letty! Don't move!" Pollack shouted, staring down at the little trench by her feet containing an exposed wire and a transformer. He couldn't tell what kind of system was buried along the fence, but it was obvious Kudirka had somehow got past it. Letty stood motionless beside the transformer, her eyes fixed on the wires that Pollack was pointing to.

She drew a breath. "Yale, is it going to hurt me?"

218

"I don't think so. You see why I wanted you to stay home? Quiet, now—let me look at it a minute."

Squatting down on the ground, he lit a match to peer into the trench. Then he saw the other small depression off to the right. A flicker of light from the match glanced off what looked like a round, flat piece of metal about the size of a quarter stuck down in the hole. Pollack tried to remember the things he'd learned at Army demolition school about antipersonnel land mines and detonators. They came in a large range of size, types, and degrees of deadliness, he remembered, and there were ways to disarm almost all of them, unless you had the bad luck to run across one rigged by a madman. But this button-sized buried disk didn't resemble anything he had ever seen before, not even in the literature, and the transformer, now that he thought about it, had to be pure defensive work.

"Okay, Letty, I think you're all right," he said carefully. "It's probably just an alarm system of some kind —I don't think it can hurt you, but we don't want to wake up any unfriendlies inside the plant. Anyway, Kudirka obviously disconnected the thing somehow, because otherwise he wouldn't have been able to get the ladder up there on the fence. Are you okay?"

"I guess so—when I start breathing again."

"Good. We have two choices—stay here and wait, or go over the fence after him. I'm going over."

Letty nodded. "I'll make it," she whispered. "Who goes first?"

"You do—you're already halfway there. I'll follow behind and catch you if you start to fall. Up there at the top, though, you're going to have to jump over and down without touching the rolls of barbed wire, and I won't be able to help you do that. Does that scare you?"

"Not too much. I grew up in the mountains, remember?"

"Good girl. Up you go."

He followed behind her, hoping his closeness would lend moral support if nothing else. In other circumstances the way his body was pressing against hers on the ladder might have been very erotic. He started to tell her so, but decided it might distract her from her job.

When Letty neared the top of the ladder she stopped, uncertain what to do next. "Go on up a rung or two and lean over so you'll still have something to hold onto," Pollack told her. "You'll have to almost sit on the top rung and then sort of leap out away from the fence."

Slowly she moved one foot and then the other to the next rung, and balanced precariously on the very top of the ladder. She turned back toward Pollack and said, "You're sure there isn't any other choice, Yale? It looks like a long way down from here."

"Okay, okay," he said testily. "I should have known it would be too much to expect a sissy Colorado mountain girl to make a little six-foot jump."

Letty said something under her breath that sounded like "Sonofabitch!" and then leaped off the ladder, Pollack just behind her. When they were both on the ground inside the fence she turned to him and said contritely, "I didn't mean that," and he rubbed the back of her neck and said, "Yes you did, but it's okay. I deserved it."

When he stood up something stung deep inside his ankle and he cried out, grabbing Letty's shoulder for support.

"Yale, what's the matter? Are you all right?"

"I don't know. It appears I'm not the world's greatest jumper myself." He tested the ankle and found that although it hurt badly he could probably bear to walk on it, which was something. "Stay here, Letty, and no arguments," he said. "I'm going over to check the entrance."

He half ran, half hobbled in a direct line to the ominously massive concrete door through which he remembered passing once before. There was no handle, no knob, nothing on its smooth cold surface that could be used to open it. He remembered the guide using a magnetic card to open the door. Pollack felt around the perimeter of the doorway until his fingers found the slot for the card, if he had had one. Stupid, to have come this far and be stopped by the lack of something that looked like the rectangular piece of plastic he charged gasoline with back in D.C. Half-heartedly he pounded on the door with his fist and then lunged at it with his shoulder, but the concrete gave back not even a sound.

He jogged painfully around the building looking for some other way to gain entrance, but there were only solid concrete walls. That made a certain kind of sense, of course—he even seemed to remember the guide or Kudirka or someone telling him there was only one door. With something as potentially lethal as a nuclear generating plant you apparently sacrificed a few conventional safety precautions, like multiple exits, for other more important ones.

He came back to where Letty stood watching him and shook his head. "Nothing . . . no way in without a special little card that I don't happen to have. I don't suppose they gave you one?"

"No, I'm sorry, Yale. They barely trusted me with the correspondence files. What do we do now?"

"That's easy," Pollack said, sinking heavily to the ground. "We sit here shivering and wait for God knows who to show up. Let's hope they don't shoot first and observe social amenities later."

"I like your optimism," Letty said. "You *could* put your arm around me—for warmth."

"Of course," he said. "Why didn't I think of that?" He did as she asked, but his attention remained focused on the building fifty feet away and the probability that Andres Kudirka was inside it, alone with several tons of nuclear fuel.

27

THEY HEARD THE SIREN FIRST, coming toward them on the road from the south. It was some minutes before they could make out the flashing red lights through the swirling haze, and then suddenly a Colorado State Patrol car screeched to a stop outside the gate in the fence and two patrolmen leaped out. An unmarked sedan braked just behind the patrol car and two men in civilian dress tumbled out and stood looking up at the towering building.

"It's Mr. Richardson!" Letty said, standing up.

Pollack nodded. "I'll bet the other one, the one with the tie, is G-whiz-man Browning . . . special agent in charge of the world."

Behind the fence he and Letty ran over to intercept the four men, who had now congregated around the heavy gate. Richardson looked in at them and smiled, though the smile seemed rather forced. "Well, well," he said, "you two always seem to be where you have no business being. How do you manage?"

"We'll take that up later," Pollack said, studying Richardson's expression. "Right now we have to get Kudirka out of there—assuming, of course, that he's *in* there."

"*We* doesn't necessarily include you, Pollack," Browning the agent said. "I've heard all about you from Mr. Richardson here."

"Really? I'm glad we're all so friendly. You should know, then, that where Henry goes, there I go. Right, Henry?"

Richardson was pointing to a button hidden at the extreme right edge of the gate. "If you'll just hit that button and hold it down while I work the cypher lock we may not become barbecues," he told Browning, "though I suppose that will disappoint Mr. Pollack."

"I always like a good show," Pollack said.

The F.B.I. agent did as he was told and Richardson punched four of the ten cypher keys in rapid succession. The gate swung open easily and stayed open.

"It's a four-digit sequence code," Pollack explained to Letty. "We might have had to run through ten thousand different sets before we'd have guessed the right one."

Richardson smiled. "Yes . . . oh, I suppose you *could* do it, but what burglar has that kind of time?"

"And although Kudirka undoubtedly knew the cypher, he couldn't reach the lock and the voltage shut-off at the same time," Pollack said.

"Ingenious!" Browning said, genuinely impressed. "Was this one of Mr. Kudirka's inventions?"

Richardson snorted. "Hardly. Hurry it up, will you?"

The four men came through the gate and joined Pollack and Letty in the courtyard. Richardson led them straight to the outer concrete door. "Steel-impregnated," he said automatically, tapping the concrete as one of his tour guides might have done. He produced a magnetic card from his wallet and slipped it into the slot, and the door rumbled upward out of sight. Both state patrolmen drew their service revolvers as Richardson allowed them to lead the way into the glistening white air-lock tunnel.

One of the patrolmen reached the door at the other

end of the tunnel and stopped, puzzled. "How do you open this thing?" he asked Richardson.

"That wheel—to the left."

The patrolman struggled with the wheel until Richardson put his card in the second slot. The wheel turned then, but the door remained resolutely closed. "He's obviously locked it from inside," Richardson said. "Here, let me take a look."

He squeezed past the patrolman to the reinforced glass porthole in the inner door. Pollack was immediately behind him. By pressing their noses up close they could see into a portion of the central control room. "It's Kudirka, all right," Pollack said. "Looks like he's hurt—his arm's bleeding all over the floor."

"I very much hope he bleeds to death," Richardson muttered. "What on earth could have happened to Wayne? Oh God, there he is, lying on the floor!"

"Is he dead?"

"He isn't moving. I *knew* we should have left more guards on duty. 'Round the clock,' I told them, 'at least three men.' No one *listens* these days."

"Gee, that's tough, Mr. Richardson. Is that what saved Letty and me—George Davis didn't listen while you were explaining your game plan?"

"I don't know what you're talking about, Pollack, and I don't *want* to know."

Browning pushed his way up to where they stood beside the door, brandishing a snub-nosed .38 revolver he had produced from a shoulder holster under his suit jacket. "What's the verdict?" he asked Richardson. "Do we get in or not?"

Richardson shrugged. "We seem to be stymied for the moment."

One of the patrolmen held his revolver by the barrel and waved the heavy handle at the porthole. "Maybe I could break through with this," he suggested.

Richardson laughed derisively. "Not in a million years. Our structural engineers broke three carbide drill bits testing that glass."

Pollack went back through the tunnel to where Letty was standing watching the others, and gently held her arm. "All these guns," she said. "I'm scared someone's going to get hurt, Yale."

He nodded. "So am I. Somehow I feel terribly sorry for Andres Kudirka, in there by himself and probably feeling the entire world is against him. I wish I knew what to do."

"Maybe," Letty said, "you ought to try to get him on that telephone. He *might* listen."

"I doubt it, not in his present condition," Pollack said, staring down the tunnel where, halfway up the white wall, the bright red emergency telephone hung like a wounded animal. "But that gives me an idea, brainy lady," he said, and went back through the tunnel to where the others were clustered.

"Richardson, isn't there some kind of emergency signal you could send through the telephone that would open this door even though it's locked from inside? Surely something like that was built into the system."

Richardson looked at him with what might have been grudging admiration. "Shrewd guess, Pollack . . . I seem to have underestimated you. There *is* a way, an emergency fire signal that will override the locking system and open the doors; but unfortunately it also turns on the fire suppressant system in the corridor out here, and if I remember correctly it flashes a red warning light on the console inside. If Kudirka sees it he can manually reverse our signal with a control button from the board."

"So what? We don't have much choice now, do we?"

"He's right," Browning added. "Better try it."

Richardson nodded to the patrolmen. "Have your guns ready, boys, and shoot to kill!"

"There's no *need* for that," Pollack said.

Richardson whirled to face Pollack. "Don't be a fool. Kudirka's obviously a maniac—his life doesn't matter to me at all. The only thing that matters is saving the plant. *That* matters a great deal."

Pollack shook his head angrily in disbelief. "You're really a nice guy, you know that, Henry?"

Ignoring him, Richardson lifted the red telephone receiver and pushed a succession of buttons. The moment he replaced the receiver in its cradle the inner door began to rumble upward and thick white globs of gelatinlike foam sprayed from hundreds of nozzles set into the tunnel walls, covering their faces, clothes, and hair.

"That way!" Browning shouted to the patrolmen, who were already ducking through under the door. Pollack grabbed Letty's hand but it was slick with foam and she slipped away from him. "Quick!" he shouted at her. "Through the door!"

From the control panel Kudirka spotted them rushing into the central areaway and slapped his palm down on the button to counteract the telephone signal. The inner door began descending just as Pollack eased Letty and himself through. "Kudirka!" he shouted, afraid one of the patrolmen or Browning would shoot at any moment. "Kudirka, listen to me!"

The scientist, his arm still bleeding from the jagged wound, stared at them wild-eyed and open-mouthed. "No," he said faintly, "oh God, not yet . . ."

He turned back to the console and appeared to hesitate momentarily, then shoved the main power lever full forward.

Richardson, blinking dazedly, suddenly realized what Kudirka was doing. In a frenzy he rushed to the fallen guard and grabbed the gun from his holster. Without aiming he began firing wildly in the general direction of Kudirka, both index fingers working the trigger as he shouted incoherent threats.

Instantly behind him, Pollack aimed a well-placed kick at Richardson's elbow and felt the bone shatter beneath his shoe. Finally, he thought, there'd been a practical application for his N.S.S. training.

"You *fool!*" Richardson screamed, clutching his arm. "The control rods . . ." He ran toward the panels of blinking lights and surging dials, his good arm outstretched and ready to grasp the offending lever. But Kudirka had snatched up a piece of scrap metal from a work table beside the console. With the flat side of a large, heavy wrench he pounded the thin edge of the metal wedge deep into the slot behind the control-rod lever, sealing it into position. Then, eying the large letters below the *Manual Scram* switch, he put his back into a mighty arc of the wrench that sent it crashing into the console, knocking the scram switch and its electrical connections completely off the board in a flash of short-circuited wiring.

Staring from Kudirka's manic eyes to the immobilized controls, Richardson froze when he saw what had happened. "My God . . . you *are* a lunatic!" he shouted. "You'll kill us all!"

"Yes!" Kudirka shouted at Richardson as he backed out of the control room. "Yes, yes! Murderers . . . thieves . . . baby mutilators! All of you!"

He bolted and ran for the open iron stairway leading to the upper levels of the plant. The patrolmen looked to the F.B.I. agent for guidance. Browning, visibly nervous about the extent of his authority here, held his .38 out in front of him in the standard television crouch, sighting on Kudirka's retreating back. He looked at Richardson. "Do I snuff him now, or what?

Speak up, man! Is there any way he can get out up there?"

Richardson waved his uninjured arm vaguely in the air. "No . . . there's only the one door. He *built* this place—how could he want to destroy it, destroy *me?*"

"Browning," Pollack said, "let me try to talk to him—I think I can convince him to surrender."

"All right. He can't get past us here, that's for sure."

Richardson pulled ineffectually at the jammed control level and shook his head. "The *fool*. Now we'll have to wait for the automatic scram system to shut it down for us."

"Just like at Neutron One, you mean?" Pollack said. "When you killed five people, including Letty's family?"

His normally pink face bright red, Richardson looked suddenly murderous. "You can't accuse me of having anything to do with that, Pollack."

Letty stared at Richardson in horrified disbelief, until gradually she realized that it must be true. "You!" she shouted in a strangled cry. "You . . . murderer! All this time you've been lying to me."

"He's been lying to lots of people, Letty," Pollack said. "Richardson, I want some straight answers."

"Wait a minute," Browning cut in, "you don't have jurisdiction—"

"And you do? Keep out of this, Browning, or so help me I'll take you apart." He turned back to Richardson. "Now tell me in words I can understand—if the automatic shutdown system works will the plant stay in one piece?"

Richardson, distrusting Letty, backed away so that Pollack was between them. "Yes, it should be safe, unless something happens to the coolant—the liquid sodium. In that case the reactor core could melt rapidly and become supercritical."

"Meaning what? Could some kind of reaction with the coolant blow the plant apart?"

"It might," Richardson admitted. He was sweating now, the glistening drops rolling down his pink forehead onto his nose. "Because of the expense involved and the unlikeliness of anything happening, we've never bothered to test it out. We just don't know."

"So the situation here now is similar to what happened at Neutron One?"

Richardson surveyed the wrecked control panel. "Neutron One was a baby. This plant has at least a thousand times the potential explosive force of that experimental reactor up at Greenrock, and considerably more than a thousand times the plutonium fuel load."

Pollack stared at him in utter disbelief. "And you've never bothered to test the containment structure for this kind of potential accident?"

"No. I told you, there were the engineering studies, thorough statistical analyses by the computer—"

"But no *test!* No actual goddamned test, because it's too expensive and it would chip away at your stockholders' quarterly dividends. Is that about it, Richardson?"

The older man looked up sharply. "You don't know what you're saying, Pollack. You don't understand anything at all about our operations. Who the hell do you think you are, making these unfounded charges against me and the entire Rocky Mountain Power Company corporate entity? Don't you think we've had to deal with your kind before? You don't bother me, Pollack, not in the least."

Pollack gripped Richardson's broken arm so tightly that he cried out. "You listen to me, Richardson. If we live through this night—and there's some doubt about that now, isn't there?—if we live through it I promise you I'm going to see to it that you spend about ten thousand years in a very dark cell."

Pollack's threat was interrupted by a large red light at one end of the control room which began to flash slowly on and off, bathing all of them in an eerie crimson light. "What the hell is that?" Browning shouted.

Richardson quickly checked the dials on the control panel. "It's the automatic alert—the temperature and pressure in the reactor core are building up tremendously and the rate of power increase is too fast for the normal controls. In a minute we should be getting the audio beeper signal that's transmitted throughout the plant . . . There, you hear it?"

There was no way they could have missed the slow beeping sound that seemed to come at them out of the very walls. "What an awful sound!" Letty said, shuddering.

"Those audio tones will occur closer together and the light will flash faster the closer the reactor gets to supercriticality," Richardson told them. "If either the flashing red light or the beeping becomes a steady signal, that will mean the automatic system has failed."

No one said anything as the full meaning of Richardson's ominous words sunk into their minds. Finally Pollack looked up at the maze of pipes and catwalks and gleaming white machinery above them, and said, "I'm going after Kudirka—I want to know what he's doing up there. Browning, I'm holding you responsible for Letty's safety. And keep your eye on Richardson —no matter what he's told you, he's not to be trusted."

Browning, too, looked up at the soaring interior spaces of the plant, his expression acknowledging the obvious—that Kudirka could be anywhere. "Go with him, boys," he said to the two patrolmen, who ran

231

to catch up with Pollack on the open grillwork stairway.

The stairs led to a storage area with partitioned-off rooms filled with boxes and wiring and surplus pipes and machinery. Pollack and the two state patrolmen slowed and began to creep stealthily along the hallway, stopping to peer into each storage cubicle. The interiors were murky, very little light reaching them from the central lighting system. At one point Pollack looked up toward a junction of passageways where a large red light, like the one on the control panel down below, was winking scarlet showers at him. He could hear the beeper, too, from somewhere further down the hall, and both seemed to be cycling faster than they had a few minutes ago. "Come on!" he called to his two gun-wielding companions.

At the sound of Pollack's voice, Kudirka suddenly burst into view from behind a huge boiler tank and sprinted ahead of them along the main corridor circling the plant's open interior. At this point the corridor, gleaming with reflections of white so bright that Pollack's eyes hurt, was much like the main entrance tunnel down on the first level. The ankle Pollack had twisted dropping over the fence throbbed with pain each time it hit the metal floor, and he wondered how much longer he could run after Kudirka without his leg buckling beneath him. "Kudirka!" he shouted. "Wait . . . I want to talk to you. Please!"

But Kudirka, glancing behind him as he ran, darted through the corridor as if he knew exactly where he was headed and had no intention of stopping.

"Don't shoot him," Pollack yelled to the patrolmen. "Let me talk to him first."

They were almost on him now. Suddenly Kudirka reached out and grabbed at a handle set into the wall. Immediately a foot-thick door exactly like the main air-lock seal at the plant's entrance rumbled down from its resting place above the corridor between Kudirka and his pursuers. Kudirka slowed to watch their reactions as the corridor quickly sealed itself off.

Calculating his chances, Pollack dove at the floor just below where the door would soon meet it and rolled out of the way on the other side. The nearest patrolman attempted to duplicate Pollack's tumbling act but his timing was a fraction of a second off; the bottom edge of the door caught his back just above the wide black-leather belt, crushing his spine and compressing his internal organs to a jellylike consistency. A brief, agonized scream escaped from his mouth, which lay pressed into the white steel floor along with the upper half of his torso. Bright ribbons of blood spurted from his nose and eyes, soaking the sleeve of his right arm, which was extended alongside his head, the lifeless fingers still clutching his unused revolver.

"Oh God!" Kudirka said, an expression of genuine horror contorting his face. He came back along the corridor to stand beside Pollack, neither of them able to take their eyes from the grisly mass of flesh by their feet.

"I did not mean for that to happen—you must believe me," Kudirka said.

Pollack nodded, thinking that only in a kind of technical sense could it be considered murder. "I'm sure the authorities will understand that," he said.

Frowning, Kudirka knelt beside the body. Suddenly he snatched the revolver from the dead patrolman's curled fingers and pointed it at Pollack. "What authorities?" he demanded. "There will be *no* authorities, *no* trials, *no* juries. My wife Mariko—what chance did she have? I have killed too many people now, there is no turning back for me. Surely you must see that."

He backed along the corridor in the direction he had been running, warning, "Do not follow me, Mr. Pollack. Believe me, I will kill you if you attempt to stop me."

Turning, he began to run toward the flight of stairs leading up to the next level. As Kudirka's foot touched the first step Pollack made a scrambling sound to suggest he was rushing him and then ducked into a side passage of the corridor. Kudirka wheeled and fired at the disappearing Pollack, and each time Pollack showed himself around the corner of the passage he fired again until the cylinder clicked and was empty. Cursing, he threw the gun toward Pollack's head and bolted up the steps two at a time.

Pollack raced to catch up with him, hurting himself each time his foot came down hard on one of the metal grille steps. The stairway was long and bent back on itself; it emerged onto a painted white catwalk, and through the evenly spaced floor girders he could look down far below to the control-room area. He thought he saw Letty staring up at them, but maybe she was looking instead at the reactor core, which was where they seemed to be heading. He wanted to let her know he was all right but he couldn't afford to slow down; Kudirka was desperate now and it was obvious to Pollack that he was deranged. Still, somehow he felt sorry for the scientist.

As Kudirka ran along the upper catwalks Pollack was not far behind. Glancing over the edge where a steel railing guarded their passage, he could once again see all the way to the ground floor. Letty was nowhere in sight now, and neither were Richardson, Browning, or the second patrolman who had been cut off by the falling door. The *lucky* one, Pollack thought, remembering the gruesome sight of a human being crushed to death.

Kudirka was apparently heading for the area that

bordered the top end of the reactor itself, and the forest of control rods and fuel rods above it. Here, Pollack could see massive machinery of a kind he had never known existed—huge polar cranes with arms the width of a building, their pulleys and wire cables supporting mechanical and electrical grippers to handle the various control rods and remove spent fuel elements for transportation to a reprocessing plant. Here and there were workbenches containing smaller pieces of equipment that were probably used to perform tests of one kind or another. Pipes and conduits of many sizes and materials clung to the circular walls, occasionally branching off to enter the concrete-encased reactor at odd points like randomly placed tentacles. Batteries of powerful floodlights attached high up on the walls bathed the top of the reactor in ghostly brilliance, and Pollack noticed another of the large red warning lights, now blinking much faster. The ominous beeps of the alarm signal bored their way into his consciousness as he ran, and he noted that they were now coming at a much faster rate. This whole scene, he thought, was beginning to be a madman's nightmare.

The two men's footsteps clanked on the catwalk and then began to sound different, slightly less metallic, as they reached a section where solid flooring had been laid underneath the open grillwork girders. Kudirka suddenly stopped and grabbed up a bright red can that had been left beside a generator. Swinging the can with both hands, he splashed the liquid contents across the floor behind him. Pollack slowed his pace, frowning as he attempted to understand Kudirka's new tactical move, since the substance wasn't slippery enough to cause him to fall.

Too late, he saw what was happening. Kudirka waited until Pollack was well into the soaked area and

235

then suddenly turned so that Pollack saw the lighted match, which Kudirka tossed almost casually into the center of the catwalk. With a sound like a thousand angry birds exploding off the ground, the film of fuel burst into flame, igniting the cuffs of Pollack's trousers.

Even as he backed out of the flaming barrier Pollack was removing his jacket. When he was safely away from the area touched by the fuel he fell onto the catwalk and wrapped the jacket around his legs, smothering the flames. The fabric smoldered for a while and the hairs on his shins were curled up into tight, singed little knots, but miraculously his legs had received only superficial burns. He stared at the flames still roaring on the catwalk, thinking what an effective defense they made for Kudirka and how close they had come to roasting him alive.

With all the time in the world now, Kudirka continued around the curve of the perimeter catwalk toward the reactor head. Pollack, immobilized by the flames, watched him across an arc of open space. "Kudirka!" he shouted. "You nearly killed me—is that what you want?"

"Kill you?" Kudirka answered. "Your life is of no importance to me one way or the other." He touched a button on a small control box and the giant polar crane hummed into life, moving out from the far wall and dragging its umbilicals with it.

As Pollack looked on helplessly, Kudirka worked other controls on the box that caused the crane to move into position just above the reactor head. An accessory servomechanism that looked to Pollack like an enormous drill chuck with six flat metal fingers descended from the end of the crane, slid over the hexagonal head of a two-foot bolt in the reactor head, and with a screeching whirr unscrewed the bolt and lifted it away. Kudirka expertly guided the fingers over three identical bolts and removed them just as easily as he might have removed the nut from a three-inch machine screw by hand.

"Are you watching, Mr. Pollack?" he called out. "You see how easy it is when you know what to do. The pursuit of knowledge has been my life, Mr. Pollack—a dangerous pursuit, as it turns out, but in many ways a rewarding one. Unfortunately, the possessor of such dangerous knowledge has enormous responsibility to the rest of the world to use it wisely, and that I have not always done." He broke off the confession to throw back his head, as if some cosmic message were inscribed in the air or on the ceiling of the vast building. "There comes a time when a man must decide what is most important, his life or his responsibilities. I have made that choice, Mr. Pollack, and no one must stop me. I am convinced the fate of the entire world rests on my shoulders."

Pollack stood up and leaned out around the flaming catwalk to get a better view of his adversary. "The world can't be saved anyway," he shouted across to Kudirka. "Haven't you heard? In another billion years or so the earth and everything on it will be incinerated by its own sun. But that's no reason to throw away your own life today, is it?"

"Yes!" Kudirka shouted. "I do not regret sacrificing myself, when I alone am capable of causing a holocaust so fierce that all of the world's leaders will listen in spite of their own petty aspirations. In any case, I find . . . I find that I have very little to live for. Nothing, in fact, to live for."

"Kudirka, listen to me. The point of living is life itself, don't you see that? What keeps an Asian peasant alive when, by all nutritional standards, his few grains of rice a day couldn't possibly sustain him? The answer is so *simple,* Kudirka: the one thing more important

237

to all human beings than even basic nourishment is life itself. *Life!* Don't you see that?"

"Ah, yes. *Life.* My life as compared with someone else's life, perhaps. But, you see, I have already taken many lives, I have already caused too much suffering and death to escape my conscience, Mr. Pollack. I used to dream about the horrors of war, the inhumanity of man toward man, the animal brutality of so-called civilized people. Eventually it occurred to me that I was no better, that in fact *I* was personally and directly responsible for various technologies more horrible than anything the world had previously known. Now, with what little remains of my life, I intend to make amends for my transgressions. I care little that you do not understand my motives; someday they will be understood only too well, I assure you. But now you must excuse me, Mr. Pollack, for I have work to do."

At that moment Kudirka pushed a control button that released a giant humming electromagnet by steel cable from the arm of the polar crane. The huge iron disk attached itself with a clank to a portion of the reactor head, which then began to rise in the air free of the reactor, exposing the silently raging nuclear fires down below. Walking out to the lip of the reactor on a separate catwalk angled like a spoke to the perimeter walkway, Kudirka stared down into the reactor mouth for a long time. Then he retreated back to the containment wall, to a particular niche where, coiled on a roller beneath a large red sign—so large that from where Pollack stood he could read the words DANGER, KEEP AWAY FROM SODIUM COOLANT—a standard fire hose connected to the plant's water system was stored. Kudirka jerked the hose out from the wall by its brass nozzle, the roller spinning as he backed along the secondary catwalk out to the edge of the reactor. The hose was more than long enough to reach it; he paid out a few feet more, letting the weight of the nozzle carry the hose a short distance down inside the reactor vessel.

"Kudirka! You goddamned idiot!" Pollack shouted. "You told me yourself about how violently the coolant reacts with water, and what it could do to the plant. You'll destroy us all!"

There was no response from Kudirka, who moved with his head down like a man in a trance. Pollack gripped the railing along the catwalk and in his frustration shook it until it rattled. For the first time he realized how completely he was trapped between the flames ahead and the solid concrete door down the corridor behind him. While he was thinking how he might be able to stop Kudirka and save himself he suddenly noticed beneath the railing an overhang shaped like a rain gutter that was separate from the catwalk itself. Probably, if a person were foolish enough to try, it would furnish a handhold of sorts. A picture of Tarzan swinging fearlessly through the trees flashed through his mind as he boosted his legs over the railing and lowered himself hand over hand to the ledge. Slowly he extended his legs and feet out into eight or nine stories of free space and felt the weight of his body painfully stretching the tendons in his shoulders, arms, and fingers. Trying not to dwell on what would happen to him if he hit a slick spot on the surface of the pipe and lost his grip, he began inching his hands along below the furiously blazing catwalk.

Absorbed in his own problems, Kudirka had so far failed to notice Pollack's body swinging toward him under the flooring. Checking to make sure he had passed completely under the flaming sea of fuel, Pollack called upon every ounce of strength left in his body to hoist himself back over the railing. Kudirka must have caught the movement out of the corner of his eye, for he yelped suddenly, as if struck by an arrow, and dashed toward the valve wheel beside the fire-hose connection. Pollack guessed that, turned not much more than one revolution, the valve would send gallons of water cascading down into the sodium effluent circulating among the highly radioactive fuel rods in the reactor core.

Springing to his feet on the catwalk once again, Pollack ran too, though where or for what purpose he wasn't sure because there was no chance now that he could reach Kudirka before the valve was opened. But along the wall closer to him than the hose connection he spotted a fire ax that was fortunately not enclosed in glass. He dove at it, wrenching it from the wall, and ran full speed toward the spokelike catwalk leading to the reactor's edge. Just as Kudirka gripped the wheel and put his shoulders into a full turn to release the pressure of the water behind the valve, Pollack raised the ax above his head and, still at a dead run, brought the blade crashing down at full length, cleanly cutting the hose in two.

Kudirka stared openmouthed as water spurted from the open end of the severed hose, twenty feet from where the impotent nozzle and a few yards of limp tubular canvas hung over the lip of the reactor. "You fool!" he shouted, glaring at Pollack with an expression of utter hatred. He turned and ran forward along the perimeter catwalk, quickly disappearing through an opening in a concrete wall.

Pollack leaped over the hose and followed as fast as his throbbing ankle would permit, bouncing all his weight onto his good leg and, as a consequence, running slightly tilted to one side. Kudirka wasn't hard to follow; a trail of bright-red, dime-sized splashes of blood led straight down the glaring white catwalk and off to the right behind another wall. Approaching cautiously, Pollack peered around the wall and was surprised to discover an extremely steep circular stairway winding serpentinely around a white metal pole descending through its center. Kudirka was nowhere in sight, and Pollack wondered how the scientist had gotten so far ahead of him. Perhaps by sliding down the pole, around and around in dizzying circles, instead of using the steps; even with Kudirka's gashed arm it might have been possible. But of course Kudirka had the advantage of knowing where he was going, and where he would be when he landed.

Pollack gripped the pole, hesitating for a second longer than absolutely necessary, and it was then that he saw Kudirka on a lower level, watching him.

"Kudirka!" he yelled. "Listen to the beeper . . . It's nearly a steady tone already. For God's sake, man, if you know how to do it you've got to shut down the reactor immediately."

"If I know how?" Kudirka said. There was something like a smile on his face. "Of course I know *how* —I designed her, didn't I? I am sorry, Mr. Pollack, that I cannot accede to your request. Neutron Two will explode, and there is nothing you or anyone else can do about it. The world will be a better place, after all. Take the others and leave while there is still time—I have no wish to kill again. The upwind side . . ."

"What?"

"Leave the plant immediately, stay on the upwind side, and run, Mr. Pollack, as far and as fast as you are able. Do not bother looking for me—I shall not be here. Oh yes, I am leaving you something . . ."

He stooped over and placed on the floor by his feet what looked to Pollack like a key and a slip of paper.

"The key opens a safe-deposit box," Kudirka said. "In it you will find complete documentation concerning the life and death of Neutron One . . . names, dates, photostats of orders and counterorders. Enough, I should think, to implicate several people most seriously. I trust you with this information, Mr. Pollack, as I would trust no one else—even though, as you have seen, I attempted to kill you. If times had been different we might have had some interesting talks, you and I."

"We can still talk, Andres," Pollack said, desperately stalling for time. "If you would just wait for me—"

"No! Good-bye, Mr. Pollack . . . If you are thinking of using the pole like some heroic firefighter, I advise against it. The last man who tried split his skull on one of the steps."

Pollack watched him disappear into the shadows of several enormous tanks from which, Kudirka had explained to him on the first visit, pressurized steam bred by the superheated liquid sodium flowed toward banks of turbines and generators. From the generators the main electrical conduits spread down through twelve miles of fields on tall power poles, down through the streets of the city and off the main lines through transformers to individual houses, where it was possible for a man to push a bathroom light switch in order to appraise himself in the mirror as he shaved or brushed his teeth.

Pollack glanced up once at the reactor head and then, crooking his elbow around the central pole, allowed himself to flow down the stairs in a long, dizzying spiral. When he reached the level where Kudirka had been, the scientist was nowhere in sight. Pollack picked up the key and the slip of paper and put them in his pocket, then hurried along what seemed to be the main corridor until he found a set of stairs that eventually led down to his starting place at the ground-level control room.

The plant guard knocked out by Kudirka before their arrival had regained consciousness but was still wobbly from the blow; the swelling at the back of his head was the size of a small orange. "Is he still up there?" he asked when Pollack showed up, and when Pollack nodded the guard swore. "I guess I'd better go up and try to get him."

"You're in no condition to go anywhere except maybe to a hospital," Pollack told him, and the patrolman who had been blocked off in the upper corridor agreed. "That's what I been telling him."

Letty held onto Pollack's arm fiercely. "We heard shots. I was afraid for you, Yale."

He nodded and squeezed her hand to let her know he appreciated her concern. Richardson and Browning were staring at something on the control panel, and Pollack left Letty to see what they were doing. "That's a Geiger counter," Richardson said, pointing to a gauge on which a needle bounced continually against the edge of the red danger area while the machine clicked rapidly. "The whole building's hot—our bodies will start to absorb the radiation pretty soon."

They clustered around another instrument, a videoscreen oscilloscope that was tied into the red lights and beeping warning signals. "Look at that!" Richardson said suddenly, pointing. "The signal is showing as nearly a continuous straight line." They listened consciously for a moment to the beeper, which had been going on so long now that it had become almost a normal background noise. The beeps were no longer separate and distinct, but close to a steady sound.

"What's keeping us here?" Browning said. "Let's get the hell out while we can!"

243

"No—we can't leave yet," Richardson said, nervously brushing away the perspiration from under his frightened eyes.

"Mr. Richardson is worried about saving his expensive toy," Pollack said. "And I'm worried about Kudirka—foolish as that may seem to the rest of you."

"You're beginning to sound as insane as he is," Richardson said.

Pollack took a deep breath. "We could argue all night about who is and who isn't insane around here. I happen to think saving a brilliant scientist's life is important."

The patrolman snorted. "Brilliant? He's a *murderer* —he *killed* a man up there, Pollack!"

"It was an accident and you know it. Guard, this is very important—do you know of any other way to shut the plant down? Did Kudirka ever talk to you about any special emergency measures built into this place?"

Richardson shook his head derisively. "Pollack, if anyone knows about emergency procedures it would be I. There just isn't anything we can do until the automatic shut-off system takes over, believe me."

"Beg your pardon, Mr. Richardson," the guard said, "but Mr. Kudirka did explain to me one time about this manual system he installed himself because he said he, uh, didn't trust the emergency control-board circuits. The system works off a bunch of twelve-volt car batteries wired together—he set 'em up himself in a cabinet around back of the control room, in case there was ever a fire in here or something. You want to see 'em?"

Richardson looked astounded. "Of *course* I want to see them, you idiot. Show us where they are."

They had to leave the control room and circle single-file through openings in several interior concrete walls. Finally the guard led them to a cabinet in a workshop area. Pollack, in the rear, felt drops of something wet splashing down the side of his head and onto his shoulder. Curious, he looked up into the gloomy far reaches of the building where he had been chasing Kudirka only a few minutes ago, though it seemed much longer than that, ages in fact. He saw nothing unusual, nothing to cause the dripping. But suddenly he had a vision, terrible as life, of the separated fire hose—and the water that must have been running from the connected half all this time, gradually collecting into a pool that would eventually begin to flow in bright rivulets down the catwalk toward the open mouth of the reactor. The certainty that this was happening made the muscles of his stomach tighten into hard, burning knots.

"Inside here," the guard said, about to pull open the cabinet door. As Pollack dashed over to interrupt with his alarming news there was a tremendous flash like a bolt of lightning near the upper part of the building and huge balls of molten sodium spewed from the top of the reactor, showering down around them like acres of Roman candles.

Richardson blanched, and immediately began shoving his way toward the entrance corridor. "The whole thing's going!" he screamed. "Run for it—it's our only chance!"

As the others scrambled to follow Richardson to the air-lock tunnel Pollack lunged for the open cabinet. Kudirka's emergency power supply was inside it, just as the guard had said—rows and rows of batteries, every one covered with an inch or more of brown fungus-like corrosion that, over a period of many months, had eaten away parts of the casings and most of the wires.

Cursing at the top of his voice, Pollack ran behind

the others through the inner air-lock door into the deathly white corridor leading to the outside. Something forced him to stop and turn for a last look at the flaming destruction taking place in the once-silent spaciousness of the plant. It was like an overdone science-fiction movie about the end of the world, he thought, and almost as hard to believe. The guard, duty-conscious to the end, inserted his magnetic card into the slot and brought the massive door down behind Pollack, sealing off the cataclysmic nightmare from view.

Inside, from his perch high up in the containment structure where nearly the entire ground floor was visible, Kudirka watched as ant-sized people scurried and the door to the outside closed down for the last time. The height made him dizzy, a little, as it never had before; he felt like a bird in its aerie, an eagle, perhaps, like the ones they had seen occasionally at the house near Los Alamos so many years ago. The simile, pleasing him, caused him to smile.

He mounted the white stairs to the upper catwalk near the reactor head, holding onto the railing with both hands so that the violent sodium eruptions would not shake him loose. Amazing, when he thought of it, and almost funny enough to make him laugh—the fire-hose water system, on its own, had finally rebelled and decided to cause this elaborate fireworks display. When he reached the upper level he smiled at the sheared edge of the hose from which the avenging waters flowed. He said aloud, "Good for you. Wonderful! I must thank Mr. Pollack." And then he cranked the water valve fully open so that now a torrent gushed out along the right-angle catwalk directly into the opening in the top of the reactor.

The reaction was instantaneous and marvelous.

Great clouds of steam and molten sodium belched from the small opening like a mechanical volcano gone mad, as the reactor itself rumbled and moved against its imprisoning bolts, wires, and concrete restraints. Nothing on earth could contain that power now—not steel, not concrete, not even the foot-thick walls built for just such a purpose. He had known that all along, of course, but seeing it actually happen while standing at the very lip of the dragon's mouth was enough to make a man lose his grasp on reality.

The water would be filling the reactor core by now, the intense radiation of the fuel elements under water producing the unearthly shimmering violet glow of the Cherenkov effect. He had seen it once before somewhere, he remembered, and his desire to experience again that optic thrill was so great that he hurried to the very end of the spokelike catwalk and, grabbing a steel post for support, stared directly down into the boiling, spewing cauldron of the reactor.

His tormented face suffused by the purple radiance, he thought about the people—the hundreds of thousands of people who lived in the city twelve miles to the south, the people who would shortly die in their beds and those for whom it would be a while longer: days, or weeks, or years. Men, women, and children quietly breathing the deadly spawn of Neutron Two about which most of them knew and cared nothing, ingesting with one innocent breath a particle of plutonium dust with the power of the sun in its microscopic heart. Could God ever forgive such wanton destruction of human life, even for an ultimately good cause?

His body began to shake with indecision and he gripped the upright girder with all the strength in his hands to keep from tumbling off. "Forgive me, Lord," he said, and though he had shouted his voice was so

247

small he could not hear it himself over the thunderous roar of the spectacle taking place below him. Tears of remorse and total helplessness streamed down his face as he tentatively began to recite the Lord's Prayer aloud: "Our Father which art in heaven, hallowed be Thy name. Thy kingdom come. Thy will be done, as in heaven, so in earth. Give us this day our daily bread. And forgive us our sins . . . forgive us our sins . . . forgive us . . ."

The building heaved a warning; there was no more time. Calmly he released his grip on the girder and stared down into the eye of the beast, meeting its purple wavelike undulations with his own massive resolve. He imagined he saw Mariko's face in the maelstrom of radiating fluids. Smiling, admitting finally how lonely he was without her, he pitched forward and floated silently down into her waiting arms. Within a millisecond his body was as crisp as dried toast, the juices trapped within his eyeballs causing them to explode like ripe cherries.

Outside, several hundred yards upwind on a hill behind the plant, Letty shivered in the cold, damp breeze as Pollack wrapped her in his jacket. Seconds later, the first of several tremendous explosions rocked the ground as tongues of brilliant orange flame licked up through the breached containment walls of the rapidly disintegrating plant. Watching in awe, they saw a thin, fluorescent mist begin to drift from the upper reaches of the reactor shell and move downwind toward the barely visible lights of the city of Denver.

"Look!" Letty said, pointing out what was obvious to them all.

"Radioactive plutonium. That's right, isn't it?" Pollack said.

248

Richardson glanced at him, then looked away. "Plutonium oxide. Yes."

"My God," Pollack breathed, "all those people . . ."

Letty frowned. "Yale? Mr. Richardson?" Clearly she did not wish to believe her senses. "Are you telling me there's no way the people of Denver can be warned? Why are all of you just standing there?"

"Letty . . ." Pollack began.

"No!" she shouted, wrenching away from him. "For God's sake, are you all crazy, or what? There's the patrol radio, there must be emergency alarms, plans to be put into action, *something*. Yale?"

"Ask your good friend and employer Mr. Richardson there. Go ahead—he has all the answers."

Richardson stared out over the dark, gently rolling grassy plains to the south, now rapidly being contaminated with radioactive fallout more deadly than any ever caused by a bomb. "For once Pollack's right, I'm afraid. With this breeze and the weather conditions that cloud will be over the city in a matter of minutes."

"You've done your work well," Pollack said bitterly. "All these years telling people the plant was ultra-safe and so necessary to their well-being—not one person in a thousand would believe that something in the air they can't see or smell is going to kill them in the next few minutes."

He walked to a little knoll and squatted down on the grass, watching the glimmering cloud stream away toward the doomed city. "Besides," he continued, "how many families listen to the radio at four-thirty in the morning? And how would all those hundreds of thousands of people get away even if they believed what they were hearing? No way—that kind of panic would be as deadly as the plutonium."

"The goddamned fool didn't have to wreck a two-

249

billion-dollar plant just to commit suicide!" Richardson bitched.

Pollack shook his head in disgust. "You still refuse to understand, don't you?"

"We'd better radio ahead anyway, even if it won't do any good," Browning said, sounding like a government official for the first time since he had arrived. "Go use the radio in your car, see if you can wake anybody up," he told the patrolman, then added, "Oh hell, I'd better come with you—you wouldn't know what to say."

"So many people do things because somewhere the regulations say they should," Pollack said, addressing the wind.

Browning, hearing him, turned back angrily. "So what, smartass? Those people have a right to live and it's my duty to protect them."

But they all knew perfectly well—even Letty realized it now—that no one down below in Denver would believe them in time. The awfulness of it finally dissolved Letty's control, and though she made no sound the tears began streaming down her sad, twisted face. Mortally tired, she sagged to the ground beside Pollack with her back toward the plant and the city, and stared at nothing.

Hands in his pockets, Pollack fingered the key and the slip of paper Kudirka had given him, thinking about how on some dark street of that city about to be ravaged there was a certain bank, and inside the bank was a safe-deposit box, and inside the box were papers that might or might not prove worthwhile. It seemed unlikely, given the way things worked in the real world, that whatever was in the box could make much difference one way or the other. But he would try, somehow—even if it took years—to see that Kudirka had not given up his life in vain. And, more important, to see that people like Henry Richardson did not continue to violate the human race and get away with it.

"Poor Kudirka," Pollack said after a while.

Richardson looked down at him as if he were stark, raving mad.

"Poor all of us," Letty said.

Epilogue

THE EXPLOSION and subsequent radioactive fallout from the Handley Pond Nuclear Generating Station north of Denver, Colorado, has now been confirmed as this nation's most disastrous accident of all time. Latest figures released jointly by the Colorado Department of Health and the Director of Civil Defense show the total number of dead at 87,426, those in the special radioactive treatment centers not expected to live at 4,280, and an additional 150,000 or more with some residual lung damage that may eventually cause incapacitation or death.

The mortality rate in this tragic accident has been largely attributed to instantaneous massive fibrosis of primary lung tissue, causing an inability to breathe and subsequent death by suffocation. Several thousand deaths have also been blamed on the almost total state of panic ensuing after the initial radioactive cloud had passed over the city. In a statement released to news media this morning Mr. Jed Staley, Director of Civil Defense, claimed: "Nothing worked as it was supposed to. All our emergency plans will obviously have to be scrapped. I would say that we are at ground zero as far as any comprehensive ability to deal with a disaster of this magnitude, and I place the blame squarely on the shoulders of the present leadership, or lack of leadership, in the state legislature. I believe the governor is solidly behind me in demanding to know why an adequate bill budgeting funds for these disaster-planning and -programming requirements has yet to reach the state-house floor during this session. God knows we can't help the one hundred thousand or so citizens of Denver who are already dead, but perhaps we *can* save lives in the future. It would be nothing short of criminal if we did not."

In a hastily called press conference this morning in Washington—the fourth such meeting with the press in the past three days—the President reiterated his deep and continuing sorrow for the families of Denver residents dead or dying, and at the same time reasserted his faith in nuclear power as a viable energy source for centuries to come. "My staff at the Atomic Development Agency assures me that this deplorable accident is in no way the fault of fast-breeder-reactor design or anything else except the actions of a single deranged person, a maniac, a lone terrorist, if you will," the President is quoted as saying. "I have already signed the necessary papers allocating some eight hundred million dollars in emergency relief funds for the State of Colorado, and more will be made available as necessary."

Mr. Henry Richardson, vice president of the nuclear division of the Rocky Mountain Power Company, was reached only moments ago at his summer home in Georgia. Mr. Richardson gave us this statement: "My sources within and outside the company—and I might say, this is fully corroborated by the eminent scientist and administrator Dr. J. Welles, chief of the Industrial Liaison Office at A.D.A.—my sources state *categorically* that this terrible accident was the work of a madman, that there was no physical or design reason for the accident, and that the safety features carefully built into Handley Pond, as indeed into *every* nuclear generating facility, were in no way at fault. Even in the face of this tragedy we must not look behind us, but ahead. In fact, Dr. Welles has spoken with the President in person as recently as yesterday afternoon, and has authorized me to announce to you today that plans are already being formulated to construct a new and larger fast-breeder reactor near the site of the old Handley Pond plant. This is, I believe, proof positive of our leaders' desire to continue investing this nation's vast technological resources in the full development of nuclear power for the benefit of all mankind."

Meanwhile, decontamination procedures on the largest scale ever known are even now getting underway at the outskirts of the Denver metropolitan area. According to a brief statement released earlier by the director of the Colorado Department of Health, many of the former residents of the now deserted city of Denver may one day be able to return to their homes almost as if nothing happened. Not this year, and probably not next—no one is making any promises at this point. But eventually human beings will be able to return to the area and once again take up human pursuits in the Queen City. How many will choose to do so it is impossible to surmise. Perhaps thousands will return. Perhaps only a few families, or the bravest of real estate speculators. And perhaps no one at all.

As shown by the aerial photographs viewed earlier, the city of Denver stands tonight virtually whole and untouched, certainly not destroyed and not even damaged in any visible way. But people make a city, are basic to the very concept of a modern metropolis, and tonight the city of Denver, Colorado—three days ago inhabited by over one million people—is as lonely and dead as the craters of the moon. There are many who mourn its passing.